ALEX TOXIC

KILL OR DIE

Have a nice game!
Alex Toxic

BOOK TWO

MAGIC DOME BOOKS

Kill or Die
Book # 2

Cover Design: Vladimir Manyukhin

Published by Magic Dome Books, 2024

ISBN: 978-80-7693-470-2

TABLE OF CONTENTS:

Chapter 01 1
Chapter 02 14
Chapter 03 28
Chapter 04 39
Chapter 05 51
Chapter 06 65
Chapter 07 77
Chapter 08 91
Chapter 09 105
Chapter 10 118
Chapter 11 132
Chapter 12 145
Chapter 13 158
Chapter 14 173

Chapter 15 186
Chapter 16 199
Chapter 17 213
Chapter 18 226
Chapter 19 239
Chapter 20 255
Chapter 21 270
Chapter 22 284
Chapter 23 299
Chapter 24 311
Chapter 25 327
Chapter 26 341

CHAPTER 01

I WATCH EVERYTHING HAPPEN like it's in slow motion. Yumi's face takes on a kind of dumb, doomed expression. I can't tell if she regrets what she's done or not, but frankly I don't care. She's too dumb to be on our team, choosing her own personal vengeance over our common interests.

And that means that we're not on the same path anymore. And I don't care about her pretend obedience or how skillfully she flaps her lips. She's dead to me. Yet I don't want to hand her over to the AI either. Maybe it's my intuition or maybe my conversations with the Master and Zvyagin, but I sense something sinister guiding these barking town guards with their whimsical little beards.

It's that neural network, the AI: The massacre in the town square, the quest the other day, none of that was by chance. I assumed the point was to thin out the number of beta testers. But I realize now that it was the AI learning to defend itself, as well as to kill. Observing, absorbing, assimilating. Seems like it's decided now to set its own rules. And what better way to do that than with a public display of punishment?

Shugga and T-Rex backpedal in shock. But Lance grasps what's happening and the benefits it offers.

"Guards! Guards!" he yells, grabbing Yumi by the shoulder. "The traitor is here, I've got her!"

Traitor? What a ridiculous label. If there's anyone Yumi's betrayed here, it's me.

There's no time to explain. I can only hope my party members knows what to do.

"To battle!" I yell, slamming into Lance while swiping at his wrist with my stiletto.

Lance yanks his hand away and that's enough for Yumi to break free. I use the element of surprise to the utmost, driving my second dagger into his chest.

Lance and the others wear simple quilted armor and wield newbie swords, yet even this level of gear is impressive. They must have a stash somewhere in-game. I'll need to think about this further.

My *Precise Strike* is now on cooldown, so my second and third hits are much weaker. Then Lance jumps back, getting into a defensive stance, laughing:

"Another fool! I'll get double bounties for you two."

"What makes you think I'm going to kill you?!"

I'm at the top of my game. The debuff is gone, and the stimulants raging in my physical body double my Dexterity and significantly increase my Strength. I'm Level 3, but with all the bonuses I'm as good as a Level 6 — plus my advantages in weapons and armor. Lance and I are almost evenly matched. If it weren't for the stupid no-kill rule, I'd have fragged him by now.

I dodge sharply to the right, avoiding T-Rex's thrust. It's three against one now, but not for long.

"Raaah!" Simba charges into the fray, scattering enemies like bowling pins. T-Rex, his main target, goes tumbling. He sits on his ass, shaking his head, clearly dazed. Looks like Simba used his new skill, and I can't say I don't like the outcome.

"Finish him!" I shout to Yumi. "You've got nothing to lose now, so you might as well!"

She snaps out of it and screams as she jumps on T-Rex. She mounts him as if she's going to fuck him, but instead, she slits his throat with her stiletto. There you have it, boys. We've got an outlaw killer on our side with nothing to lose. It'd be foolish not to take make the best of it while we can!

Lance's look is full of fury. He realizes we can kill them, but they can't kill us. Lovely, ain't it? He makes an effort to move faster. He's wielding two newbie swords, longer than my stilettos. And he's Level 7 now, meaning he's picked up seven surprises in the training camp.

Simba is keeping Shugga occupied. He's

already taken a few hits, but it doesn't seem to faze our new paladin much. Yumi gets up from the heap of rags that was once T-Rex. She arches her back sensually, a tremor runs through her body... Level 5! Yumi purrs with pleasure and licks the blood off her dagger, clearly off her rocker with blood lust.

In less than a minute, Lance's party is down by two, while the guards haven't covered even a third of the distance yet. Everything is happening very, very quickly. This isn't the Gladiator Games, so there's no need to put on a show.

Lance's blades are longer, but he can't keep me at bay. I'm a bit faster and I use that to my advantage. He's parrying more, getting defensive. It's a smart strategy on his part. He doesn't need to win, just to hold on until the guards arrive.

I kick him in the knee — to hell with the noble dueling etiquette! And... nothing happens. It's like kicking a bronze statue. Damn, there must be some skill to counter this, which I don't have. It seems that at the moment, our fight's more about builds and levels, not true fighting prowess.

I should've chosen the Adventurer class and not been so fancy! Also, I should have made Simba the party leader. What does it matter who makes our party? He probably has plenty of sneaky tricks up his sleeve.

A strike! Lance crosses his blades like scissors, strikes from below, and my stiletto goes flying! He smirks — here's one of his new skills, I guess. I parry the next blow with my remaining dagger, but now he's pressing.

BRRRONG! BRRRONG! BRRRONG! The jarring noise of a sword hilt hitting a shield resounds throughout the street. It's so irritating, I want to stop everything and attack the jerk making this racket. I want to rip that rotten sword from his hands, shove its hilt up his ass and twist it a few times... But, wait, it's Simba who's making this clatter! *BRRRONG!*

That's his aggro aura to draw enemies to him... This is how it works in this game! It's very effective, but indiscriminate. I probably wouldn't feel its effects if we were in the same party, but I haven't actually made our party yet... First it was one thing, then another...

BRRRONG! Shugga lunges at him like a madman. Bouncing around like a terrier in front of a bear, trying to reach him. Lance flinches at every sound, involuntarily turning his head towards Simba. It's the perfect time to crit him, but I'm doing exactly the same thing — turning to look at Simba and contemplating cynical ways to kill him.

Stacy, however, is unaffected. Maybe the aura's aggro effect decreases with distance. *Thud!* A stone from her slingshot hits Lance in the head. He freezes for a moment, his eyes rolling back. He's stunned! A smart move and a good use of her special skill! I could kiss her for that, but later... everything later. For now, I take aim and drive my stiletto into Lance's liver.

"Yumi!"

I don't need to call the psycho twice. She comes up behind Lance, as if she wants to have her way with him, plunges her stiletto into his throat, and whispers in his ear:

"Die, you freak."

I hear this only because at that very moment, I'm also intimately pressed against him from the front, busy turning Lance's stomach into a sieve. You can't do much damage with a stiletto, but during the time it takes you to land one blow with a sword, you can get three in with a dagger. The three of us make a kind of sandwich, with Lance as the filling.

He takes his time dying — about ten seconds. I barely manage to hold back, letting Yumi land the final blow.

"I'll find you, you bitch!" Lance yells before he expires.

I find this funny because in meatspace, he knows exactly where to find me, and if he does, he'll regret it.

"Ohhh, damn..." Yumi collapses into my arms. "Ahh..."

She's shaking. She gained two levels in less than a couple of minutes, and it's hitting her now. I slap her to bring her back to her senses.

Shugga is left alone against four and finishing him is just a matter of technique. I can see my reflection in the eyes of the approaching guards when Simba knocks him down with a shield bash. Then we hold him, Simba by the legs, me by the right arm, and Stacy by the left, while Yumi butchers him like a pig.

"Let's go!"

"Wait, what about the loot?" Simba worries.

"Screw it, they might charge us as accomplices."

Yumi is covered in blood from head to toe. She looks around confused, like a serial killer caught near a fresh victim. I briefly consider turning her in, if not to the guards, then at least to the nurses.

"Run, you dolt!"

We zigzag through the alleys, managing to build a lead. It can't last long, our stamina is dropping, but I don't doubt the guards' abilities. If the AI made them, they should be as good as hounds and will chase their quarries for a long time.

I know where we can hide though. It might be the only place where we can hide an outlaw from the long arm of the law. If not, then Yumi's doomed, and she deserves it.

We turn another corner and find ourselves in a square facing another spider's nest. You can't call this abandoned mansion anything else. Thick cobwebs cover the crooked, gothic structure so densely that they completely obscure its sharp angles. It might as well be a cocoon that has fat elite spiders with poison-green crosses on their backs crawling all over it.

From a distance, I can't see their levels, but they must be at least Level 5. They're big, fat with glossy black abdomens, and curved jaws, almost twice the size of the regular Level 1 spiderlings. If the spiderlings are the size of small dogs, these boys are at least the size of mastiffs, just more squat and solid.

The neighboring houses have changed too. Their windows are now covered in dense webs, so you can't see inside. There are spiders in the yards, on the porches, even on the roofs. Further down the street, however, it looks like the infestation has been stopped.

In that direction, three of the houses are surrounded by makeshift fortifications that look like giant caltrops. Sharp logs tied together. The town guard mans these makeshift battlements. I quickly manage to count up fourteen guards.

They're bristling with pikes, trying to catch the spiders as they climb over the logs. A successful hit sends a spider flying over the barrier, like a caught fish, to be finished off by the rest of the defenders. Nevertheless sometimes the spiders get lucky, leaping over the spikes and wreaking havoc among the defenders' ranks.

Both the spiders and the guards are low-level, just zeros and ones. I guess the AI is just playing with itself. Mobs vs. NPCs — though I'm not sure if the guards count as NPCs. They're no different from the mobs really, and we might have to fight them soon enough.

Some players stand in line with the guards, often covering gaps in the fortifications, facing the spiders head-on.

Further on, I see mobile squads of Level 3s and even Level 4s, probably there in case of a breakthrough. I spot one Level 5 guard, distinguished by a fancy gold sash and welding a sword with an ornate hilt instead of a pike.

The best part is that this battle lines clearly haven't shifted in a while and this stalemate seems to suit both sides. The spiders get to keep their nests and the city authorities can use the endless onslaught to train their troops.

That's all I manage to observe in the few moments we have before our pursuers' heavy footsteps break the silence of the alley behind us.

My plan was to hide ourselves right in the middle of battle, so that the aggressive spider mobs could serve as a natural defense for us. But first we have to make our way into this fray.

My party! I almost forgot! I assumed my Leadership skill would level up the classic way. Circumstances have changed, but that's no reason to abandon my plans. I stare dumbly at the word "party" in my interface. My gaze shifts from it to Simba... back to the interface... trying to mentally click...

"Targe... What're you, in a daze?" Simba asks. "Did you get another debuff?"

Targe eh? Sounds good to me. "TargetAi" is too long to pronounce and calling someone by their game name is bad manner. I force my thoughts back to the task at hand. The speed buffs are making me scatterbrained. My mind jumps from one thing to another, noticing many small details, but struggling to put it all together.

So why the hell did I have to grind to get all

my skills in the training camp, but this one, Leadership, was just given to me? No... that's not right... it wasn't just given to me... I got this Whistle along with it! As soon as I blow into it, a new menu appears.

TOUCH THE PLAYER YOU WANT TO ADD TO THE PARTY.

I put my hand on Simba's shoulder. He looks up surprised, then receives an invitation.

SIMBA HAS JOINED THE PARTY.

His portrait and status appears in my interface: his health bar, currently at 92%, and his skills, which include *Battle Cry*, *Copper Skin*, and *Shield Bash*. His portrait also has a "Daily Prayer" indicator with a barely filled bar. This seems to be a constant, voluntary debuff, not unlike my "Sexual Arousal," only requiring different actions to dispel.

I repeat this process to add AngelCake to our party. Her skills become visible, but there's no time to figure them out. The fuzz are breathing down our necks. Yumi, realizing something important is happening, looks at me with pleading eyes. No, darling, you're out of luck. I wouldn't be surprised if the whole party gets branded as outlaws if I let her in.

"I should have left you behind!" I yell at her. "You let everyone down! If you want to live, run after us, but I'm not adding you to the party... You haven't earned it!"

From an outsider's perspective, it must look funny, a Level 3 scolding a Level 7 like this, but she just listens, eyes downcast.

"Andrew..." AngelCake tries to intervene. Fine defender of the downtrodden she is. I thought she'd be at odds with Yumi, but instead, they've become buddies.

"Targe, let's get the hell out of here!" Simba interrupts, "Look at this mess!"

A wave of disquiet seems to pass over the square. Only the defenders remain at the fortifications, while everyone else looks at us, pointing. Then they start moving, breaking into a run. There must be dozens of them.

"There's the outlaw! Grab her... Take her alive!"

Trying not to think about possibly having led my party into a trap, I frantically issue orders.

"Make a break for the house on the right. Don't engage the guards —just push them away if you need to. Yumi, you bring up the rear, only get involved as a last resort. And don't you dare steal our XP. All right... Everyone ready? LET'S GO!"

We take off, heading straight towards the running guards. Luckily, they don't consider that area particularly dangerous. The main forces are concentrated around the central house's ruins, where most of the spiders are. We're facing only Level 1s and 2s, yet there are about twenty of them.

I adjust the party's XP distribution on the run. It'll be 50% for me and 25% each for Simba and AngelCake. It might not be fair, but we'll soon need more dps and that's going to be me.

Next we quickly close with the line of guards. It feels like rugby or American football or something. Two teams charging at each other, ready to collide.

I duck under one guard's hand and sidestep another. They just run past me; I'm just an obstacle, of no interest to them. Simba collides with one, not even slowing down, and the guard is knocked off to the side.

The AI doesn't react, however. I guess it merely registers it as harmless bumping. Maybe they didn't notice each other. I don't dare do the same, but why bother when my Dexterity allows me to dodge outright anyway...

I wonder what they plan to do with a Level 7 assassin when they do catch her? Politely ask her to go to jail? Or do they have guards of a corresponding level?

For now, Yumi is taking them down like standing targets, then she activates stealth. The pursuers spin around, bewildered, as their target suddenly vanishes.

The line of fortifications lies ahead. Without thinking of slowing down, I step on the logs and, turning in mid-air, fall into the writhing mass of spiders.

I roll and regain my footing. They're much too slow for me! I drive my stiletto into one creature's head, trip another, and land a hard kick on a third. The Level 1 spiders die from a single hit, but they don't yield much XP, especially now that it's shared among us all. I clear a space for the others.

"Where are you going! You can't do that! Hey, put that back!" the guards shout frantically behind me.

Simba drags one of the giant caltrops aside with two stubborn defenders hanging on it. He just pulls it and them along with it.

"Damn, why are you so heavy!" he grunts.

As I help him, I suffer two painful bites on my ass. My health drops. I never did put anything into Constitution, so I still have as much HP as a newbie. I fend off the spiders with my stilettos until our tank and archer catch up to me.

Yumi materializes beside them, causing an uproar among the guards. They rush into the breach, met by spiders. I just watch, admiring the scene. The first step of my plan is complete. Only a few dozen more stops to go.

"To battle!" roars Simba, charging into the dense pack of eight-legged creatures with his shield.

CHAPTER 02

IT WAS THE IDEAL farming setup. Think about it. No need to amass trains of monsters — they just keep coming to you non-stop. They're already at the perfect level for leveling up, just one or two below ours, so they die with a single hit. No interference, no jostling for space.

If only I had a couple AoE skills, so I wouldn't have to stab each mob individually with my stiletto. And also I wish the guards — who kept hacking through the sea of spiders, calling for the assassin to turn herself in — would shut up already.

"Surrender thyself, thou outlaw Yumi!" they cry. "Drop thy arms and come this way! Fear not, for thou shalt face fair justice, a trial with the mayor as thy judge!"

Yumi occasionally flips them the bird. Plodding and sulking behind us, you can tell she's bored — especially since I barred her from killing any mobs. Occasionally, she punts away an overly bold spider.

The reason I forbade her from farming XP with us is because she doesn't need it. She's already gorged herself up to Level 7 and I wouldn't be surprised if she's now second in the player rankings, after Anna — or third, after Lance. But most likely second. She did gank him after all — not the other way around. He was banging her, but she finished him off. And Xavier too.

She kills her mates almost like a black widow... I recall the "oral blessings" she's given me as of late. Even if we all band together, we might not be able to take her down. Seeing her lick blood off her dagger gave me the creeps. It seems like we've nurtured a psycho in our ranks.

Yet she's not showing any aggression at the moment. It seems the frenzy that drove her to wipe out Lance's squad and become an outlaw has passed and given way to whining.

"Andrew... what's going to happen now?"

"I don't know," I snap back at her. "Did you think about that when you jumped those idiots?!"

"What about them?!"

At least she didn't play the "you're a man, why didn't you say anything" card. I hate girls who get themselves into trouble, betting on others to bail them out. If Yumi had been like that, I'd have told her off right away. But though she messed up, she didn't drag anyone into it or force anyone to get involved. I got involved myself — since it was the perfect chance to screw Lance over one more time.

Too bad he got to the training camp first and set up his build. Otherwise, I could have knocked him out of the beta for good. Would have been quite a spectacle! I wonder whether MosTech would have reversed his elimination? Doubt it. This train's picking up speed every day and the rules are no longer set by the admins, the devs, or even the Master & Co. It's all up to the AI now.

On the other hand, at least Lance will have to sit out the rest of today. No XP and no loot for him. He was on top of the food chain, and now... At least he'll have to look over his shoulder more often and tread carefully.

And why am I having these thoughts in the middle of a battle? Because there's nothing more dull than farming. Except maybe weeding. Hit, twist... pull out the stiletto. Hit... twist... pull out... I alternate my strikes, top, bottom, side... aiming right at the middle of the spiders' foreheads, or whatever it is spiders have — right above their eight nasty little eyes.

Still, you quickly get bored from such labor. It's like peeling potatoes. Random thoughts creep into your head.

After my talk with Zvyagin, I took some time to look up neural networks on the internet. There wasn't much info to be found, and what was there seemed to describe neural networks as a quirky, unusual, but overall useless curiosity.

I recalled one example quite clearly. Programmers had worked on chess engines for many decades. The most successful engine could even beat a world champion, but not always. It could evaluate a position and crunch the best possible moves and choose the best strategy based on them. But if a human started improvising and purposefully playing to confound the engine, he still had a chance of creating a closed and even position that he could win from.

Neural networks changed all this. A neural net didn't know any openings or endgames. The devs would simply teach it the game rules and then had it play against itself. After a few months it had played several trillion games against itself and could rip apart both traditional chess engines and living grandmasters.

That's what the mobs training on each other reminded me of today. The AI was training itself... but what was it training itself for? That was the question.

Brrrong! Simba recast his aura. This time, to us, his fellow party members, it sounded like a regular noise — not too loud — like a spoon tapping a metal bowl.

"Gaaargh..." Yumi meanwhile clutched her ears in agony, dropping to her knees. "Tell him to stop or I'll kill him myself!"

"Just move back a bit," Stacy advised her, "it's not so bad the further you are. Worked for me."

Yumi looked back skeptically. The guards were preparing a special operation, dead set on getting Yumi's head. They had lined themselves in a long rank, phalanx-style, to push the spiders out of their way. A Level 5 officer had taken charge. Seeing their preparations, the assassin pressed closer to us instead.

Brrrong!

"Damn it..." Yumi jumped again, resisting the urge to lunge at the aggro-inducing paladin. "At least give me a heads up!"

Stacy put away her slingshot, which was useless at close quarters, took a sword in her hands, and was now chopping spiders with the methodical thoroughness of a good housewife prepping coleslaw for dinner.

Meanwhile the XP came slowly trickling in. I was already halfway to Level 4 and was happy to keep going — when Simba ran into a wall.

Well, calling it a wall would be an exaggeration: It was more of a fence and a flimsy one at that. There were large gaps in it, where its pickets had fallen and where elite spiders now clicked their jaws menacingly.

The spiders were Level 3s and there were about fifteen of them. They seemed as happy to see us as if we were their long-lost family and they immediately skittered our way in order to hug us, I suppose.

"Simba, your aggro aura!"

Brrrong!

"Oh goddamn it..."

"Hack 'em Stacy!"

I realized what it was that gave me the impression that the spiders were happy to see us:

They were squatted on their hind legs and swaying their bellies, like friendly dogs, happy to see their owners after a day apart. They didn't wag their tails, but that wasn't surprising.

"Eeek, son of a bitch!" Simba yelled. "Get this thing off me!"

It turned out the spiders weren't squatting just for show. Two of them suddenly leaped in loping jumps, aiming their jaws at our paladin's face. He managed to deflect one with his shield mid-jump, but the other clamped onto his hair, its furry legs covering his face like a facehugger from *Alien.*

"Halp..." Simba whirled in place, trying to shake the creature off, panicked more from revulsion than pain.

"Stand still, don't move!" AngelCake yelled. "I'll knock it off you!"

"No, no, not you!" Simba wailed. "You'll knock my head off along with it!"

"Fine then!" Stacy huffed, offended. "Keep it on! I hope it craps in your stupid mouth!"

I was afraid of missing and accidentally smacking Simba, so instead of using my weapon, I tried to pull the spider off by its leg — to no avail. The arthropod had latched on with a death grip. Further back, I noticed several more spiders preparing to jump.

"Yumi!"

Whaaang! The stiletto buzzed through the air next to me. The assassin had responded instantly. The weapon, not meant for throwing, plunged into the spider's bulging back with such force it ripped the creature off of Simba and flung it to the pavement.

I'm just starting to grasp what a Level 7 is capable of and I can't help but feel a pang of envy. If I had dealt with Lance myself, I wouldn't be lagging behind her now. However, her future place in this game is uncertain... How would she even be able to go on playing here? Sure, we might make it to the end of today's quest, but what about tomorrow? Won't the guards be waiting for her the next time she spawns? "Papers please, miss... What's this? Right this way." Or will the AI grant an amnesty, letting bygones be bygones? It does seem to be a bit temperamental. One day it engineers a general massacre and the next day it's a universal love-in. I'm just happy to get out alive at the moment. I'll deal with the bigger problems as they come.

"Raaaah, ya bastards!" Simba charges into the line of elite spiders.

One spider gets knocked deep into the yard, while the others circle the paladin like a ring-around-the-rosy. They snap at his unprotected legs: though his torso's clad in chain mail, he has on only leather pants below.

Meanwhile, some spiders turn to us, presenting their juicy abdomens. Not in the way you're thinking, but in the easy targets they make for our swords and stilettos. They go down pretty easily. I try a *Precise Strike* on one and one-shot it, while the rest fall after two or three stabs in the gaps between their shell and head, or shell and belly.

Stacy had it tougher, since her sword would not always pierce the spiders' armor, yet she made do. Especially since the spiders, even when almost cut in half, ignored us. Clicking and rattling their jaws furiously, they tried to get to Simba even as they died, that's how badly his aura infuriated them.

In this manner, we made our way into the yard, stepping over the bodies of dead elite spiders. Sounds epic and all, but in reality, the dead spiders just turned into a handful of dust, leaving no loot. As I entered the breach, I turned around. The phalanx of guards had begun to move, but their progress was slow. The spiders overwhelmed them with numbers, and whereas the pikes were good for defense, they were middling for attacking such small, nimble creatures. The town guard had no concept of tank or dps party roles, and consequently their advance was only gradual.

Their main weapon was their leader, a Level 5 officer. Far from cowering behind his subordinates, he bravely flanked the spiders, clearing a path for the other fighters. It seemed that the AI was beginning to learn the finer points of combat operations.

"What will become of me?" Yumi approached me. "What will they do to me when they catch me?"

She picked up her stiletto from the ground, wiped it on her pants, and looked back anxiously. Whereas the guards' maneuvers merely elicited curiosity in me, she was clearly frightened by them. And I noted that she said "*when*," not "*if*."

"I have no idea," I replied honestly. "Maybe they'll strip you down and spank you in the town square. Maybe they'll throw you in jail. Maybe they'll chop off your head. Or maybe they'll give you a medal and make you an honorary citizen. I simply have no idea what's going on in that AI's head. However, I advise you against falling into its hands. I have a bad feeling about it."

"Me too," Yumi shrugged. "It's like I'm a rabbit and they've set the hounds after me."

"You got a hell of a bite for a bunny," I laughed. "One wrong move, and the hounds are sure to pay."

I'll have plenty of opportunities to bawl her out in meatspace. In fact, I have a huge urge to just kick Yumi out of our party entirely. She's just too mental. Whereas AngelCake has put in hard work and gone from a whiny, busty girl to a full-fledged fighter, Yumi remains full of surprises and not much else.

Maybe it's the way she is: "I'm a girl so I do what I want." Or maybe what Xavier did to her has traumatized her so bad that she flips any time she sees him. If that's so, she's a time bomb waiting to explode at the worst possible moment. But that's for later. Right now, I need her to pull herself together and do her job.

"I meant, what's next for me in the game," Yumi guessed my thoughts.

She stepped closer, lowering her arms and

slightly tilting her head as if expecting a hug. Her whole posture screamed, "Save me, and I'll be grateful with all my heart and body! I surrender myself to your power and protection!" But of course she'd be sure to forget all that as soon as the next thought entered her fickle head... So, no way.

"Don't worry about what you can't control," I replied coldly. "Let's deal with problems as they come."

"What are you guys doing?" Simba peered in. "Blessing each other?"

"Not at all, you dummy..." Yumi playfully waved her hand at him, but on second thought decided to seize the chance to make sure. "You're not ready, are you Andrew?"

"Nope," I answered. "My stamina is still recovering. It's really low."

"Then let's go," Simba announced cheerfully. "It's a mess out there."

The house before us looked like an old Gothic mansion you see in adolescent horror flicks. A high triangular roof, echoed in the gables over the windows, and a covered, tall porch. Its windows were lightless voids, as if dozens of spider eyes were watching us from within. The wooden cladding was peeling and partly fallen off, making it hard to tell its original color. Now, it was mostly dirty gray.

Just four days ago, this house looked completely normal, but now it seemed to have aged twenty years. Everything happens fast in this game world. You can't miss a single day. If we were to take a day off from the beta, I wouldn't be surprised if we ran into Level 8 or even Level 10 mobs upon our return. Everything in this place seems to go on leveling up while we sleep.

The path from the gate to the porch used to be an alley. Now, the trees looked like dense dark cocoons, with something continuously wriggling inside. In fact, this narrow path, with this stuff hanging right over our heads, seemed like the worst part. However, there was no other way to the house.

"So, who's going first?" Simba asked.

"Who else? You, of course!" AngelCake exclaimed. "You're our tank. You can take it."

"But it's icky," Simba whined. "Just the thought of those spider legs in my hair makes me ick."

"Maybe it just wanted to nest in your hair?" Stacy teased. "You'd better check if it managed to lay any eggs — unless you want hatchlings crawling into your eyes, crying 'Daddy... daddy...'"

"Shut up, ya dumbass!" cried Simba, touching his hair just in case. "I won't go. Send the assassin instead. If she makes it, good — and if they eat her, that'll be that."

I had considered this. What would the guards do if the mobs simply killed Yumi? No body, no case. But sending someone to be devoured by spiders seemed... unsporting and wicked. If the mobs here would kill her with one blow or drive her off a high cliff... Or even if she committed seppuku… atoned for her crime… As a last resort, maybe I'd suggest it. But for now, we'll have to soldier on.

"You have to go, Simba," I concluded. "You're the strongest. The others will be devoured, but you'll just get bitten. Let's at least see who's hiding in there. Go as stealthily as you can, little by little. We'll back you up. Everyone, get ready."

Simba sighed, lifted his shield over his head like an umbrella, and cautiously, half a step at a time, entered under the trees' sinister canopy.

Thunk! Thunk! Two enormous spiders instantly dropped onto his shield. Simba barely managed to hold onto it. It was a good thing he held it with both hands, having stashed his sword in his inventory. *Whack!* Stacy knocked one off with a stone, while the other slipped off, unable to cling onto the smooth surface.

"Fall back to us, draw them out!"

Simba didn't need to be told twice; he quickly backpedaled, using his shield to fend off the spider. Annoyed that its clever ambush had failed, the spider kept lunging, trying to bite through the metal boss and splattering it with venom. The other spider quickly joined the fight, having recovered from the stun of Stacy's attack. They were Level 4, but they didn't last long. While Simba drew their aggro, I dispatched one and Yumi the other. Surprisingly, both spiders dropped loot in the form of slimy green sacks that were unpleasant to touch.

"Venom Gland of the Green Cross Spider," I

read in the inventory. I kept one for myself and handed the other to Yumi.

"Here, have fun with this. It's your kind of item."

"Wow," she marveled, staring off into nowhere, probably studying her interface. "This item can add poison damage to weapons."

"Any weapon?" I asked, excited.

"No, only mine," Yumi said to my disappointment. "Only assassins can use it this way."

"Well, at least it's something."

I decided not to give away the second venom gland — let's see how much I can get for it in the shop.

"So, what do we do now?" Simba asked anxiously. "If we lure them out one or two at a time, it'll take us hours to get through this path."

Whether it would really be hours or not, it would indeed take a lot of time. Plus, I was reluctant to clear such a perfect obstacle course for the guards. We'd basically be clearing their way for them.

As I walked along the fence, a thought nagged at me. The spiders had jumped from the trees... Simba had used his shield... And they had fallen on it... They hadn't been able to reach him from above...

"Can you lift it?"

One of the sections of the wooden fence lay on the ground, right where we had entered through the breach.

"Are you joking?" asked Simba.

"Too weak?"

"Not at all."

He grabbed the bars holding the planks together and strained...

"Ahh! There we go!"

"Hold it up and don't let go," I rejoiced. "Yumi, go into stealth and head to the porch. When we're close by, open the door for us."

The assassin nodded without asking questions and vanished. If only she'd been this obedient earlier!

"AngelCake, you take the right and I'll take the left... Now let's go!"

"Are you serious?!" Stacy asked, staring at me wide-eyed.

"Stop talking, his stamina is dropping!" I grabbed my side of the fence section, easing the burden for Simba, "Three, four!"

Something loud fell from above — more spiders no doubt. They were bumping into each other, falling at our feet and scurrying after us. We trotted down the path to the house like the Russian troika of yore, and when we finally reached the porch, we dumped the fence section behind us.

"Yumi, the door!"

Yumi flickered into sight like a ghost, flung open the door to the mansion, and we tumbled inside.

CHAPTER 03

THE MANSION HAD BEEN BUILT with a flair for luxury. The first floor had a large sitting room, where the owners would light the fireplace in the evenings, drink brandy and reminisce of better times. To the right, a staircase led to a spacious mezzanine while another set of stairs led to a dining room on the left. I glimpsed all this as we walked past. The furniture, walls, and balustrades were all covered in a thick gray moss, which the house's current occupants used to scurry around in packs. At the moment, the packs of spiders were scurrying our way. I guess they were happy to see us — why else would they rush to meet us so eagerly?

As the front door slammed shut behind us, dull thuds sounded on the other side. The spiders were lunging and slamming their bodies against the door. Luckily, there was a bolt in this house too. Really, what decent private home doesn't have a bolt? I wouldn't have minded shutters and a sturdier lock, preferably a padlock, but alas, you can't have everything.

At least this simplified the situation a bit, though not much. The mansion turned out to be packed with spiders on the inside. And worst of all, they were Level 5s. Well-fed, well-nourished and very, very angry. AngelCake even tucked behind me in fear. For the first time, I thought maybe I had blundered and led my party into a deathtrap.

"Aggro them, Simba!"

The paladin raises his shield, banging on it with his sword and summoning the arachnids from all over the mansion. They swarm him, crawling up to his feet, leaping from the furniture, and even falling on us from the second-floor balustrade. Simba fights them off but gets bitten once, then again. How long can he last without healing or potions?

Stacy comes to her senses and starts shooting the spiders with her slingshot from behind Simon. The spiders are momentarily stunned, twitching on the ground, but we don't even have time to finish them off. Eight creatures have already surround Simba and more are on the way. We're being hemmed in hard. I can't let us just die here.

In a frenzy, I jump onto a spider's back and skip from one to another as if they were tufts in a swamp. Their black armored backs are slippery under my feet. I end up across from Simba and with a final leap, I crouch down, driving my stilettos just behind the spider's eyes. Take that, you fucker!

A wave of ecstasy almost bowls me over. I've leveled up! I'm Level 4 at last. It's a good thing the nearby mobs aren't paying attention to me. They push and shove with their hard legs, eager to get to Simba's juicy flesh.

I want to dump all my stat points into Dexterity! With the buffs I already have, I'll be as good as Level 8 or higher. Or should I stick to my old regimen of Dexterity and Strength?

Grudgingly, I put all five points into Constitution. My HP immediately increases sixfold and my stamina triples, which is great considering it was already in the red.

But why did I dash over here in the first place? There was some idea initially, right? Whatever... I follow my intuition and take out two spiders to my right and left, clearing space in front of our tank.

"Push forward Simba, run!"

We're on the move again, now with a clear destination: the open door before us. We need a defensible room with a single choke, where we can make a stand like three hundred Spartans. Hopefully, it's a good idea, as we don't have any others.

Rather than outright slaying the spiders, we push them aside and break through the door. It turns out to be a kitchen with a stove in the corner, benches and a heavy-looking chest. I shut the door behind us and wedge my back against it.

"Clear the room!"

No time for fancy tactics here — there are only three spiders. We hunt them down and exterminate them. Yumi tries extra hard, taking down two of the three. Meanwhile Simba gathers the loot, which is all the same green glands from before.

"Yumi, you take the window."

The assassin nods, approaches the window, cuts through the web with her dagger, and looks outside. I don't think it's a great idea to remove the covering, but it's all quiet outside, with no sign of enemies. Maybe house and street spiders have different zones of aggro. If so, clearing the house should make it safe for us. The mobs hammering at the mansion's front door were an exception, aggroed by our passage.

There are no more live mobs in the kitchen. We have a moment to catch our breaths, restore stamina, and plan our tactics.

"Simba, drag that chest over here... Can you move it? Let's go!"

Together, we position the heavy chest to block the door, leaving only a narrow slit open.

"Simba, you aggro. Hold them there and don't let them through. You hold... I'll do dps... Then I'll swap with Stacy and she'll dps while I rest up."

"Can I try?" Yumi steps forward, her eyes narrow, her nostrils flaring with each breath. Wait, is she excited about killing?

"No!" I cut her off.

"Please... I'm the strongest... I can be most useful..."

"NO!" I say loudly and firmly, like giving a command to a dog.

All that's left to say is "bad" and "stay." Yumi lowers her eyes and steps back, dejected. I'm not wasting mobs on her. Spiders are not just enemies; they're experience points. That's the simple math.

"Watch the window instead," I command Yumi.

She sighs and moves to the wall, sitting down. Like me, she no longer thinks that there's any threat coming from the window.

I move away from the door I've been holding. It swings open forcefully, banging against the chest...

Brrrong! Stunned by the noise, the spiders get stuck in the doorway, clambering over each other to bite this noisy intruder. Simba keeps them at bay with his shield. I strike from the right, targeting the spiders' vulnerabilities. The first one falls after five hits, the second after four. Simba grunts but holds on. The situation is starting to resemble a normal grind, without any imminent risk to our lives.

After about ten minutes, my stamina drops, and Stacy replaces me. She kills slower with her novice sword but is equally steady.

Then Stacy reaches Level 4, moans blissfully, and takes a break from the farm. I have to replace her. Soon enough though I reach Level 5 myself.

Simba is the last to level up. The stream of mobs dries up. A considerable pile of ash forms at the kitchen's threshold, and our inventory is filled with venom glands. These had better be worth something.

"Let's clear the rest of the house," I command.

"Wait, let's check the chest," Simba suggests, unable to resist his looting nature.

Despite our best efforts, the chest remains locked. It's secured with two powerful steel hasps and a hefty lock. Neither Stacy, who has no lockpicking skills and hopelessly fiddles with the lock, nor Yumi, who tries to pick it with her stilettos ("like I saw in *Sherlock*"), nor Simba, who furiously bashes the lock with the bottom of his shield, can open it.

"You know why it won't open?" I ask, watching them struggle.

"Why?" Simba asks hopefully.

"Because it's empty," I laugh. "The AI didn't put anything in it, so it won't budge."

Simba spits in frustration.

"I'll come back for it," he says vengefully, giving the chest a light kick, careful not to hurt his foot.

The mansion greets us with a gloomy hush among which only the rustling of a myriad hairy spider legs is clearly discernible. But we're ready for them. Isolated mobs are no issue for us.

We clear the first floor. The spiders, lacking in numbers, act more cautiously and only appear after Simba tolls his "*Brrrong.*" One scares us by jumping out of the fireplace.

We carefully ascend the stairs. On the mezzanine overlooking the living room, we encounter larger spiders, almost as tall as our waists, their legs almost as thick as our arms. They're fun to kill. When the first attacks our tank, I jump onto the balustrade, run past the mob and leap onto its back. I've mounted it!

The spider spins in place, trying to throw me off or bite me, but unlike a rodeo horse, its legs aren't strong enough, and I sway like I'm in a hammock. Lacking a neck, the spider can't turn its head enough to reach me.

Meanwhile, I can gouge out any of its eight eyes or riddle its head with holes, which I do, putting it out of its misery.

The loot these mobs drop is different. I pick up an odd-looking needle named "Cross Spider Stinger." The AI seems confused about meatspace biology since only bees and wasps sting, while spiders bite. But a stinger is a stinger. It looks like an ingredient for crafting some devious weapon.

The larger spiders attack one at a time, allowing me to fully display my riding talents. They're bored; I'm entertained. In this manner, I even manage to reach Level 6.

Now I understand how Anna got so far ahead of everyone else so quickly. If you're skilled and well-armed, you can easily reach Level 15 in a mansion like this. After all, all the XP I'm getting is divided among the three of us.

There are three doors on the second floor. The

ceiling is high up and vaulted and adorned with a large, once beautiful chandelier. The second floor is full of bedrooms or maybe offices. We're about to find out.

The first door… is empty! A broken mirror, a wrecked bed, two small spiders, just Level 3s — no match for us, easy peasy. The second room is almost the same story, though it clearly used to be a child's bedroom. Cheerful wallpaper covers the walls with images of a bunny and a bear walking hand in hand, the bunny holding a red balloon. The floor is littered with indistinguishable remnants of toys which crunch under our feet. A child's bed and a tiny cradle stand nearby, all gray and lifeless.

Now naturally I understand very well that no one ever lived in this house. I've never even seen NPC women here, let alone children. By the time the spiders showed up here, the house was already empty… ugh… it was *always* empty! But still…

Where does the AI get these images from? How does it create a world that feels so real? Whose memories did it find this room in? Was it AngelCake's or Yumi's? Are these their memories or dreams? Could this be their ideal nursery? Or maybe someone else was here before us, leaving their mental imprint.

In the cradle, we find the cocoon of another Level 3 spider. I don't kill it right away; instead, I knock it to the ground and crush it underfoot with glee. A search reveals two more, under the bed and behind the door. The spiderlings are now scared of us — the level difference is starting to show. They still attack in groups but they try to run away and hide when they're alone.

I realize I'm hesitating at the last door. I've been heading towards it, yet dreading it the most. Can we handle it? Dying now, on the top floor of a spider mansion, would be a mega-fiasco.

Leaving our gear and any hope for an advantage here? We'd struggle to get them back, especially in noob gear and without the narcotic buffs Yumi injected me with. It's not like I'm going to keep abusing those substances just for this, and anyway MosTech won't let me pull today's stunt again. Marina's probably standing guard over my VR pod this very moment.

I realize that the VR pod has translated my chemical brainstorm into game stats. I'm strong, agile, fast... confident and carefree.

I remember how I felt before diving in. Interestingly, at the moment I barely feel the chemical rush that had me so fired up out in meatspace. My brain is jittery, constantly jumping from one thought to another, but not spouting nonsense. Maybe this is because only consciousness is transferred here, and all the stimulants and hormones are left in my unfortunate body outside this virtual reality.

What really bothers me is the note about stamina consuming health points. Is this just a quirky game mechanic, like a pleasant debuff, or a warning? Don't overdo it, or you'll drop dead. It's unsettling not knowing if the same also applies to meatspace.

"Yumi, you open it and stay outside... Simba and I will go in... whatever's there, aggro it immediately... then Stacy comes in and shoots to stun... Yumi, you enter last and DON'T TOUCH A THING!"

Simba and I stand at the door like elite commandos. All that's left is to gesture at each other, as if to say, "let's go in and take them down." For a laugh, I point at him, then me, then around. Simba gets I and laughs. Yumi mistakes his laughter for the order to go, opens the door... and we burst into the room still laughing.

It's empty! No furniture, no mobs. The room is utterly bare, only a web fluttering at the sole window like a creepy gothic curtain.

We've been beaten to the punch! I blew it!!! Damn it! Damn it! DAMN IT ALL! I stamp around the room, furiously punching the wall! I'm lucky I don't break my finger, just lose some HP.

How could this happen? I calculated everything! The mini-boss was in the left house, so there should be one in the right. Even if Anna decided to farm it, she'd go to the familiar place first. We had a chance!

I recall the room drenched in green spider slime. It was just like this one! If someone had been here before us, there'd be a mess. But nothing means I just drew a blank. Comforting? Not at all!

"What's wrong, Andrew? We did great! Leveled up, cleared the house..." AngelCake chimes in.

That's positive thinking for you. Add to that that we didn't get killed... also a great achievement.

"Targe!" Simba puts a hand on my shoulder. Annoyed, I shrug it off.

I go to the window and tear through the web. It overlooks the main nest. This house is higher, and from here, you can see life teeming under the web layer. Spiders carry larvae up and down, like ants trying to burrow... burrow...

"Guys!" I suddenly shout. "Quick, down to the first floor! Was there anything that resembled a cellar on the way in?"

"There was," Simba suddenly says. "I shut the trapdoor so they wouldn't come out, and so we wouldn't fall in accidentally."

I don't know whether to kill him or kiss him. We rush downstairs, and he points out the spot on the move. A large copper ring is clearly visible on the floor, though the trapdoor itself is so expertly cut you'd miss it if you weren't looking.

Simba pulls it, and the trapdoor pops open with a thud. The cellar reeks of dampness, decay, and something acidic, like vinegar. There's also a constant clicking and crackling, as if the cellar is chockfull of spiders.

"I'm going in," I nod to everyone and step down the stairs.

Chapter 04

THE CELLAR IS DARK. Sounds clichéd, but it's true. You can't see a thing. A square of light from the open trapdoor falls on the steep wooden staircase, which looks terrifying to go down. One slip or misstep and you'll tumble down into the endless darkness.

I wish I had even the most basic flashlight or a kerosene lamp. However, so far, I've seen no fire in this game world. It's a shame because I'd love to burn this creepy place down. On the other hand, I doubt I'd get any XP for doing that, so what would be the point...

I descend carefully, ready to dash back up at any moment. "Dash" is a bit of an exaggeration; I would climb back up like a blind turtle. So slowly that even a one-legged spider could catch me.

The darkness is full of rustling sounds. I already know the sounds the spiders make, and that's definitely them. At long last, my foot feels the floor. I've made it down in one piece.

"What do you see?" Simba asks from above.

Geez! He scared me. I look up. My three companions are leaning over the hatch, staring down. No wonder it's so dark!

"Move away, you're blocking the light! I can't see a damn thing."

They're curious and so am I — curious about what lurks in the dark. My companions pull back reluctantly, and it immediately gets lighter around me. It takes a while for the square of light to stop dancing before my eyes. I stand still for a few minutes, letting my eyes adjust, then slowly start to make out the shapes of objects.

The cellar is crammed with what looks like bales or bundles. I push one, and tiny spiderlings spill out onto the floor. They're the size of ordinary hairy spiders you find in the tropics — or like the ones some idiots keep in their apartments and feed cockroaches to. They're ordinary spiders really, but after the monsters we've seen here, they seem pretty small. They have thin, semi-transparent shells which reveal their pale green, glowing insides. Bah, how revolting!

I stomp on them in disgust. The crunching and clicking grow closer. I see something large moving towards me through the cocoons, lit by green hairs. It looks like an absolutely black mass in the dark gray gloom. A meter away, glowing eye spots and acid-green mandibles dripping glowing venom appear. Goddamn, this is terrifying!

I bolt up the stairs like I've got a rocket strapped to my butt, barely using my arms and legs. Hairy black spider legs try to grab at me, scratching at my legs and the staircase. I manage to escape, thanks to my agility and probably some luck.

The creature is raging below but it doesn't climb up after me. In the light, I can only see its powerful head, with hook-like jaws. It looks more like a scorpion than a spider, though I can't see the rest of its body yet.

"We need to lure it out somehow," I say.

"Do you think it's worth it?" Simba looks doubtfully down the stairs, "Maybe we should just leave it? It's down there, and we're up here. Seems like we're safer here..?"

"Exactly," Stacy agrees to my surprise. "I hate these creatures in general, and this one's the grossest yet."

"First, it's XP," I count off on my fingers, "and second, it's loot. That's why I brought you here anyway."

"Uh-huh," Stacy drawls skeptically, "I thought we were running around like headless chickens. Turns out you were leading us, huh? A great guide you are."

"That's why I'm the one doing the thinking here, not you." I raise my voice, quelling the mutiny on board. "Enough backtalk out of you. Now go ahead and lure the thing out here."

"Me?! How?!" AngelCake cries flabbergasted. "Are you going to send me down there as bait?"

"No," I slap my forehead. "Fuck, who am I dealing with here? Damage it from a distance," I explain slowly, seeing Anastasia's puzzled face. "Shoot at it with your slingshot to make it come out."

"And if it doesn't?" Stacy asks doubtfully.

"If it doesn't, you'll eventually kill it. All the better for us."

"Maybe I should try to aggro it?" Simba suggests.

"Go ahead and try," I shrug, "but I doubt you'll get its attention. It's too far away and its aggro-zone is probably just the cellar."

Indeed, no matter how much Simba bangs his shield, Yumi is the only one affected by his *Brrrongs*. First, she retreats to the farthest corner of the room, then she squats down and covers her ears, and finally she starts to quietly whimper:

"You noisy bastard... I'd kill you myself..."

Interestingly, the Simba's aggro aura isn't felt inside our party. It's just a sound, albeit a slightly unpleasant one... But I remember the feeling when I first heard it. It was like being turned inside out and wanting nothing other than to tear the source of the noise to pieces.

I imagine this kind of skill will evolve in the future and start to vary from player to player. Because if use this skill to farm in crowded areas, other players will skewer you before the mobs get a chance.

While Simba experimented, I peeked out the mansion's window. The guards had reached the fence and secured the breach in it. We had led the way and they had followed in our footsteps. But now they faced the path up to the mansion which was chockfull of surprises. For their part, they seemed to know what to expect and took their time, forming themselves into a tight formation, like a Roman *testudo*, before setting out.

They advanced slowly, systematically aggroing all the mobs lurking in the branches above them. Dozens of spiders threw themselves at the guards, gnashing their mandibles on their steel armor and trying to find a gap between the shields.

Their fun didn't last long, however, because three ranks of crossbowmen brought up the guards' rear. First rank: fire! Second rank: fire! Third rank: fire! By the time the third rank shot its bolts, the first had already reloaded. Like a jet stream, the barrage of crossbow bolts swept the mobs off the guards' armor.

Watching their progress, I felt less and less eager to tussle with these guys, let alone pick a fight with them. The town guards seemed to learn fast, adapt to any tactical challenges and were generally becoming a more formidable fighting force right before our eyes. And that meant that our time was running out. Once their formation reached us, we'd have no more time to farm XP.

"Get to it, Stacy!"

AngelCake approaches the cellar entrance, her lips puffed up at the cosmic injustice of it all, yet she does as ordered and raises her slingshot.

Thwack! Thwack! The stones strike the spider queen's head without fazing her however.

The boss seems annoyed, hissing and clicking, yet she doesn't climb up. The stones bounce off her armor like peas. I remember how thick the armor was on the Level 7s, barely penetrable even with my *Precise Strike*.

"I think her regen is greater than your damage," I rib the puzzled AngelCake.

"How about we throw Yumi down there?" Simba suggests, dead serious.

"Why the heck would we do that?" I'm bewildered.

"Maybe the spider queen will eat her," Simba takes a dramatic pause, "get poisoned by her own venom and die."

"What venom?" I'm slow to catch his drift.

"Her own," Simba triumphs, "Maybe we could feed Yumi some spider venom, just to be sure!"

"Eat it yourself!" Yumi retorts.

She never takes such teasing personally. But Simba should be careful. Not only is she three levels higher, but she's also an outlaw with nothing to lose, and he's just joking around.

The idea about the venom swirls in my head until it finally clicks.

"Stacy, can you shoot this thing at her?" I hand her a spider's venom gland.

Stacy hums skeptically, places the soft sack into her sling, draws and fires. The spider queen bellows beneath our feet. She rampages through the cellar, trampling cocoons and clicking her mandibles, a toxic green stain spreading on her head.

"Shoot her again, Stacy! You're doing it!" I hand her more venom glands.

The spider queen climbs the lower steps, almost stands upright, and leaps up. I barely manage to push Stacy who's too busy shrieking away from the edge and roll to the opposite side.

The creature thunders out of the cellar. Now I can finally see her better. She's the size of a small car, like a Nissan Leaf but twice as squat and low to the ground. Her spider legs are long and jointed, with hooks at the ends. I bet she can climb walls too.

The spider queen's jaws have grown huge and now resemble pincers. The elongated body ends in a scorpion-like egg-laying tail. This disgusting appendage is coiled over its back like a spring, with a real stinger at the end, dripping green venom.

The spider queen skids across the floor, charging at Stacy. She screams and scrambles up the stairs. The spider queen follows hot on her heels.

"Simba, aggro her!" Our tank tries to draw the enemy's attention, but the spider queen doesn't care. She's locked onto her prey.

"Stacy, jump!"

"It's too high!"

"Jump, you fool!"

AngelCake climbs over the balustrade and jumps down. She doesn't land gracefully, tumbling and hitting her shoulder hard, then lying still, probably in disbelief at being alive.

Crack! The balustrade splinters and the spider queen comes crashing down right on top of Simba! She pins him down completely, trying to snatch his shield with her legs. The stinger wiggles on her tail, looking for a spot to land a fatal blow.

"Die!" I rush at the spider queen, cross my stilettos like scissors, and with a counter-movement, cut off her egg-laying tail. Take that!

The creature shrieks! The short stump sprays venom. Some droplets hit me, burning fiercely. My life bar plummets and my HP streams away in my log.

"Get this thing off me!" Simba's muffled voice comes from under the spider queen.

She tries to bite him, starting with his face. Simba desperately pushes his shield into her jaws. Her legs beat against his body, seemingly piercing his paladin's chain mail.

I strike where a rear leg attaches to its chitinous armor. A few hacks from my sword and the leg falls off.

"Yumi, over here!" I call. "Do like I did!"

The guilt-ridden assassin has been standing quietly by the wall, not even trying to join the fight. Hearing me, she springs into action. We move along either side of the spider queen, lopping off her legs like branches. A few moments later the boss has become a vicious, but immobile, caterpillar.

I kick her off Simba and roll away. The spider

queen clicks and cracks, unable to do anything. Even writhing is beyond her now.

I approach, dodging her jaws, and start stabbing the carapace on her abdomen.

I work like a sewing machine, striking with piercing blows... left... right... left... then my *Precise Strike* resets, and I hit harder, aiming for where her eyes are.

The spider queen dies after the sixty-second hit. The wave of pleasure knocks me off my feet: Level 7... Level 8... Level 9... My body arches with delight, gaining three levels almost simultaneously. Simba, covered in dirt and spider guts, laughs joyously beside me. I can't even hear Stacy, though she got her levels too.

Still, I'm disappointed. Level 9 is good and all, but I expected more. How did Anna get to Level 15? Sure, I shared my XP with two others. But still, it doesn't add up...

Thoughtfully, I approach the loot. The spider queen's remains look like she was blown up from within. There's venom all over the floor, as well as chunks of her armor and her head. I gather the pieces, placing them in my inventory. There are eight pieces of carapace, just like last time with Anna. Not all fit into my inventory, so I hand three to Simba. When I place the ninth piece of loot in my inventory, I can read what it is: Spider Queen's Head (Quest Item: see the mayor).

I'll rush right over, as soon as I can. Maybe I can even bargain for Yumi's amnesty.

"Simba, let's head down to the cellar," I say.

"Why the heck?! We just killed it, didn't we?" Simba lies on his back, looking like he's ready to stay there until we log out of the game.

"We need to deal with the little spiderlings down there."

We go downstairs, and on a hunch, I throw a spider's venom gland on the floor. I've got plenty of these. The venom spreads out into a glowing pale green puddle, bright enough to light up the space. I throw a few more around — on the walls and even risk tossing one at the ceiling.

One... two... three... twelve cocoons. What to do with them? Using a sword or dagger to kill each spiderling is like counting grains of sand on a beach.

Drop them on the floor and stomp on them? It's an idea, but it'll take forever too. Think, brain, think! We don't have fire or water... but we do have spider venom. The queen didn't like it — it made her roaring mad.

I approach a cocoon, take out a clump of venom gland from my inventory, and smear it on the cocoon.

"Simba, squash this thing with your shield."

He doesn't need to be told twice. Simba smashes the cocoon with his shield, spreading the green goo all over it. The cocoon starts glowing from the inside... something squirms and runs around in there. It's disgusting. The next cocoon goes faster, and then we get into a rhythm.

Once we're done with the last cocoon, it hits me:

YOU HAVE DESTROYED A GREEN-CROSS SPIDER NEST.

+10,000 XP.

I collapse on the dirty floor, the levels washing over me until I hit Level 12. My nails scrape the concrete, my hand lands in a poisonous puddle, and my life ticks down. Get up... get up, you rag! You're the strongest now, the King of the Hill. The Alpha and the top of the food chain. I've got thirty unallocated stat points. I throw five into Constitution, just in case, as I won't be able to carry loot otherwise. Fifteen more go into Dexterity. Ten into Strength.

My body feels weightless. I'm light as a feather on the wind. I leap up the stairs, doing a somersault on the way. I'd never manage this in real life, but here, easy!

Simba and Stacy are at Level 8. We congratulate each other. I even think about adjusting the XP distribution next time, giving each 30%. No need for them to lag too far behind; it'll make farming inconvenient.

Yumi has turned from a leader into a weakling. There's envy in her eyes. I ignore her. She chose her fate. I peek out the window again. The guards have covered at least half the distance to the house. The crossbowmen have leveled up as well — they're already at Level 4. They're methodically and relentlessly following the outlaw's trail.

The ground floor is unbearable, with remnants of the dead spider queen everywhere. We go upstairs, dragging all sorts of junk onto the staircase on the way: wardrobes, chairs, a tea table, and even a couch higher up. I don't know if this will slow down the guards much, but we've got nothing better to do. We've fully completed today's quest. All that's left is to wait for it to end, and it's somewhat entertaining.

There are about twenty minutes left of the two hours given to us by the AI. Just need to sit them out calmly.

I choose the third room, the one with no furniture and barely any spiders. Just bare walls. We jam the door from the inside. I head to the window to see if any surprises are coming, and as I approach, a powerful blow knocks me back and slams me into the opposite wall.

What the hell?! That's when, I realize that we're not they only ones in this room.

Chapter 05

ANNA MAKES A DRAMATIC entrance, that's for sure. She slams me into the wall, taking a third of my HP in the process. I mentally pat myself on the back for boosting my Constitution stats. If I hadn't, I'd be crawling now, or worse, dead.

Anna's already moving on however: Recovering from her strike, she enters a low defensive stance, her eyes wild, scanning the room for threats. There's a big hole in the web that covered the window, so I guess our guest swung in from the roof. Just need to figure out her intentions — doesn't look like she's here for a friendly chat.

In real life, such a blow would've broken my spine. But here, it's just some HP and so I'm ready to fight. I lunge at her, pressing her with a flurry of attacks, my stilettos matched up against her twin Japanese swords. A katana isn't that fast. It's a two-handed sword, heavy with a lot of inertia. Good for powerful slashes, but not quick enough for close combat.

Anna is currently at Level 19. I had expected more, though I know the higher you go, the harder it gets to level up. I'm Level 12, but thanks to how the game buffed my stats based on the drugs in my system out in meatspace, I'm as strong as a Level 15 and as agile as a Level 20.

Anna was like an unstoppable force of nature for me earlier, deadly and relentless. But now we're almost equals. I can time her thrusts and counters, anticipate where her sword will go before she even moves. I even have to hold back, unwilling to give away my true capabilities too soon. That's my ace in the hole, never know when it might come in handy.

Finally, Anna strikes, slashing wide from 1 o'clock. It's a typical kendo move, which is frequently enough to start and end a duel. If it connects, no further strikes will be necessary. The katana will simply cleave me from shoulder to waist.

I dodge to the right, blocking her katana with my left-hand stiletto, forcing Anna to turn and exposing her unprotected right side. I strike!

I won't kill her with this hit; the level difference is too great, but drawing blood is a point of pride for me. I've been running, cowering and bargaining with her for too long. The time has come to reevaluate our relationship.

Pop! Anna vanishes... A kick to my back lets

me know where she went. A combat teleport! Short but insanely effective. I go tumbling again. Anna has at least eighteen skills against my three. No amount of boosted stats can beat a good build.

She hovers over me... to finish me off?!

Brrrong! Brrrong! Brrrong! Simba starts his racket.

"Will you stop this racket!" Anna leaves me, shifts quickly to Simba, and strikes him on the head with the hilt of her sword.

The blow, which is probably another skill of hers, sends Simba flying into the wall — no small feat considering he's a tank.

I regain my feet while Anna's distracted and attack her, but she switches to defense. It's all about speed now, while technique takes a back seat. Strike, dodge, block, strike...strike...block...I'm not hiding my power anymore, and Anna has to fight on equal terms. I relish the look of her shock on her face. Surprise!

"What's with the puny katana?" I strike up a conversation, like in the movies. "Couldn't find anything bigger? Or is it a woman's katana? Lightweight?... It's not kid-sized, is it?"

"Better than your toothpicks," Anna snaps back.

Her swords are quite curious actually. Shorter than traditional katanas, about a meter long, with an almost straight, thin blade. Two red tassels on their shortened hilts flare with every strike or block, distracting and confusing her opponent.

Suddenly Anna explodes in a flurry of slashes, creating an almost opaque cocoon around herself with her blades.

Zing! A dagger thrown by Yumi from stealth at close range ricochets off Anna. She deflects it in mid-air, sending it flying into the wall. Its blade glints green and smokes, while Anna quickly spins and elbows Yumi in the face. Yumi falls with her nose smashed, blood gushing on the floor.

"Tell that fool I can still see her," Anna informs me for some reason. And as she does so, she misses the incoming stone from AngelCake's slingshot, which whacks her in the head. The stun is brief, but long enough for me. Instead of striking, I duck down, grab Anna by the waist, and slam her into the wall. Revenge is what I'm after.

The first thing Anna sees after my move is the tip of my stiletto near her eye.

"You won't kill me," she says. "You're not allowed to today."

"And neither will you," I smirk. "You think I didn't realize that?"

How she handled Simba and Yumi… If she wanted to, she would have just killed them.

"So… a draw?"

"Not exactly…" I nod towards Yumi, who's just getting up from the floor, wiping bloodied snot with her sleeve. "I can't kill you. But she can."

"That's the outlaw assassin?" Anna looks at Yumi curiously — not afraid, just interested. She lowers her sword from where she'd pointed it at my liver, and I realize we're pressed right up against each other. And she's wearing only...

DEBUFF RECEIVED (SEXUAL AROUSAL): -20% to ALL STATS.

Damn! Damn! Damn! I pull away from Anna and start looking around to distract myself. The wall... Simba lying knocked out... the dagger with the green blade, it looks like it's starting to rot and crumble... such a waste of good weaponry... need to calculate the cost with Yumi... Anna's chest popping from her corset... A pool of blood... The pattern in Anna's lace stockings...

"What the hell do you dress like that for?! Couldn't you find something more decent?" I blurt out.

"To mesmerize dummies like you," Anna smiles for the first time. "I use every advantage. If you're drooling, you're already dead."

"I'm not dead," I grumble. "I got a debuff from staring at you."

"What?! No way." Anna doesn't believe me. "There's no such debuff."

"I have it. I'm unique."

I tell her about my satyriasis and Anna guffaws loudly, deliberately pulling up her stockings. She's having a blast.

"Come here," she says. "Let me see."

I'm curious. I now understand that this girl knows more about the game than Marina, the Master, and Benjamin Zvyagin combined. Every word she says is worth its weight in gold.

Anna takes my face in her hands and looks into my eyes.

"Why you're dosed out of your mind!" she says, astonished. "How did they even let you connect?"

"I'm charming," I bluster.

Anna snorts, clearly not believing me.

"What are you looking for here? I'm sure it's not us."

"The spider queen," Anna confesses. "A mini-boss. I thought there'd be a nest of these creatures here like in the house opposite. Turns out, you guys found a dud."

"No, ma'am, no duds here," AngelCake interjects, "the spider queen was down in the cellar. Emphasis on *was*."

What a dumbass. I really want to give her a piece of my mind, but that will have to wait till we're back in meatspace. Anna smirks cunningly. I bet she'll be back here nice and early tomorrow and she certainly won't start clearing this house from the top floors. I can't help regretting that Anna didn't knock out Stacy along with the others. At least we could have had a peaceful, leak-free conversation.

DEBUFF RECEIVED (SEXUAL AROUSAL): -40% to ALL STATS.

Waterfalls... It's been so long since I thought of waterfalls...

"What's with the odd katana?" I ask to distract myself.

"It's not a katana at all."

"Then what is it?"

"A Korean sword, a hanja. It's shorter, lighter

and easier to wield. Katanas weren't really used for dueling, you know."

"Yeah right," I disagree, "what about Miyamoto Musashi?"

"Who's ever even seen your Musashi?" Anna heats up. "Maybe he's just a legend."

"Right, sure. So where'd you get this sword?" I ask. "And not one, but two."

Anna has two swords, the second one just as thin but shorter. In their flat wooden scabbards, they look like two canes. Elegant and effective — I saw it for myself.

"The shop's got it all, as long as you've got the money to buy it... And by the way, you owe me," she suddenly changes topics.

I realize we really do owe her a bunch of money, but I'm bad with numbers, and Simba, who's best at bargaining, is currently knocked out.

"Will this do as a trade?" I hand her a piece of the spider queen's carapace. "Are we even?"

"Yes, perfect." She's pleased. Looks like I sold it cheap.

"And what do you mean 'the shop's got it all?'" I persist.

"The AI knows our innermost desires," Anna grows heated as she speaks. "Don't you understand how it works?! It uploads us into itself. We're an open book for it, practically a part of it. Just like these spiders or guards. It just can't command us — and that annoys it to no end."

Quickly storing the carapace in her inventory, she walks to the window. Got what she wanted, time to leave. But at the last moment, she turns to us, or more precisely, to Yumi.

"Don't let the guards catch you... and don't get killed... You're better off not connecting anymore, not entering this game. It all started this way last time too. Exactly the same way." And with that she vanishes as suddenly as she appeared.

"Hey, what do you mean it all started?! What 'last time?!'" I rush to the window, trying to stop her, but Anna's already gone.

DEBUFF RECEIVED (SEXUAL AROUSAL): -60% to ALL STATS.

"I got another debuff, Stacy," I announce.

"What's that got to do with me?" AngelCake replies.

"We need to remove it..."

"Let Yumi do it," Stacy digs in.

Yumi jumps up, ready to act.

"Yumi is punished," I say. "She can't do it."

The assassin immediately slumps and returns to the wall like a beaten dog.

"Like I said, what's that got do with me?" Stacy stands her ground.

"Well I can't ask Simba, can I?!"

"Nah bro..." Simba laughs awkwardly. "I got this vow of celibacy. You handle it."

"I can't do it myself. It won't work," I lie blatantly. "Come on Stacy, aren't you ashamed? Think about our squad's combat readiness."

Stacy looks around suspiciously, probably sensing she's being watched. She approaches closely and tells me in a sultry tone: "Take off your pants."

She doesn't go down for a blowjob, just strokes me with her hand from below, biting her lip in concentration.

"Show me your boobs at least, Stacy..."

"No way..."

"I won't come otherwise, Stacy..."

She stashes her leather jacket in the inventory with the same look of concentration on her face. Freed, her supple breasts begin to bounce with each movement of her hand.

"M-m-m-m!"

At some point, her plump bustiness and skilled hand movements remind me of milkmaids, and I come, bending over laughing. Andrew the tribal bull has been milked.

There's a little more than twenty minutes left until the end of the quest. This time the AI gave us two hours. Each immersion is getting longer, and I wouldn't be surprised if we soon spend entire days in VR. As long as it's well paid, I don't mind.

We just sit and begin waiting out the time that remains. Yumi starts whining.

"Andrew... Why are you bothering to save me? This is all my fault... You should have turned me in right away..."

"Enough!" I cut her off. "We just need to hold out a little longer..."

Just then, dull thuds sound from the floor below, there's a crash as the mansion's front door flies off its hinges and we can hear the guards come stomping in.

"Don't resist," I instruct my party. "Don't attack the guards, just try to BUY US TIME."

Now noise comes from behind our door, the sound of furniture being moved. Something falls heavily down the stairs, maybe a wardrobe. The steps get closer...

Knock... knock... knock... A polite knocking on our door.

"Who's there?" I answer mechanically.

"Town guard! We're here to take the outlaw to the mayor to face justice..."

"Just a minute, the lock is jammed."

I pull the door towards me while the guards try to open it. Simba helps, or rather, he's mainly the one pulling, while I argue with the guards.

The guards' patience is wearing thin. Or maybe they, like us, feel that time is running out. Could the AI be telling them how long the quest will last? They knock on the door again, louder now in warning, and then yank it open. The door swings open and four guards burst in with a large log that they were using as a battering ram. It immediately gets crowded in our room. Ungainly, they try to turn around while we stand by, not helping.

When the guards with the battering ram are pushed out, a Level 5 officer appears with four pikemen. He scans our faces sternly, especially AngelCake's, then turns his attention to the window with the hole in the web. The implication is clear — everything suggests that the assassin escaped through the window.

But the Level 5 doesn't let up, he first examines the windowsill, almost sniffing it. Then he takes out a snuffbox, grabs a pinch of powder and tosses it into the air.

"*Aaah-choo!*" comes from the void, "*Ahchoo... Ahchoo...*"

As the dust falls, it settles over a semi-transparent silhouette, bringing it gradually into focus like a Polaroid. Yumi is revealed standing among us, desperately wiping her nose and sneezing.

"There she is, the outlaw! Seize her!" the officer orders and the pikemen approach Yumi.

They're pretty cautious, however. After all, they are Level 3s and their prisoner is Level 7. The officer realizes this too. He takes out a whistle hanging on his chest, just like mine, blows it, and four crossbowmen enter the room.

These guys are Level 6-7. Were they just hanging out in the alley outside? These guys can turn us into pincushions with their bolts. The officer also draws his sword, just in case.

Seeing that things are going south, I wedge myself between the officer and Yumi.

"Officer! I have urgent business with the mayor."

"What business?" he grumbles.

I pull out the spider queen's head from my inventory. It's clearly a quest item, and to complete the mission, I need to go to the mayor. The guards should respond to that.

The officer's eyes grow wide. Slaying a

monster like that is no ordinary feat.

"We'll escort you," he offers, "but this... this girl will go with us."

Whether she'll go or not, what's the difference. The main thing is not to hurry. We're buying time here...

The pathway in front of the mansion is completely cleared. There are piles of dust on the ground that were spiders, tendrils of web on the trees. I wouldn't be surprised if after the mansion is completely cleared, the hardworking guards will even make some repairs, do some painting, whitewashing, and so on.

We walk as if we're being escorted by a guard of honor. Yumi's with the rest of us. The guards don't even look back at us, but the other players in the area stop what they're doing, watch, and whisper.

"There goes the outlaw... The outlaw is being led away..."

"That guy in black ratted her out... Must be raking in the dough now..."

"No, she's in black too... they're all in the same party..."

"They say they killed a bunch of people... horrible."

"Psychos..."

The mayor's residence turns out to be a big edifice right next to the town square. Just yesterday, it was like any other building, surrounded by a high fence. Now, it's all lit up, there's music's playing, and it's swarming with guards and civilians.

"Welcome, oh brave warriors!" a voice booms from the heavens.

Everyone on our way stops, looks, and applauds. I'm sure that after such a reception, they might go easy on Yumi, or maybe even grant her amnesty.

The mayor's enjoying his wine, immersed in conversation. He's sitting at a small table with two non-player characters, one of whom, to my surprise, is the merchant. Who's running the shop, then?

Seeing us, the mayor jumps to his feet and launches into his speech as he approaches.

"You alone weren't afraid to fight the monster, and you managed to defeat it," he says pompously but quickly. "This town is grateful to you and ready to reward you generously."

"What about this girl?" I ask, pointing to Yumi.

"What about her?" the mayor asks naively.

"She won't be punished, right?"

The mayor frowns, as if it's hard for him to hold more than one thought in his head at a time.

"Let's deal with you first, then we'll talk about the outlaw. You're entitled to a gift from the town's treasury. Take your time choosing and be sure to choose wisely."

Having concluded his speech, the mayor sits back down at the table. The merchant stands up in his place.

"Come, I'll show you to the treasury."

Yumi starts to follow us, but pikes cross to bar her way.

"What's the problem?"

"Well, she's not entitled to any rewards," explains the merchant. "Don't worry, she'll wait for you here."

Here or not... the main thing is that time's about to run out, and we're all about to pop back into reality in our VR pods.

The treasury turns out not to be in the basement, as I initially thought. They've dedicated a whole separate hall in the adjacent wing to it. And when I walk in, the only thing I can manage to say is "Whoa!"

Chapter 06

THE HUGE HALL is brightly lit. Several massive chandeliers hang from the high, vaulted ceilings. Below them stand tables, sturdy and very long. A single one could host several wedding parties. There are no chairs, however. Instead, the tables serve as huge display counters to showcase the goods.

It's like I've walked into Aladdin's or Ali Baba's cave — I don't remember which had the greater treasures. And there's no silly gold, nor trinkets — only weapons and gear. There are simple noob swords, Level 1 dirks, my familiar stilettos, heavy rapiers with daggers, cavalry sabers and shashkas, ferocious-looking bastard swords and Zweihanders with flaming blades, Lance's beloved "cat skinners," timeless Carolingians, and classic Roman gladii. Halberds, bardiches and glaives stand in neat rows by the tables. Heavy cavalry pikes stand close by, though for what, I have no idea, since I haven't seen a single horse or other mount in this game yet. However, the AI loves surprises, so who knows what's coming down the line.

This place is a sword nerd's wet dream. Further on are Eastern specimens: Chinese dao swords and bō staffs, Japanese sai and naginatas. I see Anna's Korean swords with red tassels, but I've already forgotten their name. And there's a daishō too, a pair of Japanese swords. I almost rub my eyes in disbelief. Right there on the counter is my tournament set from the Gladiator Games — black octagonal scabbards with bright red hilt wrapping... I thought these swords had been deleted long ago, along with the rest of my combat gear. Removed after I was kicked out of the esports league. I thought they only existed in my head, in my memory.

Swish... the blade leaves the scabbard with a whisper as quiet as rustling leaves. Reflections from hundreds of candles on the chandeliers stream along the blade. It's still razor-sharp... I guess, you don't have to sharpen blades in VR. +20% to damage, +20% to evasion, +20% to critical hit chance. How I want to try them out... and the sooner, the better...

I never truly liked kendo, that silly art of ritual dances with wooden sticks, yet now my body naturally assumes the "middle stance." The sword moves like an extension of my arm, like a part of me, matching the balance that my body still remembers.

I look around. Do these tables really contain the dreams of all the players who've entered the beta? Are these the very Katzbalgers Lance used in the arena? All these Carolingians, sai, and glaives living in someone's imagination, waiting for their rightful owners. I wonder what else the AI can pull from our memories, if we're so transparent to it?

"TargetAi, loooook," AngelCake almost squeals, "Can I have this? Please? Please?!"

All her sulking and pouting is gone in a flash. Stacy coyly sticks out her leg, showing off her figure. She's wearing a short, gold metallic dress that clings to her curves like a glove. It makes her look like a jazz singer with a full on big band to back her up.

"Is that armor?!"

"Yeah, can you imagine? It's scalable too! +10% to Dexterity, and -25% to all incoming damage!" AngelCake begins rambling, trying to persuade me.

Only now do I observe that this sexy little number on her is actually chain mail, woven from the finest rings of golden metal. I don't know what could possess such marvelous protective properties, mithril or adamantium, maybe...

Time to get used to the fact that things aren't always what they seem in here. Even a swimsuit can have protective properties if it has the right stats. It makes the skin itself tougher. Offensive skills work the same way. My *Precise Strike* can crit even a knight clad in full armor: Either my sword will find a weak spot on its own, or if not, it will burn its way through the metal.

Of course this is obvious in any video game, but here where everything looks so real, the laws of MMORPGs seem wild. I need to reacclimate, to live by these rules. My brain needs reformatting.

"Oh, there are shoes to match!" Stacy starts changing shoes, arching her back and sticking out her butt. Like a call girl Cinderella getting ready for her royal ball...

The hem of her tiny dress creeps up...

DEBUFF RECEIVED (SEXUAL AROUSAL): -20% to ALL STATS.

Damn! Not now! This cursed debuff will end up ruining sex for me entirely. Get it on, let off steam, and back into battle I go. Thanks, buddy, but we gotta go, I'll hold them, you do the damage... Ugh! I'll kill Yumi when we get out of here... Or maybe first have my way with her, then kill her... damn!

Just have to hold out till the end... What's left? 1:32... 1:31... I can make it. Just need to pick a prize. Can't miss this chance because of some fluke debuff. Opportunities like this don't come twice. And I'm not even sure that any status effects will remain with us next time we enter the game. The "town authorities" might not even recognize us next time.

"Andrew, look!" Simba's ecstatic, holding a powerful riot shield over his head. "+100% to armor, +150% to throwing, +10% to deflection! Why this thing's a portable fortress!"

Simba is a born tank. Even his dreams are... unbreakable.

"Stacy, isn't there anything more decent in there?" I try not to even look her way, to keep my debuff from getting worse.

"You always liked the indecent stuff before," Stacy retorts pluckily.

I don't get it — is she flirting or what? And I thought she was still mad at me. Maybe if she hadn't come across that nightgown... uh... chain mail, she might still be sulking. But circumstances have changed.

"We've made our choice," I turn around and encounter the merchant's calm, even sympathetic smile.

But, I mean, is he really a mere merchant anymore? His doublet is embroidered with gold, he's got rings with stones on his fingers, and a ridiculously massive chain with a multi-rayed star pendant around his neck. Must be some kind of treasurer now. That's what drinking with the mayor does for you. The operation expands, and the right people take the key positions. The AI even copies this. Wonder whose brain it pulled it from...

"One item," the merchant's smile widens. "Your reward is one item. Or one set, like these swords count as one set. Or the chain mail and shoes of this young lady..."

ONE?! Out of all these amazing choices, I have to pick just one thing! What a dilemma. Though logically, I get it, one quest — one reward. But how do you figure out in... 40 seconds, what's going to be the most useful for my team? And do it without making mortal enemies out of your FORMER friends? Surely, they could still turn on me.

"Andreeeew!" Stacy whines, pursing her lips.

"Andryusha!" Simba shouts, brandishing the shield he wants in the air.

What's the best decision for my party? Clarity — as clear as a diamond and as pure as mountain air — comes to me as the quest timer counts down its last seconds...

* * *

"Is he alive in there?"

"His vitals are normal, his blood pressure a bit high and his pulse is quick though..."

"Open it already!"

"Don't rush us, lady, we have protocols here..."

"Don't you call me 'lady!'"

"Well, you sure look like one..."

"Jerk! I'll be reporting you for that!"

The voices outside are irritating. More than irritating, they're infuriating! They're getting into my head, making my hands tremble and fumble inside this pod... Bastards... How much longer do I have to be trapped in here? I knock from the inside... Gently, I think, but the pod's lid rattles loudly. Oh that's right, I have a strength buff... but wait, what buff?! This is meatspace... Damn it, how long do I have to wait here...?

"Help him! Help him! Open the pod! He's in trouble!" I recognize AngelCake's voice.

"Come on, Sergio, open it, he's gonna puke in there..." says an older, male voice.

Damn it, I'll give him a piece of my mind once I get out. He's worried about his precious pod while I'm suffocating in here. I'll beat that Sergio for being too slow too and the "I'm no lady to you" lady for her annoying voice. So whiny, as if everyone owes her something. The others better stay quiet and keep their heads down and then maybe I'll leave them alone.

The pod lid hisses and slides upwards. There's a whole welcoming committee waiting for me. Two techs — Sergio, whom I'm familiar with, and his grumpy older partner. I feel like punching his gloomy face.

Simba and AngelCake are there, in robes, like they just came from a bathhouse. They didn't even change before rushing over to me. Curiously, Yumi is not here. Scared to show her face, the bitch. Good, I'll kick her off our team and she can play on her own.

I hate losers like her, always causing problems and leaving others to clean up their mess. In the game, I felt sorry for her because she had nowhere to go, and because her situation was advantageous for me. But I won't be protecting her anymore. She can kick rocks.

I climb out of the VR pod, not bothering to cover up. They've seen it all in the game anyway. I stand up, searching for my slippers with my bare feet, and suddenly the floor tilts and shifts. I grab the pod's edge to keep my balance.

An older technician rushes to help me.

"Fuck off," I growl at him to back off.

Everyone else takes a step back with him just in case. It must have been a convincing growl indeed. Sergio looks panicky. Probably forgot to prepare a syringe. Lucky him. I would've shoved that syringe up his ass.

Marina is also not here, which surprises me. She should have been the one to meet me, since she's the one who stuffed me into the pod. Instead, there's this skinny chick, model-like with a doll face. Why is she here instead of Marina? She's dressed in the office uniform: a white blouse, and a skirt that's a bit too short. Marina's not here and this girl is... It's easy to add two and two.

"Hello, Mr. Andrew." She tries to keep a straight face, but keeps glancing down, "My name is Christina, I'm ready to assist you in any way..."

"Really? In any way?" I smirk.

I get why she's blushing and fidgeting, but I don't sympathize. Nobody asked Christina to come here and why she did remains unclear.

I grab a robe from the hanger and casually wrap myself in it. Finally, I slip my feet into my slippers. I look almost presentable now. Time to head to the locker room. But first, one question.

"Where's Marina?"

"You mean Marina Skvortsova?" the skinny girl asks. "She's been fired... for incompetence!" Her face cycles through a range of emotions, from malice to triumph. “You may address any inquiries you have to me from now on. Senior management has put me in charge of… Ah!”

She yelps in surprise as I shove her aside and stalk out into the hallway.

“Where are you going, Mr. Andrew?!” she calls after me. “She’s already packed up and left. You won’t catch her… And I’m much more professional… Just give me a chance, and you’ll see!”

“Andryusha, wait! You need to go to the locker room first!”

“You need to rest, Andrew…”

The rage inside of me has now found a purpose and a target. I rush down the hallway, skidding in front of the guards near the stairs and elevator. They’re all wearing sunglasses again. I guess the guy whose glasses I borrowed has changed shifts or stolen new ones from someone else.

As I pass them, I slow down and push the elevator call button.

“Hey, where do you think you’re going?!” One of them steps forward. “This area is off-limits!”

“Off limits, eh? All right… I thought I’d take a shortcut… I’ll go around then…”

I wait until the elevator behind the security guy opens, and then, as it starts to close, I dart under the guard’s arm, outstretched to stop me. But I’m faster… stronger…

The second guard lunges at me. I land an oblique kick on his knee, leaving him flailing on the floor. Bunch of noobs! They're big guys all right, but the bigger they are, the harder they fall.

First, I think of checking if Marina is still in the building. But the new doll's last words make me change my mind. "Packed up" means "gone for good." I'm not sure what irritates me more, that Marina promised me sex in a nurse's outfit and now that won't happen, or that the bigwigs fired an employee willing to do anything for her damn job.

Third floor... fourth... fifth. The elevator stops and I dart between the opening doors. The guards are stomping and panting like rhinos up the stairs behind me. I can hear them even several floors above them.

Out of habit, I want to jam the door with something, but realize that there aren't any convenient locks or furniture to create obstacles out here in reality. So, I storm into the Master's office instead.

The secretary at the reception desk just glances at me. As if I pose no threat and there's no need to stop me.

The Master is there, as usual, fiddling with something on his computer, huffing and puffing like a cartoon hedgehog. There's no sign of alarm from him either.

"Why did you fire Marina?" I start. "She did everything you asked. She really tried her best. And you just tossed her out like trash!"

"What's it to you?" he replies. "She's our employee, not yours."

Riddle me this, riddle me that. What do I say? Because Marina is the only person I trust in this corporation? Because she's nice to my mom? Because my balls ache to fuck her again, especially in stockings and a white coat? Because she helped me, took risks for me? Because I'm just used to her?

"Because I WANT it that way!" I growl.

And at that moment, I don't care what the right answer is. My right shoulder starts to rise, ready to wipe that smug smile off his face. This so-called Master of Destinies!

"Now, now..." the Master says soothingly, placing a hand on my shoulder, "Don't make a mess. Why are you so upset?.. I thought you'd like Christina... picked her for you myself... like for my own son."

"I don't like her!"

"Then why come to me? I don't make firing decisions."

He grabs my wrist and pulls me along briskly.

"Where are we going?" I ask, stunned.

"Why to the HR department, where else?"

We pass the unflappable secretary and nearly collide with the panting guards and their telescopic batons. The Master stops them and sends them back to their posts with a grand gesture.

We don't have far to go, practically to the next office. The room, more like a small conference hall, is so bland, there's nothing to catch the eye. Standard tables and chairs, a nondescript screen on the wall...

However, the people sitting there are anything but ordinary. Out of the three present, I only personally know Benjamin Zvyagin, but for obvious reasons, I don't approach him to shake hands. Everyone in here seems busy anyway. Benjamin Zvyagin is intently speaking on his smartphone, making notes on his tablet and laptop. A woman, probably the psychologist Dr. Skuratova, is watching a live stream from inside the game on her screen and doodling flowers in her old-fashioned paper notebook.

And finally, there, at the head of the table, sits none other than Dr. Dmitry Kotov, the mere mention of whose name made Marina's palms sweat and her heart race. Kotov is attentively studying something on his laptop, occasionally smiling at something that occurs to him. I don't introduce myself or even say hello. Instead, I walk the length of the conference table, grab Kotov's laptop, and hurl it against the wall. Just like that. To get their attention, so that we can have a conversation.

CHAPTER 07

"WHAT THE HELL do you think you're doing, kid!" Doc shot up from the table and got into my face. We stood there, eyeing each other like two true Alphas ready to tear each other to pieces over prey or territory. One experienced and cunning — the other young, brash and pissed. We may as well have been baring our fangs into each other's faces.

My brain felt like it was splitting in two. One part, still in control, urged me to punch this arrogant jerk in the nose and watch his blood splatter across his pristine white shirt. The other, more rational but timid part of my brain was insisting quietly that I was doing something very wrong to put it mildly and that I'd soon deeply regret it.

Laughter, boisterous and goofy, out of place in this tense moment, made both of us turn around. The Master was braying like a donkey, gasping for breath.

"What now, Doc? Looks like you've created yourself a real Terminator," he said through his braying. "Didn't you know that fighting dogs sometimes bite back? Especially when something tasty is taken from them. Be careful he doesn't give you a black eye. And remember, if you guys start a fight, I'm on his side! You really pushed the kid too far, you engineers of human souls!" And he doubled over laughing again.

The Master's laughter was like a bucket of cold water over my head. I felt like a complete clown. Dr. Kotov seemed to feel similarly because he deflated like a balloon and sitting back down.

"Sorry," I muttered.

"It happens," Doc replied, just as flatly.

"I've never seen you fight, Dmitry," said the only lady in the room, who, judging by Marina's gossip, was Dr. Skuratova, and who was looking at us with lively curiosity. "You must be good."

"Do you really need Marina?" Doc asked, changing the subject.

"She makes me feel comfortable," I replied. "I'm used to her."

"How is her performance overall?" Doc glanced around the room, addressing no one in particular.

"Well, she's a dummy all right, but she is a hard worker," Benjamin unexpectedly defended Marina.

"She's just young," added Dr. Skuratova, as if that explained everything.

Doc pulled out his smartphone, fiddled with it disdainfully, and put it to his ear: "Listen, about Marina... Yeah, the blonde one... We haven't hired a replacement yet, right...? Great, then I want you to reinstate her... What's that? Are you an idiot? You don't know how? Just ignore the firing document and that's it... I don't care where you took her, bring her back... That's right. I ordered you to fire her and now I'm ordering you to reverse that order... Give her the day off today... for health reasons... She wasn't herself today... A sick day... uh-huh..."

"They even moved the furniture out of her office," he chuckled, ending the call. "Good thing they didn't call a priest to sprinkle holy water over the floor. Your Marina seems to have many friends around the office."

I shrugged. Everyone loves the weak, while those who go their own way are mostly hated. So, this bit of sarcasm only spoke in Marina's favor.

"Maybe Andrew should tell her?" The Master put a hand on my shoulder. "You know where she lives, right?" He winked at me.

Six pairs of eyes stared at me with curiosity.

"I do," I confirmed.

I knew these childish games already... I'd been playing them for five days now. My life had split abruptly into "before" and "after," making it feel like I'd been on this project forever. So many things had happened in such a short, compressed amount of time. I had more money than I'd ever had and women too... if not in quantity, then certainly in quality. As a result, I felt no need to be shy about anything here.

"Just change your clothes first, otherwise it'll be too… romantic," Dr. Skuratova interjected.

I realized that I was still in my robe and slippers, looking like a fugitive from a psych ward. The standoff had passed, and I wasn't about to entertain anyone, so I silently turned and walked towards the exit. The funniest part was that I had nothing to change into. My clothes were back in the hospital.

"Take the car in the parking lot," the Master called after me, "one of the white Camrys."

I nodded without looking back. I was running out of energy like a dying battery, but I wanted to hold on as long as possible.

* * *

"Dear colleagues, remind me again why we're messing around with this child's play?" Doc asked patiently. "Why the hell are we wasting time on all this?"

"Teenagers are malleable…" said Dr. Skuratova.

"So what? What's so special about this damn malleability?" Doc lost his cool. "We have data analysts, IT folks, R&D guys, even armed security! We have enough resources to stage a coup in a medium-sized country without the locals even noticing!"

"Doc," the Master leaned over the table, "if we

threw you naked and empty-handed into a hostile environment, you'd be a goner for sure. And so would all your IT guys and analysts. Even your armed security. Heck, even I would. But kids, they survive. SURVIVE! And not only do they manage to stay alive, but they learn to devour others along the way. Not all of them, but those are the ones we're looking for. Remember, humans are the most dangerous animals on Earth because they adapt. But using children for our purposes is... let's just say, illegal. Teenagers, on the other hand, are fair game. Adult bodies, childish minds. Shake them up a bit, and the beast comes out."

"You're oversimplifying," Dr. Skuratova frowned. "There are psychological tools and methods..."

"I'm a pragmatist," the Master spread his hands. "I work to get results, not dissertations."

"Just make sure you can control your little monsters," Benjamin chimed in. As a technically minded person, he couldn't stand such discussions and was actually somewhat afraid of the malleable teenagers.

"We have specialists for that, right, Dr. Skuratova?" the Master said to the psychologist.

She merely smiled and nodded.

* * *

I knew how to drive, but I didn't have a license. With all the required driving classes, it was too expensive to get one in my previous life. So the

Master's offer puzzled me more than it pleased me. Sure, I could take the risk and just go for a drive, but driving without a license could easily get messy with all the unknown drugs still in my system and a DUI is not something you can easily wriggle out of.

I was also a bit concerned about clothes, but in the locker room, I found jeans, a turtleneck, high boots with thick soles, and a black, fur-lined jacket. I didn't recognize the brands, but the clothes were comfortable and, most importantly, fit perfectly. I wasn't sure whom to thank for this bit of thoughtfulness.

It turned out, however, that the Camry came with a driver. He knew the way, so I just shut my eyes and fell into a heavy drowsy state, aware of everything happening but unable to pry my eyes open.

Marina didn't open the door right away. I had to ring the doorbell for a long time, and when that didn't work, I knocked and even kicked at the door.

"Go away!" I heard Marina's voice clearly from the other side.

"Marina, it's me!"

"Go away, you," Marina was adamant. "I'll call the police."

"Ms. Skvortsova, your pipes are leaking and flooding our apartment!" I hammered the door with my palm.

The deadbolts turned and Marina's face appeared in the cracked door.

"What pipes?" She saw me and looked vaguely surprised. "Oh, it's you? Come in. Why didn't you say it was you?"

She was a little tipsy. Even a very abstentious person wouldn't call her drunk, but her klutzy movements and slightly wild eyes gave her away. That kind of look in a girl's eyes means she's calm at the moment, but could do something utterly unpredictable the next.

She was only wearing a short silk robe, carelessly fastened, and I could easily see that she had on semi-transparent, black, lace panties and no bra at all.

"Come in," Marina repeated. "Why are you standing there like a stranger?"

Her kitchen confirmed my suspicions. A bottle of red wine stood open on the bar and another empty one was on the floor. Next to the first one, there was a big chocolate cake with a fork stuck in it. Having lost her job, Marina had plunged head first into self-destruction.

"Want some?" Marina gestured at the wine.

I shook my head. I was feeling worse and worse, and I had no idea how alcohol would react with Yumi's drug cocktail in my bloodstream.

"Did you come to pity me?" Marina briskly filled her glass and downed half of it in a couple of gulps. "Or to comfort me? You guys are good at that..."

I decided I wouldn't let her spoil the moment. I was there to surprise her after all.

"Ms. Skvortsova," I began, carefully

mimicking her tone from five days ago. “I came in order to apologize on behalf of MosTech Incorporated...”

Marina’s eyes grew wide. She was starting to guess where I was going with this but still refused to believe it.

“...Your dismissal was an error, a technical glitch,” I went on. “The company requests that you return to your previous position. Keep in mind, I have to get you back by any means, so...,” I paused for effect... “You’ll have to blow me.”

“You’re not kidding?!” Marina put her glass down sharply, spilling wine. “You can’t joke about these things... I won’t forgive you if you’re messing with me now... but you’re serious, right?!” she yelped in excitement, like a kid who got a puppy for her birthday.

I nodded slowly and seriously.

“Who put you up to this?” Marina jumped up to me, grabbed my shoulders, and started shaking me. “Who? The Master? Dr. Kotov?!”

“All four of them,” I confirmed. “You were never officially dismissed. At the moment, you’re just on leave.”

Marina clung to me, squealed, and then, without loosening her grip, started kissing my neck and pulling off my turtleneck.

“Oh, I... I’d... blow you... you silly... I’d do anything...”

The turtleneck flew aside. Marina kissed down my chest, then knelt in front of me, unfastening my belt. I lowered my head, and at that moment, everything blurred before my eyes, Marina's blond hair merged into a whirlpool that swept me away, engulfing me. My battery was completely dead.

* * *

My new hospital room could not be any different than my earlier one — as different as a hotel penthouse from a homeless shelter. A bed that could be raised into any position, massaging any part of the body separately or all together. Doctors as caring as loving uncles and nurses straight out of pornos.

The nurses didn't stick around for long, however. Marina refused to leave my bedside for a second, watching their every move and chasing them away as soon as they had finished their procedures. She fed me with a spoon, changed TV channels for me, and even read me stories aloud.

Simba and AngelCake also visited. My bro brought me a new iPhone with wireless earbuds ("A replica, just like the 'Pro', no one can tell the difference"). Stacy brought me an apple pie.

Marina almost ate the whole pie, citing stress and the need for happy hormones. I didn't mind; I couldn't swallow a bite, whether from exhaustion or the meds. My IV was changed almost continuously, and according to Marina, by the next morning, I should be as fresh as a cucumber and just as green and bumpy.

One wall of the room was glass through which

I could see the visitors who weren't allowed to come inside. The Master came, talked to the doctors, and left. The head of security came. With a couple of tough guys, he walked around the hospital corridors, glaring everywhere, and then left one of the guards right outside my door. I guess they got in big trouble for attacking me, especially the second time around.

The most unexpected visitor turned out to be Anna. She burst into my room in her motorcycle gear, smelling of snow and wind. She nodded at Marina, who to my surprise, obediently left the room and shut the door behind her.

"So, you're not a junkie, huh?" Anna said. "I thought you were a druggie. I was amazed the tech people even let you enter the game in that state."

"As you can see," I gestured around the hospital room, "it was a matter of last resort."

"And did the game really hit you with the horny debuff?" Anna snorted into her fist.

She seemed a lot younger when she did that. Like she was my age, or maybe even younger. I took a good look at her, taking advantage of my status as a hospital patient. What else is there to do when you're sick and there happen to be pretty girls around? They say it even helps you recover faster.

Anna was beautiful. But it wasn't immediately obvious. She didn't have AngelCake's luxurious chest, Yumi's plump lips, or Marina's in your face sexuality. In her coveralls, she seemed boyish at first glance.

Yet the features of her face could easily be described as aristocratic. I had never seen real aristocrats, but for some reason, I thought they looked just like her. An elegant nose, big dark eyes with long eyelashes, sensual lips that a plastic surgeon could only ruin. Her figure was sculpted like an Italian statue, and her hair was wild and unruly.

“Yep, it was unbearable,” I confirmed. “All my stats were impaired until I could... umm... release the tension.”

“And is it gone now?” Anna asked curiously.

I didn’t know what to say until I realized she was teasing me.

“Unfortunately,” I nodded.

“The AI loves you,” Anna said oddly. “If she’s playing pranks on you, it means you’re special.”

“You talk as if it’s alive.”

“Why wouldn’t it be?” she seemed surprised. “She grows, learns, thinks. Of course, she’s alive.”

“That’s good, right? That it loves me?” I asked, guessing.

“It’s bad,” Anna replied. “It means she wants to claim you for herself.”

Her words rattled in my head for a long time. The mayor, the merchant, even the five-star officer all seemed like living people to me. They had personalities. I wonder what they thought of me?

Later in the evening, when normal hospitals would call lights out, Marina got a phone call. She talked on the phone behind the glass partition for a long time and then came back in looking gloomy and puzzled.

“We have to go,” she said.

“Where?!” I was hoping they’d let me be sick at least until morning.

“They’ve called an emergency meeting in Dr. Kotov’s office. We’re needed... you’re needed,” she corrected herself.

She seemed to have accepted that I was now her main project. Like an agent to a writer or singer, she looked after me, hoping for profit down the line. What exactly she wanted, I didn’t know. I wasn’t very savvy when it came to office politics. I could tell now, however, that Marina was not hiding her intentions but rather displaying them openly.

We were silent in the car for almost the entire ride. Only near the destination did Marina find my hand and squeeze it tightly.

“Andrew, I’m scared,” she confessed.

“What are you afraid of?” I was surprised. “They seem like nice people on the whole. And working with them is fun.”

“You just don’t understand who you’re dealing with,” Marina wrapped herself in her fur coat, even though it was warm in the car. “Did you see Dr. Kotov’s watch? I googled it. It’s a Patek Philippe — one such watch costs 1.5 million euros. That’s more than we’ll earn in our lifetimes. These people don’t think about money anymore — only power matters to them. And you think they’re nice people?!” She squeezed my fingers painfully. “If they treat you like their equal, it means they need something from you. And the nicer and more normal they seem, the more dangerous that something they need is."

Despite the late hour, the MosTech tower was lit up like daytime. Technicians were running through the corridors, exchanging phrases in their respective argots. Employees who hadn't managed to get home were brewing coffee in buckets for their bosses who were working late.

Still smarting from her recent humiliation, Marina walked through the corridors like a queen to her throne. Guards straightened up and forgot to breathe at the sight of her, while office bitches ducked into their offices as she approached.

Entering the reception, Marina dropped her fur coat into the curly-haired secretary's arms, checked herself in the mirror, and, exhaling as if before a jump into the water, approached the door.

She needn't have bothered; no one paid any attention to her arrival. All four were focused on the screen which had a feed from inside the game. It was a view of the town square. The platform that had been erected there had had new additions made to it. One of them was stocks.

Two large, rough boards with holes cut out of them in order to clamp down on a penitent's neck and wrists. Right now, there was a girl locked in them. Her tiny braids trembled on her helpless head which stuck out of the stocks between her two limp hands. Yumi! But how... What in the hell was this?!

"She's on your team, right, Andrew?" asked

Benjamin Zvyagin.

That wasn't quite right; I hadn't officially accepted her into our party, but I nodded anyway.

"Today, when the beta round ended, the AI refused to let player Zoya Menshova disconnect," Kotov said without looking at me. "Her consciousness remained in VR. Her physical body is now in a coma."

CHAPTER 08

"HOW COULD THIS HAVE happened?" I asked, unable to calm down. "What's going on? Is it a power surge? A system failure?! How can someone not come out of VR?"

And in my head, I kept picturing the merchant's cunning smile as he told me, "Don't worry, she'll wait for you here." He had deceived me, played me like a fool, bought me off with some trinkets, some gadgets — a valuable prize. It seemed like complete nonsense, but I was sure it wasn't a problem with the technology. And now too Anna's words to Yumi seemed ominous: "Don't let the guards catch you…" she had said, "and don't get killed…" Had she known this would happen? There was something else I wanted to know first, however:

"Why did you find out about this just now?" I asked.

Benjamin winced painfully as if this was his fault and he had already been scolded for it.

"The technicians bungled it," he said. "They thought it was their error — that either they ran the wrong config or they got the immersion parameters wrong. So they tried to fix it themselves first and then called their supervisor. And they kept it quiet until they saw this mess on their control panel," Zvyagin pointed at the stockades. "If the morons had reported it immediately, there wouldn't have been any consequences. Now the whole crew is packing their bags."

"So, whose fault is it?" I peered into their faces, fearing that the answer would be "yours." There must be a reason they brought me here in the middle of the night. Maybe they just needed a scapegoat? I handed her over to the NPCs, brought her to the mayor's residence... and then left her alone in a dangerous situation...

I mean, what a bunch of nonsense! This is a GAME! NPCs can't kidnap a player!

"Please go make us some tea, Marina," the Master told my companion. "It seems like we're in for a long conversation."

"I'll warn you right away, Andrew," began Doc when we sat down at the table, "when you walk out of here, you'll have to sign some very serious documents, which amount to an NDA. What we're about to tell you constitutes an important trade secret and you could easily end up behind bars if you disclose any of this information. Your other option is to walk out of here right now, leave, and never come back. In that case, you'll be able to say whatever you want to whomever you want. Though no one will believe you. You'll have no proof, and our lawyers will crush you for slander. The choice is yours."

Why had they sent Marina away? Did they think her presence would stop me? I don't care about her advice! She was terrified as it was after spending a few hours without work, facing car loans and a mortgage that she had to pay. I, on the other hand, have lived like this my whole life. I've never known anything else as long as I remember.

Even if there was a risk of getting trapped in this game, that just meant that the rewards must be worth it. "Blue pill or red pill, Neo?" asks Morpheus and I reply, "Who cares? Give me the one that pays better."

"Why me?" I asked Doc, genuinely curious. "Am I the chosen one? Do I have something the others don't?"

"We had to start with someone," Doc brought me back down to earth. "You would have found out about this sooner or later anyway. You're all playing together and you talk to each other. You would have lost her — if not today, then tomorrow. You would have found out everything in the game eventually. We'd rather prepare you in advance."

"Did you know this would happen?" My question arose naturally, prompted by their hints, the things they didn't say, the slips of their tongues.

"We were expecting it," the Master nodded. "We waited and moved as quickly as we could in the meantime. And still, we were too late."

"We lost a whole day," Benjamin piped up. "The first round of the beta was a flop and that put us too far behind. The neural network had already begun to develop. Everything was supposed to happen a day or two later. We would have been prepared... We could have warned everyone... But who could anticipate that that girl would go rogue?"

Marina brought in tea, silently set the cups in front of everyone, and sat down again. She wanted to appear as inconspicuous as possible. Everyone calmly poured their tea and boiling water, added sugar, tinkled their spoons — as if not wishing to continue the conversation, to stir up something dark, big, and foul that had long been buried away from the world. Suddenly, Zvyagin spoke up again.

"Eight years ago, my father, Sergei Zvyagin, began developing the first fully-immersive MMORPG. The problem with all earlier, similar games was their...," he hesitated, searching for the right word, "clunkiness. To render a simple village hut realistically at the resolution and level of detail that VR requires, you need a server farm that could just as well handle all the cell phone service in an entire city. And there has to be hundreds of such huts, to say nothing of trees, animals and, most importantly, people."

It's one thing to render an avatar on a flat screen and quite another to see NPCs with your own eyes, to touch them, to talk to them. Any incongruity, any error of representation, immediately becomes obvious. In clothes, in gestures, in words. It's nigh impossible to model a daisy faithfully, let alone a human.

Sergei Zvyagin's solution was to use a neural network. The world was very rudimentary initially and sourced from the players themselves. The AI guessed their expectations and embodied them for each person. How a flower looks, how the wind howls, how a damp pine smells after a summer rain... The software generated whatever was expected of it, becoming more advanced and more natural every day. The neural network learned. The characters it created became indistinguishable from people. Many of them were based on real individuals, but their character traits were mixed so that even the "originals" couldn't recognize their depiction in-game.

The project was called *Lutetia*. Zvyagin was fascinated by medieval France and the European middle ages in general. However, Sergei Zvyagin died soon after the alpha's launch, never to see the full realization of his brainchild.

The first testers to play the alpha were ecstatic. The new game world was more vivid, more palpable and certainly more interesting than reality. However, then *Lutetia* began behaving strangely. It began issuing odd quests, pitting players against each other, provoking them to murder each other, to go to war against one another. And it was at that point that the developers, not knowing what to look for, missed a critical moment.

"As if it's any different now," muttered the Master. "Come on, Benny, stop making excuses."

"One day," Zvyagin went on, "none of the players came out of their VR pods. Every single one remained in VR, trapped in the game world."

"All of them?!" I couldn't believe what I was hearing.

"To the last man," he confirmed. "Every single one. Five thousand people remained in the game as their bodies turned into vegetables."

Five thousand?! The number made me light-headed. How can you cover up five thousand people lying in comas?

"Now we need to figure out what is going on," Dr. Kotov interrupted Benny quickly, not letting him finish his sentence. It seemed he was afraid that the tech guru would reveal too much.

It occurred to me quite clearly that he was lying. They had told me before that the object of the beta was to test the players, not the neural network. And this means that it wasn't our skills, or behaviors that they were interested in. It was us ourselves.

"So why go to all this trouble?" I was surprised. "Why create a whole new game if you could just monitor the old one?"

"The AI won't let us in," the Master shook his head. "Since all the players ended up inside, the connection with the server simply broke. We have no idea what's happening in there."

"This happened four years ago, and we're still fending off lawyers, paying compensation to the families, covering up any indications that five thousand people are now locked up I don't even know where," Doc summed up.

"What if you just unplug their VR pods?" I asked.

"Then they'll all die."

* * *

"Will you stay in the beta?" Marina asked me.

We were lying on the bed in her bedroom, finishing the wine and cake. Just lying there. She claimed it was harmful for me to overexert myself, and I was so exhausted that I didn't bother to object. We watched some silly comedy, then turned off the light and just lay there chatting in the darkness.

The day had rolled over us like a tractor with heavy wheels. I was physically tired, and Marina seemed to have lost her backbone, and with it her self-sufficient nastiness. It was just for a moment, no doubt, but it was a moment worth remembering.

"Of course, I'll stay," I said, surprised. "Has anything changed?"

"You're risking your life, and even worse..." Marina twirled an empty glass in the air. "You could lose your soul."

"Cut it out with the mysticism," I laughed. "The important part is that it's a risk and taking that risk pays more. And I'd like to end up very rich."

Finally, I pulled Marina toward me, and we made love — as decent people do, for the first time, unhurriedly, in bed, on silk sheets. Marina sat on top, straddling me, arched her back and began to move her hips smoothly, caressing me somewhere inside her own body, tantalizingly... agonizingly slowly... as if adding tension drop by drop.

I watched her body in the darkness of the bedroom, the perfect contour of her waist, how her breasts rose, how the moonlight softly traced her in the darkness, and it was like I could see the two of us from without. I savored my new image and status. This is my woman, I defended her today, and now all of this... the bed, the place in her bedroom, and she herself are my reward.

And then we simply fell asleep.

I dreamed of the locker room at the Moscow Region Cup of the Gladiator Games again. Lance, skinny and lanky, stands with a broken nose, scooping up bloody snot with his palm. The coach is yelling at me, Lance is being led away... And then again there was Lance and me in the corridor. The walls are carelessly painted in a runny, splotchy green. We stand in front of a large white door. Certificates hang on the wall, some of them mine. "Snitch," I say to Lance. "It wasn't me," he shakes his head as if it's about to fall off. "Snitch," a sharp, prickly word. It scrapes my tongue to say it. Yelling comes from behind the closed door. It's growing louder. They're deciding my fate in there.

"I've explained everything to my parents. They won't file a complaint," Lance mutters. There's a crook now on his straight, patrician nose, a reminder of the punch I landed. The door opens revealing my coach, his face red with anger, and my mom. Why her? Why not Lance's parents?! Why does she always have to meddle in everything?!

She grabs my wrist and pulls me after her. I try to keep up, but it's awkward to walk, the corridor is narrow, and she just pulls and pulls... "It wasn't me, Ratmir!" Lance shouts after us. His voice reverberates from the painted walls and follows us out into the street.

It's summer outside, hot. Swifts screech piercingly. Children run and eat ice cream. There's an ice cream truck nearby, so there are lots of children and they're all eating ice cream. After the darkness of the corridor, the colors are so bright they hurt my eyes. Mom turns to me and says, "Now remember this: You will never play with your silly toys ever again. No more fighting! NO MORE!"

* * *

Marina gets up in the morning before me. There's not much morning at 6 a.m. in the winter anyway. In the summer at least there's light, but in winter it's still dreary night out and creaky snow in the spotty streetlight.

At least this dreary winter morning I awake to the hissing of the coffee maker, the intoxicating aroma of coffee and fried toast.

"Didn't you say that you don't cook?" I remind her.

"There was no need," Marina waves her hand, munching on a piece of toast.

She skillfully spreads cream cheese on another piece of toast, tops it with a slice of tomato and hands it to me.

This is our second breakfast in her kitchen, but this time I feel much cozier. I'm even starting to get used to Marina's voice, to the scent that washes over me when she passes me, to the firmness of her body when she wriggles out of my arms and says "Stop, we'll be late." And I already want to come back here in the evening and it seems she's not opposed to the idea.

Warmed-up, the Mazda purrs contently. Something clubby plays from the speakers. I've never liked clubbing, but now I can easily imagine Marina on the dance floor in tight pants, or even better, in short shorts.

We enter the building, greeting the guards as usual. Marina is in high spirits, clicking her heels and shaking snow off her fluffy coat.

"Andryusha!" I hear a voice behind me.

I turn around to see Simba.

"Wow, what are you doing here?" I look at my friend in bewilderment.

I have the feeling that I haven't even thought of his existence since last night.

"I've been looking for you! Imagine that?!" Simba starts getting worked up. "The hospital says you left last night. You're not picking up the phone… and neither is Marina."

I take out Simon's present from my pocket. I even forgot to insert a SIM card into it yesterday. Marina doesn't react to Simon's words at all.

"Sorry," I awkwardly apologize. "I didn't feel good yesterday, so I slept in."

Simba forgives me easily. Happy to have found me and that I'm okay, he quickly changes the subject.

"Yumi is missing. Stacy says she never came back to their apartment last night. And she's not answering her phone either." Simba looks at Marina. "We figured you two might have been hanging out together, but I guess not…"

Marina snorts disdainfully, scoffing at the idea of me hanging out with someone like Yumi.

"Andrew, I need to go." She kisses me lightly on the cheek, as if to let all the other girls in the area know that I'm hers and leaves.

"So you haven't seen Yumi?" Simba persists.

How can I explain the situation to him without violating the NDA I signed yesterday? The execs told me that they'd reveal everything to the other beta testers tomorrow. And if they don't? I can't keep my friend in the dark and risk him getting stuck in the game forever, can I?

"Let's go eat," I say. "There's supposed to be a cafeteria that opens at seven around here somewhere."

"Seven? They must be maniacs," Simba says, surprised. "Of course, maniacs can be useful too."

I didn't tell him everything. Only a tenth. Not about Zvyagin, or the experiment, or how the neural network gets into our brains. Only that Yumi is stuck inside, and there's danger ahead if we keep going in.

"Of course I'll go in," Simba replies without hesitation. "Maybe we can pull her out."

Damn altruist. I'm not going to talk him out of it. No point in persuading him that rescuing the unfortunate prisoner would be a waste of time and energy. I mean, I get it, of course — Yumi deserves our sympathy at the moment — but then again... Who asked her to cause trouble? And now we'll have to expend energy to rescue her, while the others are leveling up... It's a bad deal any way you look at it.

AngelCake arrives at nine. She sniffs me like a hound dog, comes to her own conclusions, and kisses me on my other cheek. She's wearing a tracksuit again today, expensive even at first glance. The dark fabric shimmers in a matte-gray, and a Versace logo nestles at the collar. She reacts to the news of possibly getting stuck in the game forever with absolute calm.

"Well, you guys wouldn't leave me in there," she says.

Actually, I'm beginning to think that both of my friends aren't taking this new danger very seriously. They just believe that Yumi is to blame for her predicament and if we behave properly, nothing like that will happen. And then again, don't I believe the same thing?

I shower, put on my robe and shuffle in my slippers down the corridor to the VR pod. Sergio is there, but it looks like his technician buddy's been laid off. It's not that I care, but I take it as a good omen.

The spiral spins before me, loading the game... Everything is normal again... There aren't any bonuses or debuffs... It's all just the way I remember it.

I look for the familiar fence but it's nowhere to be seen. Instead, I'm surrounded by paintings, chandeliers, and moldings on the walls. I'm in the mayor's residence. Simba and AngelCake blink their eyes beside me. We spawned together this time and even in the exact same place we logged out yesterday.

Well, almost — the treasury's door is now behind us and firmly shut. But my daishō — my twin swords — are in my hands, and I still have no doubt that I made the right choice. Choose strength first — ensure your safety — and see to the rest of it all later.

I can't wait to read the new quest description. What does the AI have in store for us today? Will it be more farming or more killing? Maybe a new crafting or magic mechanic will appear... And I need to urgently visit the training camp and pick up some new skills for the levels I've gained since I was there last. To my surprise, however, the quest log is empty. All there is, is a countdown timer. Today's round of the beta will last two and a half hours.

We head for the exit, Simba on point with Stacy and me covering the rear. Although I don't anticipate any threats here, we should work on moving in formation and also communicating properly — without calling each other "Andryusha" or "Simon" or "Stacy."

The hallway brings us to a large hall, which is clearly used for receptions and entertaining visitors. Like every other part of the residence now, it's empty.

"Esteemed adventurers!"

We turn towards the voice. The mayor is descending towards us down the central staircase. He wears a luxurious hat, holds a cane, and has the most affable of smiles on his face.

"Esteemed adventurers," he repeats. "Be not in a rush to take your leave. How would you like to work with the town guard?"

Chapter 09

"ARE YOU REALLY GOING to give him the time of day?" Simba nudged me with his elbow. "That bastard kidnapped Yumi."

"And now he's mocking us," AngelCake chimed in supportively. "Just wait, I'll give him a piece of my mind! He's in for it now... the creep!"

"Quiet!" I silenced both of them, "This 'creep' is the chief authority in this place. As for Yumi — let's be honest — she got herself into the mess she's in. And besides, don't you want your nightie... err, your chain mail, I mean?"

AngelCake puffed up but nodded obediently.

"Well if you do still want it, then you'll smile and nod and play nice. And that goes for you too, Simba."

Simba frowned. "Bending over backwards for some gear..."

"Simon, are you an idiot?" I whispered. "Are you planning to storm their dungeon or jail or wherever they're holding her? We need to figure out what's going on first and only then start cracking heads."

"You're right," Simba relented. "We should talk to him first."

We headed toward the mayor and I finally got a good look at the city's main NPC. The mayor had changed significantly since the first day. He looked younger; his wrinkles had smoothed out and the wart on his nose had turned into a small mole. His doublet, though seemingly the same, looked as if it had been tailored or resown out of finer cloth. White lace could be seen peeking at the collar from under his suit, and there were lace cuffs on his sleeves. He wore a massive rectangular ring on one finger, and as he spoke, his voice oozed such cloying sweetness that it was a wonder the NPC didn't stick to the floor with every step.

"Dear TargetAi," the mayor said, approaching. He pronounced my name as if it were a title. "And you, his faithful companions. Would you be so kind as to join me for breakfast?"

At the mention of "faithful companions," Stacy shot me a suspicious glance, but I chose to ignore it.

"Thank you, Your Highness," I replied, "but we're in a hurry. We need to get stronger and our sojourn here is limited."

"I recognize a hero when I see one," the mayor replied, not at all offended. "Heroes don't waste time idly. They seek feats and glory. But I advise you not to decline. I'm sure it will benefit you."

He gestured towards a small table, already set. The reception hall now resembled an upscale restaurant. Tapestries, moldings, and mirrors on the walls, chandeliers on the ceiling. Bright, light, and festive. Yet there was only one table, specially prepared for us. Fruits, appetizers, wine... Why such luxury?

We sat around the table, expecting some servants to appear, but the mayor uncorked a bottle himself and poured the red wine into large goblets for us. This was the second time someone offered me wine recently, and the second time I wanted to refuse. Either because I've come to value a clear mind or because I don't trust those who offer me drinks.

Could an NPC poison or drug me? Have a sip and then wake up with Yumi in the neighboring cell? It's possible. The AI gets trickier every day, and I recalled Marina's words yesterday about the kindness of influential people. This fox was no different from the real-life execs of MosTech.

On the other hand, if this is a game, any debuff would be immediately visible, were it sleep or poisoning.

"Stacy, have a sip, please."

"What?" AngelCake asked, taken aback.

"Take a sip of wine and tell me the result," I said without taking my eyes off the mayor.

He met my gaze and smiled back slyly.

"Mmm... tasty." Stacy smacked her lips in delight. "And it grants a buff! Plus 10% to all stats for half an hour... Why do I have to be the first to drink?”

“To check if you pass out,” chuckled Simba tactfully.

“Ohh... You’re terrible!” Stacy protested. “Don’t you care about me?!”

“On the contrary, I care for you more than anyone else!” I finally turned to look at her. “If something happened to you, Simba and I could protect your body and keep it safe...” I glanced at the mayor. “However, if it was me who passed out, it would be that much harder for you two to do the same for me.”

Stacy pouted and glared, unsure whether to argue with me or not, but eventually decided to say nothing.

“Well, you see,” the mayor waved diplomatically, having observed our deliberations with interest. “We do no harm to young ladies.”

“Really?!” I challenged. “I’ve heard otherwise.”

“Perhaps you mean the outlaw...” the NPC smiled again. “That’s a different matter. ‘The law is harsh, but it is the law,’” he proudly quipped.

Damn, where did he pick all this up from? I had a strong feeling that I was talking to a real person. Oddly dressed and in a strange setting, maybe an actor or roleplayer, but alive and with a definite personality.

He reminded me of a shrewd lawyer, like those who took all the retirement savings from my mom during my father’s trial. They took the money and promised a lot but guaranteed nothing. Just like this one. He was smiling and offering us all kinds of opportunities — yet I knew instinctively that this was no friend.

"Still, I'm curious," I feigned as much indifference as possible. "Curious as to the fate that awaits her..."

"I don't condone violence," said the mayor. "You have been seen committing slaughter and affray on our fine town's noble streets. I don't mean you personally — please understand — TargetAi. By *you*, I mean all *you* newcomers. When *you* adventurers descended on our town, we were afraid to leave our homes because death reigned in the streets. *You* slaughtered each other like beasts! What else can we expect from you?"

How do I explain to this fellow that the players were just fulfilling a quest his own creator had set? That those murders were provoked by the AI, of which he himself was a part? I doubt a medieval NPC would understand.

"If we're beasts, why meddle in our affairs?" I retorted. "Yumi killed another adventurer, not one of your... subjects."

"I draw no distinction between us residents and you immortals! This is my town and it falls to me to guard the laws here!" The mayor knocked the table with his fist, so gently however that even the glasses didn't wobble.

"Immortals": The word rang out with special resonance. This was clearly what the NPCs called us players. To them, we were "immortals." An interesting way to put it.

"Why do you call us 'immortals?'" I asked.

Since we're having such a cultured conversation with one of the AI's own official representatives, I should try to find out more. Especially since the mayor wasn't any old NPC. He had been in the game since its inception. Surely, the AI had dedicated extra resources to shaping his "personality." I remembered very well how he used to stand around with a big red exclamation mark above his head. More of a subroutine than a man. And now he sits across from me at the breakfast table, serves me wine, converses, barters and plies intrigues known to him alone.

"You lot don't value your own lives or the lives of others," said the NPC, shaking his head. "You die agonizing deaths, yet the next day you appear again as if nothing happened. You respect only strength and your life's sole purpose is to grow stronger. If we wish to survive, we have to be like you, whether we want to or not. There's just no other way."

I was about to object but then tried to see things from his perspective. We really did show up here unannounced and immediately started to beat, smash and kill everything in sight. And it didn't matter whether it was each other or mobs. We always had weapons in our hands and we were always running around with murderous intent. Any bystander would indeed take us for aggressive psychos. No wonder the town authorities want to ensure...

Damn! I even shook my head to clear my mind. For a second, I was about to agree with this bot, this bit of code. I almost understood his point of view... But come on now, Andrew: This is a *game* and I'm talking to a *script*. It may be complex and unusual, but it's not *intelligent!*

"So what will happen to Yumi?" I asked again.

"She will be tried," the mayor declared pompously. "Not immediately, but later. Why? Do you wish to help her? I heard she was your friend? Was she in your band of immortals?"

"Nope," I shook my head as indifferently as possible. "She just happened to be nearby... It was a random encounter."

"Ow! Owie!" AngelCake yelped suddenly.

The ninny tried to kick me under the table and got back twofold in return. Maybe she'll think again before trying to interfere during a negotiation.

"Am I to understand then... that you're not interested in freeing her?" This time the NPC genuinely seemed surprised.

"Why would I be?" I said, turning away from Simba, who was winking at me.

"*Andrew, what are you doing?*"

Look at that, my party members remembered the chat.

"*Both of you, zip it,*" I replied. "*I'll explain later.*"

"The hell do I need her for?" I asked the NPC sincerely. "Here's the only thing I'm interested in."

I held up my twin swords before the mayor.

"These are indeed fine weapons," he nodded. "Did you enjoy my... modest collection?"

"Yes," I didn't deny it. "And we've already set our sights on some items in there. Especially Dame AngelCake here. As you know, a lady's wish is as good as law."

At the moment, Stacy's face was filled with resentment and was even growing outright angry... a whole spectrum of emotions.

"I understand," nodded the NPC.

"Tell me, though, I've never seen a single lady around here," I said, my curiosity getting the best of me. "There doesn't seem to be even a single woman in your town. Surely this can't be a place of just men?"

"It's simply too dangerous around here," said the mayor, cool and collected. "We've hidden the women away from the newcomers. Trust me when I say that you'll meet them soon enough. But let's get back to the rewards. Are you willing to serve our town?"

"If the reward's good enough," I nodded.

"How about another item from my collection?" the mayor offered. "At first, I thought you'd want to free your friend. But turns out you're more of a... business-minded person."

"You were wrong to call me a hero," I smirked. "I'm not a hero, I'm a mercenary. I only believe in useful things and cold, hard cash is the most useful thing of all."

Interesting situation. I felt bad for Yumi, of course. Lucky my friends didn't see the image of her locked in the stockade, or they'd be giving me hell right now. "Rescue that poor girl this instant," they'd be yammering. "Dry her tears and take her home."

That's what the four execs at MosTech were hinting at, too. Obviously they didn't drag me out of the hospital so late at night only to break me some bad news. Why else would they share this information with me anyway? They brought me there, showed me around... stood next to me, oohing and aahing. They scared the hell out of me with that tale of the 5,000 human vegetables languishing around here somewhere.

The hell did I need any of this for anyway? I had spent the whole morning thinking about it, and it all came down to one thing: They were manipulating me to go rescue Yumi — playing on my pity, my sense of duty...

Why me, though? I'm pretty sure I'm the highest-ranking player in the beta at the moment. Well, except for Anna, of course. But she wouldn't give a damn about that cocky brat Yumi. So, it falls to me to try and rescue the rogue assassin. And if I succeed, then the MosTech top brass will have a recipe for saving their own "lost" flock. Andrew will show them how, just 'cause he's such a nice guy.

Only a week ago, I'd have jumped at the chance to rescue a damsel from medieval distress. But these last few days have changed something inside of me. I understood now that there was another game being played beyond the confines of this VR sandbox. A game in meatspace. And to the big bosses in meatspace, we're no different than the NPCs and mobs are to the AI in here.

Here's a simple example. As a kid, my dad used to say, "Want to do something nice? Mess it up first, then fix it." They fired Marina... then hired her back... and now I'm supposed to thank the bosses, and Marina's grateful to me. But in reality, nothing's changed!

Even now there are thousands of people trapped in some instance of this virtual world, but those who are truly responsible for them have dumped the rescue operation on me — without even the courtesy of telling me what they were doing outright. I had walked out of the board room feeling like I've got a *mission!* Like I'm the chosen one. Like I'm gonna save the world...

Then I banged Marina, got some rest, and... it all faded away. I had better play dumb, let them tell me openly what they want, so that we could talk business in earnest. They want a job done? Good. I want cash money.

"So listen up," the mayor finally got to the point. "My scouts have uncovered five wyvern nests in the countryside around the town. These are rare and dangerous predators. But they're also very valuable. Especially their eggs. Each nest should have one such egg by now, and these eggs will in time hatch into lizards that can be trained as mounts. Bring me those eggs, and you'll get a generous reward!"

"Whoa..." Simba's eyes bulged.

He grasped the situation just as I did. Have we grown our reputation with the town so much that we're getting personal quests now? This is a great opportunity to not only strengthen our lead but to leave everyone else in the dust.

"Thank you for entrusting us with such an important quest," I bowed my head. "We appreciate your confidence..."

"Fie! You believe this quest is for you alone?" snorted the pesky NPC. "In half an hour, every immortal will have it too. I just wish to remind you of one important condition. The greatest reward — another item from my treasury — shall go to whomever collects all five eggs!"

"But that's impossible!" I protested. "We can't possibly hit all five nests at the same time!"

"You're forgetting an important detail..." the mayor leaned in and whispered dramatically. "Beyond the town limits, there are no restrictions on eliminating your competition."

* * *

"Go, go, go!" I hurried my party like every drill sergeant in every movie ever. "Move it, people! We've got half an hour! Let's light the tires and kick the fires!"

"But we're headed the wrong way!" wailed Simba as we ran.

"We need to stock up and level up our skills," I countered. "You'd have to be an idiot to take on a boss unprepared."

"Guess we were idiots last time then, huh?" Stacy grumbled, but I didn't even bother to respond. Bunch of whiners.

The shopkeeper was new. The old one must've gotten a promotion. This one was young, chubby and balding. The first thing I did was dump all the obsolete junk I had on me on the counter — and then topped that off with four pieces of the Spider Queen's carapace.

"You wish to identify these?" the merchant looked surprised.

"I'm selling them," I replied.

Legendary ingredients are great and all, but who knows when crafting will be available in the game. Until then, I wasn't about to sit on a pile of treasure like some dragon. Equipment could make us stronger here and now, and we could always get more carapaces later.

"820 gold pieces," the NPC quickly swept the gear off the counter.

"That's a nice sum," Simba rubbed his hands. "Now we've got some startup capital to work with."

We bought Simba a round shield made of iron-bound wood, with a solid boss in the middle. It granted bonuses to his *Shield Bash* skill, so it was the perfect choice for what we'd already been through.

Our paladin wanted a full set of steel armor, but I talked him out of it. It was a real stamina sink, and we needed to be quick today. We settled on lamellar armor, long chain mail gloves, and high, steel-clad boots with greaves. In his new getup, Simba looked like a proper tank. Practically bulletproof.

All in all, he got a 20% boost to his armor, and

that meant that any weapon doing less than twenty percent of his health in damage wouldn't even scratch him. Moreover, if the damage was higher, the armor value was subtracted from it.

For Simba's weapon, we chose a bastard sword. It looked awesome for his size and almost matched a Zweihander in damage. Of course, damage output was a secondary consideration for a tank. But we hadn't advanced that far in class specialization yet. And at Level 7, Simba could really hold his own, even in one-on-one combat. The bastard sword would let him keep his distance and it packed a punch when it landed too.

For Stacy, we picked out a large repeating crossbow. Interestingly, using a bow in the game required strength, probably because of the draw weight. But I was planning to boost AngelCake's Agility and Constitution. Let her be quick and hard to kill. The crossbow came with a cool-looking five-shot magazine that was operated by a single lever action for quick reloading. It seemed more steampunk or post-apocalyptic, but paired with our archer's busty charm, the crossbow looked freaking awesome.

I looked over AngelCake from head to toe, thoughtfully.

"Now, Stacy, pick something really slutty from the gear..."

"Why would I do that?!" AngelCake's eyes bulged in outrage, steam nearly whistling from her ears.

"Because we're going to use you as bait."

Chapter 10

EVER SINCE KINDERGARTEN, Vitek Sutugin dreamed of being the tough guy. The kind that made everyone go quiet when he entered the room, the kind who could shove anyone he didn't like, take their chocolate bar, and maybe even kick them while they were down. Alas, this dream remained elusive for little Vitek. His bigger classmates were always the ones doing the shoving and taking, while he stood aside, averting his eyes. He grew up small and scrawny, never cut out to be the aggressor.

Even his nickname wasn't intimidating. When Vitek's baby teeth fell, the ones that grew in their place stuck out so prominently that he earned the nickname "Bunny," and unfortunately for him, the nickname stuck.

Bunny hated his teeth. But when a pediatric dentist suggested braces to his parents, Bunny's dad declared that "only fags wear that crap," dooming his son to eternal outcast status. Plus, Bunny was slightly cross-eyed. It was hardly noticeable, but together with his teeth, the effect was devastating.

The only place Bunny felt good was in multiplayer computer games. That's where he discovered how to gank.

To gank is to kill noobs, to backstab players busy with farming, to gang up on solo players. Bunny killed for loot, for frags, and often just for fun. He could spend days "shooting fish in a barrel" without it ever getting old for him.

The ultimate thrill was cornering some noob at a respawn point and repeatedly killing them, listening to them whine in chat. In those moments, Bunny felt big and important, the master of some poor soul's destiny. The best was when the victim was an "oldfag" — some dad playing after a dreary day at work — only to keep dying at respawn. In those moments, Bunny imagined his own dad, and it made him feel really good.

His gamer tag, "CryBitches," was well-known and reviled throughout many game servers. In some locations, the rule was to kill CryBitches on sight, PK penalties be damned.

Bunny found his way into MosTech's beta thanks to his buddy Dimon Grechin, whose nickname (for some reason known only in his hood) was "Millet." Millet offered Bunny the chance to make some money, and they hit the jackpot right from the start. While the other idiots were busy with stupid quests, Bunny and Millet lured a dumb girl in a slutty skirt into an alley, promising to show her a shortcut to the spider's lair. They couldn't actually have sex with her — their bodies were like those of dolls in children's stores, smooth between the legs. But they had their fun, tearing off her clothes and then strangling her with her own top.

Bunny even earned some XP for this sordid deed.

Taking this as a cue, the buddies started racking up experience by preying on weaklings and loners.

They had a blast during "the Purge" round of the beta — as it came to be known among the beta testers. The clueless newbies hid in alleyways and didn't even try to fight back. They just squatted down, covered their heads with their hands, and begged to be left alone. There were plenty of pelts to harvest that day, but the two buddies, crazed with bloodlust and pumped up by their rising levels, just took them out along with everyone else. That's when a third member joined their crew.

At first, Bunny figured him for a total loser. He was skinny and twitchy, with long black hair. The guys didn't expect any fight from him, but the dark-haired guy fought like crazy, while screeching like a psycho. Then Bunny, who was pretty practical, suggested that this weirdo join their party.

The gloomy and taciturn guy with the handle "NOANGEL" turned out to be a great addition. He loved killing and wasn't afraid to scrap. This was especially useful because Bunny and Millet were kind of cowards and preferred to fight from range. So, when the game started handing out classes, they both became archers. It's easy to shoot from afar and run if things go south. Plus, shooting someone in the back is also a smart move.

NOANGEL chose the "Punisher" class — a hybrid between a slow dps and a light tank — so he could easily cover his cautious friends from an opponent who turned out tougher than they reckoned.

That's when Bunny came up with a simple philosophy for his party: There were the wolves and there were the sheep. Wolves were strong and cunning, sheep were weak and dumb. Naturally, they would be the wolves, and the sheep were all the other players who brought their silly meatspace preconceptions with them into the game.

The previous round of the beta, in which the mayor had banned any killing, had really thrown off Bunny. He hadn't seen that one coming and hoped it was just temporary. And his hopes were not misplaced.

"What's up?" drawled Millet, whose in-game handle was "Murderator."

"It's all quiet," replied Bunny, peeking out from under an ample bush.

Bunny's trio set their ambush on the road to the first wyvern nest. While the other beta testers ogled at the quest notice that had been pasted on the big board outside the mayor's residence, while they squawked and formed parties, discussing what gear to bring and how they'd divvy up the loot — the three cutthroats rushed to get a head start. They didn't attack the wyvern itself, a big old beast with an 18 foot wingspan and claws the length of a bastard sword. The thing was twice the size of NOANGEL, which didn't exactly inspire optimism.

Instead, the trio doubled back along the road and picked a suitable spot to waylay the others. The country road made a sharp "S" here, concealing the spot from either direction, and this meant they could "welcome" a lone traveler quietly, without anyone else noticing.

Bunny and Millet were both Level 5 and had hardened steel-tipped arrows for piercing armor and *Stun Shot* in their arsenal. NOANGEL was Level 6 and all together they made for a tight little band of cutthroats.

Their first victim was a lone Level 6. It wasn't clear what the bald guy with a quarterstaff and wool cloak was planning on accomplishing. Maybe he thought he could beat the boss alone, or maybe he wanted to join a party near the wyvern, or distract the beast somehow and steal its egg. No one would ever know because he never made it to his destination. Instead, he ate two arrows, one with stun, and then faced off against NOANGEL while getting peppered with more arrows in his back.

The next victims to appear from around the bend were a couple — a guy and a girl, both Level

4s. These loons were walking like they were on a picnic date. Holding hands, chatting, not even looking around. The girl had a garland of daisies on her head.

They could have killed them without leaving their hiding spot, but the guys couldn't resist showing off. Two jumped out in front, one from behind.

"Run darling!" the boyfriend yelled, brandishing his little stick. "Save yourself!"

Dumb move. They would have lasted longer together. And if they hadn't freaked out, they might have been able to retreat together too — if the girl had really tried, as unlikely as that was. XP is XP after all.

Either way, "darling" got a stun arrow in the back and took a short break, while her knight in shining armor got hammered by arrows and a bastard sword. Bunny wanted to keep him alive so he could see what they'd do to his girl. But NOANGEL, screeching like a bobcat, went for his throat.

So they had to have fun with the girl without an audience. They took turns with their whimpering prey, but didn't take much pleasure in it. A lesson for the future, so that she'd remember what real men were like. Then they ganked her.

Three parties passed by after that — numbering five, seven, and again five members. They all had good equipment and high levels... The wolves were no match for sheep like that and just pressed themselves into the ground so they wouldn't be noticed. And after that...

"Damn..." Millet whispered quietly. It was his turn to keep watch. "Holy shit... I can't believe it!"

"Where... what?" Bunny joined him, "Damn, look at that chick..."

Even the usually impassive NOANGEL got curious and poked his nose between the bushes, to see what was happening below.

A girl was walking along the road. Her lively curls bounced with every step and so did her impressive breasts. All she wore was a skirt and a top made of golden chains. The top's chains were fixed at the top and bottom to her collar and belt and therefore parted with every movement to reveal her supple skin. The skirt's chains hung from the waist like a thick fringe. Her slender legs were clad in golden boots, confidently stepping along the dusty road.

"Wow... where did she find those clothes?" Bunny wondered, amazed.

"Who cares? Wherever she got them, they're about to be ours," Millet replied nonchalantly.

He already considered the girl and everything she wore as good as his.

"I bet that armor's stats are amazing too..."

"Then we'll give it to NOANGEL!" Millet laughed. "He'll really put the fear in the sheep with a get-up like that!"

He laughed even louder when he caught NOANGEL's smoldering glare. They had blown their cover a long time ago, but the girl kept walking, humming to herself, seemingly oblivious to them. She carried a large crossbow on her shoulder, currently undrawn and pointed skyward.

"That's a kickass crossbow too," Bunny went on.

"How can you think about the crossbow when she's got those boobs?!" Millet was indignant, "I call dibs!"

"No way!"

Just then, NOANGEL darted down through the bushes next to them. His buddies hurried after him.

"Madam! Oh madam! Do hang on a second!" Bunny bowed mockingly. "You've trespassed on private property, there's a toll for using this road and now there's a fine for trespassing too!"

"Oh, I didn't know it was toll road," the girl acted surprised, opening her mouth wide and batting her eyelids. "How much is the toll?"

"The rate for chicks like you is three blowjobs each!" Millet announced. "And all the clothes you're wearing. Then you can pass!"

"Oh, I'll give you my clothes..." the foolish girl actually put down her crossbow. "Just please don't hurt me."

"Don't worry, we'll be gentle," Bunny chuckled.

The thugs relaxed, lowering their weapons and preparing to have some fun. Even NOANGEL stopped looking around cautiously and stared at the girl's exposed ass.

Pop! Another player suddenly appeared beside NOANGEL. It wasn't a matter of stealth — Bunny had taken the skill to see invisible enemies right away. The stranger just moved so fast that his movements were a blur. He had just appeared at the bend in the path, and in an instant, covering about ten meters, he was standing next to their punisher.

Snicker-snack! A short sword flashed red and stabbed right through NEANGEL's armor from behind, under his shoulder blade. He twitched and collapsed into a pile of loot. A one-shot.

Bunny drew his bow. He had leveled up his *Stun Shot* to Level 3. This was an excellent skill for a ganker, which could immobilize a victim, or if needed, stop a pursuer and buy time to escape. Thanks to its relatively high level, the skill almost never failed.

Whomp! As his arrow flew towards the stranger, Bunny finally got a good look at him: He had short dark hair, he wore black leather armor and he wielded two Japanese swords, a long one and a short one.

The stranger exploded into a flurry of strikes, forming a solid steel cocoon around his body with his swords. Some freaking skill! He was a Level 12! Oh sheeeit!

Without thinking twice, Bunny turned tail and fled. He managed two steps before feeling a blunt pain in his back. "The crossbow," he thought. "The girl had a crossbow on her."

* * *

The second time, Stacy aimed longer. The bolt whistled as it flew and when it hit the thug, he was thrown into the air as if he got a powerful kick from behind. He fell to the ground already a bundle of loot.

"That's my *Air Ram*," boasted AngelCake. "Double damage with knockdown."

"Why you're a regular Valkyrie," I said, "An Amazon! A Xena, Warrior Princess!"

"Okay, that last one's too much!"

"Why?" I laughed. "Your outfit fits about the same!"

Stacy snorted but without resentment. A short bit ago, she threw a huge tantrum in the shop. "I'm not wearing this slutty thing..." "My whole butt is hanging out..." "I'm not your whore..." I had to threaten to kick her out of the party and then bribe her with a very expensive crossbow.

She's totally used to her, uh... armor now though, which, by the way, grants +5 to Dexterity and +10% armor against melee weapons. I have no idea how that's supposed to work... Maybe if someone tries to kill Stacy, they can only stare at her boobs... and they swing their sword where they're looking... and there are those chains there, so bang goes the edge on the chains and... Well it's just ridiculous! Better not overthink it. It's just stats on gear.

"He's getting away!" Stacy shouted.

Preoccupied with our banter, we almost forgot about the last cutthroat. He didn't waste time trying to kill us and bolted straight for the forest.

"GET OOOVER HERE!" roared Simba suddenly.

The PK-er stopped as if he tripped mid-step. He was shaking, desperately trying to run away, but his legs were bringing him back to us. One step... then another... a third... and now he was running towards Simba with his bow raised.

"GET OOOVER HERE!" Simba roared again in exactly the same tone.

"Man, couldn't you have chosen a different trigger for that spell? Are we going to have to hear this line every time now?"

"I thought it was funny," Simba shrugged guiltily.

We had swung through the training camp before setting out for the wyverns' nests. There'd been no crowds of players to push through and the clerk literally jumped up from his desk and ran to meet us. Whether it was the status that came with being Level 12 or our reputation with the mayor, we didn't have to wait.

Simba finally got his targeted aggro spell and chose Scorpion's immortal phrase as the trigger for activating it. I'd already heard it five time over the last twenty minutes and was starting to get annoyed. He also got the *Iron Life* skill, which at its base level increased HP by 10%, improved incoming damage absorption and even increased our paladin's pain tolerance.

Stacy, on my advice, learned to detect traps and stealthed enemies and also picked up several archery skills, focusing on shot speed and power.

The best stuff went to me, but that's a story for another time...

"Gaaaarhgh..." The remaining thug charged at Simba, so crazed with aggression that he tried to hit our tank with his bow like it was a club.

Bonk! Simba knocked him down with his shield and put his bastard sword to the guy's throat.

"See this sword? Do you see it?! Look at me, damn it!" Simba looked at him fiercely. "I'm gonna shove this sword up your ass and twist it, you scum! Where'd you stash the loot you took off the others?"

"Over there... there... in the clearing under a bush..." stammered the cutthroat. "I'll show you..."

Once Simba transferred the loot stash to his inventory and finished off the thug, we moved on. Though my companions were eager to start hunting for the precious wyvern eggs, I wasn't in a hurry. First, I stocked up at the shop, trained thoroughly at the camp, and only then headed to the first wyvern nest. By that time, natural selection had already begun thinning out our competitors.

Stacy made a great decoy. I even caught myself checking her out. The first PK-er just burst out of the bushes screaming "Woo-hoo!" and tried to grab AngelCake's boobs. Startled and caught off guard, she went into fight or flight mode — in this case, fight — and took him down before we even got there.

Then we had to deal with a party of seven Level 3s, which took some effort. Simba drew them in with mass aggro, and we cut them down one by one. It was nice that no one took AngelCake seriously. All the brigands wanted to mess with her first before getting down to business.

The landscape was getting hillier and the road began to climb steadily uphill. The quest marker on the map was getting closer, but we still couldn't see through the trees. At last, we overcame the last hilltop and entered a ravine. Cliffs walled it in from all sides and high off the ground, on a precarious craggy ledge, we beheld a long-necked creature with a crocodile's head hissing aggressively.

Ten players were smoothly maneuvering in front of it. I even admired their coordination for a minute — it was that beautiful. Two tanks held the creature's aggro, while five dps tried to hit it with swords and spears and three archers showered it with arrows and stones. Bundles of loot and piles of ash lay strewn over the rocks in front of the wyvern. Not all of the party's members had survived to see our arrival.

We got closer and were noticed.

"Over here!" a tall blonde warrior in steel chain mail waved at us. "Come join us!"

I waved back with a smile and whispered to AngelCake:

"On my mark... Let's go!"

Stacy furrowed her brow and raised her crossbow.

CHAPTER 11

THE SKILL WAS CALLED *Rapid Fire*. I laughed at the name, but I appreciated its effect. At its current first level, ten bolts from Stacy's crossbow shot out like a machine gun. The cooldown was long, a whole five minutes, but its effect was powerful.

The archers died first. Three shots took down one; the other took four. Another three bolts hit a tall, skinny spearmen, slowing his movements. His health must have dropped into the red. We had to take care of the rest at a normal pace.

"You fuckers!"

"What are you doing, you bastards?!"

"Filthy gankers!"

When there were only three dps left, they realized that we were more of a threat than the wyvern. The fighters finally disengaged the monster and turned on us. Stacy gritted her teeth and fought them off at close range. Two got close and died immediately. I met the armored blonde with a piercing chest strike, then *Dashed* behind a stocky swordsman, showing off a bit for AngelCake, and beheaded him.

That left the two tanks. They glared back at us angrily but couldn't turn their backs on the wyvern. The creature spread its wings, hissed menacingly, and struck at their shields with a clangor. They were in a tight spot: Turn around and die instantly or wait for us to come and stab them in the back. Eventually, the tanks slowly backed away, still defending, hoping to draw the wyvern onto us as we got closer. This gave them a slim chance of escaping. And it gave us a couple of minutes to calmly assess the situation.

"Maybe we shouldn't have killed them?" Simba grumbled. "Feels kind of wrong."

He didn't like my plan from the start. For a born businessman, Simon was too principled and kind-hearted.

"We've talked about this," I shook my head, "It's a matter of XP. Experience doesn't just fall into your lap. We could have just waited for the creature to finish them. But then it would get the XP, not us. And if they had killed it, we'd miss out on the loot."

"What if we joined them?" Simba persisted.

"And then what? Draw straws for the goods? 'Eenie, meenie, miny, moe?'" I laughed. "You may as well have suggested a fair fight."

"How are we any better than those we've killed along the way?"

"We don't torture them and we're killing them for the XP. We're doing what's allowed by the rules and what the mayor himself hinted at. Don't worry, there aren't any pacifists left around here. Those were purged the day before yesterday," I replied, but to my surprise, I soon found out how wrong I was.

When we got closer, I noticed another player, a girl, still alive. Strange that I hadn't seen her before. She was squatting down, fearfully covering her head with her hands. That's how we found her.

"Why did you spare her?" I asked AngelCake sternly.

"She was unarmed," AngelCake snapped back.

The girl was indeed unarmed. Short, thin, but shapely in the right places, with light straight hair, she looked quite young. Hmm... is she even eighteen? How did she get here? She was barefoot and dressed in a long shapeless dress or tunic — something like a chlamys. The most surprising thing, however, was that she was only at Level 2!

What the hell is she doing here?! Who brought her and why? At her level and without any gear, she's useless in a fight. My first thought was that someone had brought her along for their sexual needs, but then I dismissed this idea. The girl looked... innocent, somehow. No wonder AngelCake had spared her.

"Who are you?" I asked.

"My name is Sibyl..." The girl realized we weren't going to kill her that instant and peeked out from her fingers with a mix of hope and curiosity.

"You have no weapon?"

"Nope... none..." she even shook her head for emphasis.

"Alright, get out of here, Sibyl, run away..." I said, convincing myself that I was letting her go because of her low level and the small amount of experience she'd give, and definitely not because I liked the girl and felt sorry for her. "Hurry up before I change my mind!"

"I can't!"

Sibyl held up her arm. Tied to her wrist was a thick, long rope which stretched twenty or so feet to the belt of one of the tanks.

"Now you can!" Simba cut the rope decisively. "Those lowlifes!"

His mood and attitude towards people changed like a weather vane. Now, suddenly, the unfortunate victims of our treacherous attack had become the bad guys. It's dangerous to be so hot-tempered at his size. Dangerous for others, I mean. He grabbed the loose end of the rope and yanked it with all his might.

The unsuspecting tank lost his footing and landed on his butt. The wyvern clucked approvingly, like a chicken laying an egg, and pinned him to the ground. Seeing this, Sibyl burst out in laughter — as clear and resonant as a ringing bell.

"Are you a sex slave?" I asked bluntly.

"No!" She blushed from indignation. "I'm a

healer!"

My jaw dropped.

"But there aren't any healers around here! There's no magic... no mana..."

"But that's what I am!"

Encountering a healer in here was just... unreal! Even one as small and skinny as this one — and a mere Level 2! Yet binding her to us with a rope was not our style. It would be better to gently persuade her of the benefits of joining us, hinting at the advantages of cooperating...

"Will you take me with you?" Sibyl asked before I could.

She stood up lightly and her thin dress cascaded over her shapely figure. Not so skinny after all... and the dress not so shapeless... yeah, a long skirt, but with a slit up to mid-thigh, and how it clung to her... damn... I really didn't want to pass up such a... such a...

"Have you thought this through?" I managed to say. "We're not exactly the good guys..."

"You freed me, and I like you..." she said flippantly.

Then all of a sudden, Sibyl stretched so sweetly that it seemed like she had just woken up, standing on her tiptoes and reaching up with her hands balled into fists, just like a kitten. The fabric of her tunic stretched along with her movement, forcing me swallow hard.

"Let's take her, what do you say?" AngelCake chimed in unexpectedly, "She's been through enough..."

The last thing I expected was Stacy's approval. She should have been jealous of a potential rival, but instead, it seems she felt sympathy for the girl.

"You're in," I pointed at Sibyl, prompting further giggling from her.

"Wow, you're all at full health!" she said, probably seeing the party interface that had popped up before her.

"That won't last long," I replied. "Simba, aggro that wyvern!"

"GET OOOVER HERE!" resounded through the ravine. Sibyl rolled with laughter. She really did seem to be chipper.

"Quick, explain how your healing mechanic works!" I leaned in. "What do you use instead of mana?"

We were already in battle, the seconds counting down.

"Stamina! One point of my stamina gives ten points of health to whomever I heal."

Yet she was only Level 2. Even if she had put all her stat points into Constitution, she wouldn't last long. I decisively changed the party's XP distribution, giving Sibyl 100%.

"AngelCake, finish that tank there on the ground!"

Stacy nodded, knelt down, and took careful aim. The wyvern was stomping on the knight, unable to finish him due to the other tank distracting it.

I didn't want to pull the monster's aggro too

soon either. If the wyvern got hit by Stacy's arrow now, it might chase her all over the ravine...

However, AngelCake took her shot like a true sniper.

"Aaaah..." Sibyl let out a half-sigh, half-moan. A blissful smile spread across her face as she reached Level 3. Just you wait — there's more to come.

The creature, having lost its prey, flapped its wings unhappily and turned its head, choosing between the tasty old tank and the equally tasty but new Simba. The former wanted to escape but had accumulated so much aggro he was afraid to turn his back on the wyvern. Finally, seeing Simba nearby, he decided to go for it, turned around and made a dash for it.

Crunch! The wyvern's jaws clamped down on the knight's backside. It flung him into the air like a dog playing with a stick, then smashed him to the ground. With a *Dash*, I was right there, on the spot. What a great skill. It's basically an instant, short-range teleport.

I couldn't appear behind him because the player was lying flat on the ground, so I ended up right on top of him. Nearly slipping on his armored back, I finished off our last human opponent and feel the stench of the wyvern's breath wafting into my face. It's hovering right above me. Damn, weren't you just spawned? How could you stink so bad so soon?!

"GET OOOVER HERE!"

Our paladin finally drew the creature's

attention. It turned around, nearly clobbering me with its tail, and crawled his way. The wyvern fought cautiously, hiding on the rocky ledges, preferring quick counterattacks. I was really tempted to hit it from behind, but I wasn't sure if Simba had enough aggro to hold it. And even at Level 12, it'd be foolish to go one-on-one with a Level 20 winged lizard.

A wyvern's pretty much a mini-dragon. The difference is, dragons usually have four legs, and wyverns have two, making them more bird-like, like demon geese or something. Its small but toothy head swiveled on a long, agile neck. Wyverns didn't breathe fire. At least, this one didn't try, though if it could, it probably would have used it by now.

I glanced back and got a satisfied smile from Sibyl. Too satisfied, actually — she was already at Level 4.

"Put all your points into Constitution!" I yelled and she nodded in reply.

Now I changed our party's XP distribution back to what it had been before. We had fattened up this girl enough. Actually, since there were four of us now, I kept 40% for myself and gave 20% to each of the other three. Unfair? Let them try farming solo — I'd love to see how far they'd get.

Simba was fighting like a lion. Claws clanging against his shield, sword gleaming in the air, both the wyvern and the paladin screaming at each other — it was almost a shame to interfere.

"Stacy, blast that thing with all the skills you

got. Let's see what works."

Air Ram didn't do much. *Piercing Shot* was better — the bolt glowed red and seemed to burn through the dark scales, embedding itself halfway. The creature roared and headbutted Simba's shield. *Rapid Fire* was still on cooldown. It was clear that slaying the wyvern with ordinary attacks would be a long and uncertain grind.

I kept looking back towards the treeline where we came from. There was no guarantee that another party wouldn't show up on the horizon and stab us in the back.

"I'm trying!" AngelCake took my pensive look for a reproach and started aiming more carefully at the wyvern's elusive head.

Sibyl also nodded at me, as if to say, "all good." Yet, she was noticeably pale and biting her lip, beads of sweat streaming down her temples. Healing wasn't as easy as it seemed. Still, I could see on the interface that Simba's health was dropping and then quickly recovering to the green. This girl really was a wonder weapon.

The most frustrating part was not knowing how much more we had to hit the wyvern. The *Life Sense* skill, which revealed a target's current HP, came in two varieties, one for mobs and one for players. I chose the one for players, and now regretted not splurging on both. The customary HP bar did not appear over this creature, so we could only guess how much it had left.

I took a moment to scan the ravine we were fighting in. It was almost circular, a big round clearing surrounded by cliffs with only one narrow, steep path leading in. The cliffs rose about 15 feet overhead, too steep to climb even with my Dexterity. The thick forest covered them on both sides, and the path was more like a crag, but I didn't see any real precipices. Just a slight rise, then a descent. Struck by a new idea, I turned around and headed back along the path.

To my companions' credit, none of them seemed to think their slightly crazy leader had just run off, abandoning them to their fate. I returned to where the path started descending, chose the highest point and turned right.

The trees thinned out and the rocks got bigger. At first, I had to jump from ledge to ledge, then climb, gripping with my fingertips. Eventually, I hit a ten foot rock face. It was smooth and slippery. Not too tall, but with no features to hold onto. What narrow cracks there were, were too small even for my fingers.

Climb a tree and *Dash* across its branch like a ninja? There weren't any suitable trees nearby unfortunately, only saplings. Throw a rope up? I now regretted not bringing the rope used to tie up Sibyl. What else could I use in my inventory? Aha!

I took my stilettos out of my inventory. *Shank!* The narrow blade delved deep into the thin crack, sinking almost to the hilt. I tugged at it. It was stuck tight. I grabbed it with one hand, pulled myself up, and reached as high as I could with the other hand. *Shank!* Another step for my ascent...

I stretched even further. I had no more thin,

sharp objects left. I heaved my torso up, searching for the handle of the first stiletto with my foot. Got it! I was standing on the stilettos driven into the rock a good six feet off the ground. If I stretched, I could see the edge of the cliff... just a bit more...

How long had I been wandering in the forest? Had I missed the action? Maybe more "adventurers" had already reached the ravine. Simba might already be dead and the girls...

I shook off my doubts through force of will. Squatting down, I coiled up my body and then pulled up on my outstretched arms, flinging myself into the rock face, letting go, reaching up, and flying vertically until I grabbed the edge, my hands slipping on the grass and clay... My foot found the top stiletto, pushed off it and I grabbed a tuft of grass with my other hand, slowly pulling myself up inch by inch.

Having caught my breath, I took off running! The stilettos remained in the stone, handholds for future climbers, while I raced among the boulders along the cusp of the ravine, round like a volcanic crater.

There was my team, all safe after all. AngelCake was focused, firing bolts, her chains clinking, her tits bouncing. A true Valkyrie. Sibyl, pale as a sheet, sat on the ground, her eyes fixed on Simba, barely blinking. Fully committed to her role in the party.

And there right below me was the wyvern — about nine feet away. Without much thought, I pushed off the rock and jumped straight onto its neck.

Precise Strike! My wakizashi glowed red-hot and sliced through the black armor on the creature's neck like butter. I hung there, holding the hilt, dangling off the wyvern like a leech. The demon goose hissed, trying to reach me with its teeth, but couldn't — I'd calculated correctly. I hacked at its neck, heavily, like with a butcher's cleaver. It wasn't the intended use for my noble weapon, but it worked perfectly.

The wyvern howled, piercingly and pitifully. It flapped its wings, trying to take off, but the extra weight kept it grounded. Another strike, and its heavy, bony head fell to the ground, blood spurting like a fountain, its neck flailing like a fire hose in old comedies. The impact against the rocks knocked the wind out of me, and I just lay there, staring at the sky, waiting for it all to end.

Clouds... I wonder who decides what they look like in here? Does the AI take the images of the most beautiful clouds from each player's memories? Or does it create them itself, once it's learned what a cloud is? Does it make them look like animals or ships on purpose? Does it enjoy what it does? The god-child of this little toy world. Are you mad at me for breaking one of your toys? Or are you laughing with glee at how fun it all was?

A cool hand touches my forehead.

"Want me to heal you?" Sibyl asks. "It's easier when I touch."

When I don't reply, she starts healing me on her own. A coolness flows into my body from her palm, refreshing and invigorating me, as satisfying as drinking spring water on a sweltering day.

Clap. Clap. Clap... At first, I don't understand the sound I'm hearing, but then it comes to me — a golf clap — sarcastic applause. A tall, light-haired warrior, his long hair tied back, is doing the clapping. He is wearing an animal hide over his shoulders and he has a Zweihander on his back. A Level 8 barbarian and already quite cocky by the way he's acting.

"Bravo," he says. "What a touching scene. Thou hast brought a tear to my eye. Now, put down your weapons and line up — the lot of ye. Perchance, then, you shall be spared."

Other warriors appear behind him, emerging from the treeline. I lose count by the second dozen.

Chapter 12

I JUMPED TO MY FEET, instinctively shielding Sibyl.

"Oh! I know him, that's Arthur!" The girl peered curiously from behind me. "Hi, Arthur!" she waved.

Arthur the Barbarian turned away arrogantly. To me, his name seemed more fitting for a knight. Although he was definitely the leader here — he even had a banner flying over his head. The samurai class also had leadership skills available to it, but I mostly ignored them in favor of my own combat abilities.

Arthur's banner granted +10% damage to his party; however one of the members had to be the standard-bearer, constantly lugging the rag around. It seemed like a waste to me, but it did look impressive.

"Arthur was recruiting people in the town

square for his crusade!" Sibyl went on nonchalantly. "He was even going to rescue me."

"And then?" I grew curious.

The adrenaline rush I felt before the imminent battle was starting to fade now. Sibyl didn't seem at all concerned about this armed mob, clearly here to reap our souls and loot. Either she was naive or she had a lot of faith in me — and that seemed more flattering.

"Marcus told him to kick rocks!" Sibyl laughed out loud, seemingly unaffected by her recent captivity. "And he got scared of the guards."

"Thou liest, wench! Never did that happen!" Arthur protested. "'Tis naught but foul lies and calumny! Arthur the Barbarian fears no man!"

"Whatever you say. She's free now, though, see?" I got up and sarcastically spread my arms. "So you can be on your way!"

"We have journeyed here to vanquish that vile creature!" The barbarian raised his sword.

The mob behind him roared incoherently: "Kill it!"

"Well, the creature's dead too," I replied, amused. "Everyone can go home now."

Lucky me, bumping into a role-player. He thinks himself a great lord, showing off before his host.

"We require greater proof than thy mere word!" Arthur demanded. "Hand over the egg, and I'll let thee go."

Oh but of course. That's what he's really here for. I guess he's negotiating because my Level 13 seems too much for his herd. That's right — I had gained my thirteenth level for slaying the wyvern. Simba and AngelCake were now Level 8s and Sibyl was Level 5. The demon goose had generously rewarded us with XP.

Meanwhile, Arthur's Level 8 was the highest among our uninvited guests. The rest were mostly Level 5s, 4s and even some 3s. I guess he'd gathered whoever he could persuade in the town square and set out.

"What's the range on your healing skill, Sibyl?" I asked.

"All the way to the forest," she nodded understandingly.

"You planning to fight him?" Simba asked, moving closer.

"What, you want me to surrender to these zerglings?"

"No, but..." Simba glanced at the enemies lining up, "there are too many of them."

The whole time that I distracted Arthur with small talk, he was arranging his mini-army and my party was slowly backing up — until we were against the cliffs. The barbarian noted our maneuver but merely sneered, thinking we were retreating in fear.

Right behind us was the ledge where the wyvern had perched. I thought about how we hadn't found its nest yet. The egg must be somewhere here, on the high ground, in a well-protected, safe spot...

"Simba, raise your shield."

I crouched down, offering my back. Light as a feather, Sibyl climbed up, then onto Simba's shoulders, then onto his shield and up to the cliff's edge.

She disappeared for a moment but soon peeked over the top.

"A nest!" she shouted joyfully. "There's a nest back here!"

"I know," I waved back. "AngelCake, you're next!"

"Why?" she was confused. "I'm not afraid of anyone."

"So you can shoot from a good vantage," I explained patiently. "The enemies will be in your field of fire, while you'll be far from them."

Comprehending my plan, Stacy quickly climbed up as well.

"Fleeing like rats will do thee no good!" Arthur declaimed dramatically. "Thou would'st be better served surrendering to thy victor's mercy! I PROMISE TO SPARE THY WENCHES IN EXCHANGE!"

"What a moron," Simba snorted.

"Sibyl..."

"Sibi..." the girl replied, smiling from above. "You can call me Sibi..."

"Sibi," I started giving instructions, "heal me. Only me. You can heal Simba only if he's at critical HP. Otherwise, all your focus is on me, got it?"

She nodded, no questions asked. I was increasingly pleased with our new recruit. It felt like Sibyl had been part of our party for a long time, it was that easy to communicate with her. Stacy always argued about everything, but Sibyl just listened, smiled and nodded.

"Stacy, don't let anyone get close. Prioritize those who approach. Start with the weak ones, especially those you can one-shot," I waited for her nod and continued. "Simba, you stay here... your job is to protect the girls. Don't move forward. Make sure no one gets up here."

Arthur wasn't giving us time to prepare out of mercy or chivalry. He was arranging his troops, directing four heavily armored guys to the front of his line. I figured they were tanks, although in this game the role of a tank wasn't too glamorous, and finding such players among loners was almost impossible.

A tank isn't great solo. Despite their ability to take hits, their damage output is minimal. For such aggro-focused fighters, a partner is needed to take down controlled mobs. And for balanced experience sharing in a party, you also need a leader...

The main fighting force behind the tanks was a motley crew. Levels ranging from 4 to 2, armed with swords, spears, halberds, glaives — you name it.

And of course, there was the classic rank of archers in the back. They'd shoot over the heads of their own troops. In real life, this formation would have made sense. Arthur was either a history buff or a strategy game enthusiast, so he got that right. Except he forgot that this wasn't

Agincourt, but a fantasy game.

Having issued my final orders, I turned and faced the enemy.

"Thy time for deliberation hath EXPIRED!" Arthur shouted as if anyone cared about his threats.

"Good luck, TargetAi!" I heard from behind.

Wonder who that was? Stacy or Sibi?

I started walking faster, picking up speed with each step. Back in the VR pod, my body pumped adrenaline, making my ears pound... *Boom! Boom!* like war drums. Let this be the metronome for the dance I'm about to perform.

Numerical superiority means something everywhere but in the arena. Here, it's just fodder for my swords... appetizers for the main course.

I broke into a sprint, my katana and wakizashi spread to the sides, heading straight for their tanks as if I wanted a hug.

"ARCHERS! NOCK YOUR ARROWS!"

What a clown!

BRRRONG! The annoying clangor of four shields. Mass first-level aggro only works up close. The others wouldn't be affected, so I was here to draw their fire.

Immediately, the sounds of wind, raindrops and rustling leaves filled my ears, cleansing them of the annoying, resonating noise. This was *Nirvana*, a skill I'd upgraded to Level 3 just in case. A passive skill that allowed me to completely ignore all forms of control. Aggro auras included.

Mid-stride, a second before hitting the tanks'

shields, I vanished. I'm no assassin — I don't have stealth — but I have something even better! I perform a *Dash* and reappear behind the enemy tanks, right in the midst of their archers. Then I cast *Whirlwind*, a skill for mass-PvE which sends me spinning like a possessed lawnmower. A good way to quickly dispatch dumb, low-level mobs.

Screams, curses, the sound of wood and metal clashing... I couldn't even keep track of the carnage my blades were causing — chopping bows, slicing armor, lopping off hands and fingers, slitting open unprotected throats.

One... two... three... four... five...

The skill lasted five seconds. I stopped in a dramatic combat pose, kneeling, my swords close to the ground. Around me, the minced meat quickly dissolved to ash. No more archers for the enemy. Were there six or seven of them?

The idiots who still hadn't noticed me got backstabbed. Every hit from me was a one-shot for a Level 4 player.

"IN OUR REAR!" Arthur was screaming frantically. "HE'S IN OUR REAR!"

"They've surrounded us!" clamored his minions. "It's an ambush!"

They were running my way not to attack me, but to save their lives. They fought desperately, but cowardly. *Tiger Knee...* I finished one... chopped off a hand... finished another... *Precise Strike...* another one-shot!

AngelCake was raining death into the rabble from above. I saw her bolts turning one warrior after another into dust. Advancing for our assailants was like charging a machine gun nest. But I was even more dangerous.

"GET OOOVER HERE!"

Wow, did they already break through to Simba, or is he just bored? I can't see from here, so I try to hurry and grow careless in the process.

Bong! My katana rings like a metal gong in a Buddhist temple. The fencer deflects it, and immediately swipes at with the dagger in his other hand. Only my upgraded Dexterity saves me. I dodge aside at the last moment as the dagger glows red, slicing through my armor and stabbing into my shoulder instead of my ribs. My HP drops to yellow and my arm goes limp.

My opponent quickly jumps back. He's got intelligent eyes and a quirky goatee. Level 6. He salutes me with his rapier and switches to a counterattack. He's playing an unusual class, maybe even the adventurer one I passed over. I parry his quick strikes with my katana, forced to defend myself. Did he really put all his points in Dexterity?

A pleasant coolness envelops me. Sibyl reaches me with her healing touch. Surprise, bitch! My left arm comes back to life, and I thrust my wakizashi into fencer's sternum, ripping open his chest cavity in one move.

All of a sudden, there are no more enemies. Just a moment ago, I was cutting through them like a hot knife through butter, and now I've got nothing to do. Ahead, near the cliffs, Simba is fighting the three tanks. Each one is as riddled with bolts as a pin cushion.

I rush to help him — when Arthur blocks my path.

"Let us settle this like men, with a duel!" he proclaims. "And let the winner take all the, erm, winnings!"

"Are you stupid?" I ask. "First, you gang up on us with your mob, wanting to rob and maybe even kill us, and now you want me to indulge your sense of honor?"

Instead of answering, the barbarian swings his Zweihander, bringing it down on my head. It's clearly some special skill because the heavy sword moves through the air like a twig, tracing a figure-eight and striking not from above, but from the right.

I don't even want to try blocking a strike like that with my swords. His heavy Zweihander could knock all the durability off my fragile blades with one hit. Instead, miraculously, I dodge to the side and we end up facing each other.

There's five levels' difference between us. If he were Level 1 and I Level 5, this disparity would be catastrophic for him. Conversely, between a Level 95 and a Level 100, it's barely noticeable. Right now, it's just enough to give Arthur a slim chance of winning. With his long Zweihander, he keeps me at bay, while I circle him, looking for an opening.

This idiot likes to lead, so he must have taken plenty of leadership skills, and that's good because it means he'll have less surprises for me in a duel.

I used my own skills quite generously in the initial battle, and now have to wait for the cooldown to expire.

Arthur extends his sword forward, as if marking his personal space. The blade tip points at my chest. It's trembling. The barbarian is nervous. We're evenly matched until my skills come back, but he's too scared to commit, and that suits me fine. I go on circling him, keeping my distance from his giant sword, until my cooldowns expire. Then I act.

Dash! I reappear behind Arthur and thrust my wakizashi into his throat with a *Precise Strike.* Arthur gurgles something unintelligible, falls to his knees and dies. His crusade ends here.

Left alone, the remaining tanks abandon their fight with Simba and make a break for it. Stacy takes down two from behind, and I have to chase down the third.

The first thing I see when I approach the cliffs is Sibyl's cheerful face. She peeks from above and extends something white and oval to me:

"Catch!"

"Wait, don't!" I yell.

Sibyl laughs heartily. She got me, the rascal.

Her laughter turns the page, leaving behind the blood, guts, and other gory detritus of battle. Everything looks too realistic, in this place. It's difficult to remember that it's a game. Ordinary morals — with injunctions like "thou shalt not kill," "thou shalt not covet thy neighbor's ass" and "hold the elevator door, please" — always intrude at the worst possible moment.

Meanwhile, this game only has one commandment: woe to the vanquished! Then again, I'm starting to believe that it's no different in meatspace. Its true nature is just more carefully hidden from us.

There was a whole mountain of loot left after the battle. We took the most valuable stuff, and had to hide the rest in a cache. We set it up to the right of the ravine's entrance, near the cliff where I left my stilettos. We wanted to put it in the ravine itself, but then thought, what if the wyvern respawns? That might make it difficult to reach our stash.

The wyvern itself, besides the egg, which we treated as a great treasure, dropped a dozen scales and a claw. I took all of it with me.

I wanted to pick out some new armor for Sibyl from the loot, but it turned out that any metal blocked her healing ability. And here I was, thinking of disguising her as a second-line fighter. No need for the others to know we had a healer. Better to keep her as the ace up our sleeve.

"How did you manage to get this class anyway?" I asked her.

"I just… took it…" Sibyl replied.

We were walking and chatting. Stacy had gone ahead, playing the role of bait. Simba, on the other hand, lagged behind a bit, covering our backs.

"No one else could simply 'take it,'" I objected. "I asked around."

"Maybe someone just liked me?" Sibyl flirtatiously batted her eyelashes, then laughed at herself. "I mean, look at me, who could say no to this?"

She twirled around in front of me, and I had to agree — she was irresistible. Even NPCs wouldn't be able to resist such charm. Sibyl no longer looked like a teenage girl. Her light hair was braided into a loose, voluminous braid — not the kind you'd see on a first-grader but more like something out of a fashion magazine. Her stride was light and graceful, her face constantly changing, either from the way the light hit it or her ever-changing emotions.

At times she reminded me of Marina, a blonde like her, or my neighbor Olga, or some actress, but whatever it was, with every glance, Sibyl just kept getting prettier.

"It's true," I smiled. "No one could..."

"Why do you play?" Sibyl changed the subject. "What are you here for?"

"For cash money, of course!" I replied without hesitation.

"Ugh, you're so greedy," she teased, "but I don't believe you."

"Why's that?" I was caught off guard.

"For people like you, money's not the main thing," Sibyl said seriously. "I bet you don't even count it. How much coins do you have right now?"

"I don't know," I said, a bit flustered. "Simba has it all, he's our treasurer."

"You see?" She raised a finger triumphantly

as if she had just scored an important point.

Surprisingly, talking with Sibyl was really enjoyable. Around AngelCake, I was comfortable, knowing I could get anything from her and she'd always give in. Interacting with Marina was like a duel I'd learned to win, savoring my victories each time. But this was different.

I didn't just like her. I liked the way she saw me, talked about me. Her words made me seem important, interesting, and cool — just as I had always wanted to be.

"Why do you play?" I turned the question back on her.

"I like it here," she replied thoughtfully. "Everything's so different: the air's clean… there's big trees… the town… it's all so beautiful!"

"And are the spiders beautiful too?" I teased.

"The spiders too!" laughed Sibyl. "Have you seen their green fur? I'd love to pet them! Oh!"

She looked back anxiously. A bellowing roar sounded from the forest behind us, very close, just a few dozen feet away. Damn! Simba's supposed to be back there!

But the roar grew closer and louder — until Simba himself burst out from the undergrowth behind us — bellowing, roaring. His eyes were glassed over and empty — just two blank pupils. He growled hoarsely, raised his sword, and charged directly at us.

Chapter 13

"LOOK OUT!" I barely manage to push Sibyl to one side of the path while I jump to the other.

Growling like a bear, Simba rushes past us oblivious to our presence. He's holding his sword like a club and seems utterly unaware of what he's doing. But damn! AngelCake is further ahead! What the hell is happening?!

"AngelCake — Stacy — watch out!" I yell, taking off after our crazed tank.

"Stop... Don't come closer! Stop, you idiot or I'll shoot! Aaah!" Stacy's voice gives way to a frantic shriek.

"Raaah!"

Damn, what am I doing?! *Dash!* I hop forward, hoping I'll land on the path and not among the trees that grow thickly on either side. Luckily, the *Dash* brings me right up behind Simba.

He's already lost his sword and is simply trudging towards AngelCake, who is pointing her crossbow at him, pale with fear.

"Targe, what's wrong with him?!" Fear blends with concern for Simba in Stacy's voice.

I kick our paladin behind the knee, and he flops on his back. I pounce, holding his right arm, and Stacy, realizing what I'm trying to do without me having to say it, grabs his left.

Sibyl appears from around the corner. She's not even out of breath. No surprise there, with her athletic build, she could run cross-country races with plenty of stamina to spare. Thankfully, her physique doesn't make her look like a muscle-bound bodybuilder. I quickly shake off *that* mental image.

Sibi deftly sits on Simba's legs. Our paladin tries to break free, but the three of us hold him down firmly. He shows no rational reaction at all. His pupils are dilated; did he get high on something? When did that happen?

"Here, take this!" says the healer, handing me a rope. The same one they had used to tie her up earlier. She's always prepared.

Simba struggles as hard as he can, but we manage to tie up his hands and then his legs. Wrapped up like a package, he lies under the bushes, occasionally twitching and growling in discontent.

I'm furious. Not only are we wasting time, but I also have no clue what's happened to Simba and what to do next. Should we just leave him here and come back later? I don't want to. First, it'll be harder to kill the wyvern without our tank. And second, I just don't want to. He's not like Yumi, who joined us with her own agenda and couldn't care less about our party.

"Sibi, you're a healer," I say. "Can you check him out, maybe see what's afflicted him?"

In some games, healing classes can not only restore health but also remove debuffs. Who knows what abilities healers have here. Sibi might not be able to remove a debuff, that would require special skills, but maybe she can see something...

Sibyl's gaze freezes, like a psychic from one of those TV shows. I know she's browsing her interface, but it still looks funny.

"His health is fine... the bar is full..." she says, "He's got a debuff. It's class-related... What class is he?"

"Paladin."

What debuffs could a paladin have? Of all the classes, they're usually the most stable, the Holy Warrior. Did he see a witch? I glance suspiciously at Sibyl, who with her frozen gaze does look a bit witchy.

But if he had seen a witch, he'd be trying to kill her, not us. What else is part of a paladin's duties? A "Vow of Celibacy"... Did he break that already?! When?! And with whom?!

There's something else I remember about the paladin's requirements, though it's less memorable than the amusing vow. That's right! Prayer! Paladins are supposed to pray for ten minutes a day.

"Stacy, did you see Simba praying to anyone?"

"No... Whom would he pray to?" AngelCake shrugs. "There aren't even any temples here. We thought we'd wait until some gods show up."

So there are no gods, and he decided not to pray. But the AI thinks otherwise, and now he's suffering from "Holy Madness," according to Sibyl.

How did religions start? Unexpectedly, my most useless college major, sociology, comes in handy. Before there were temples, people prayed to idols. They would craft them by hand and place them in sacred groves. Why can't we do the same?

Working together, we drag the resistant paladin off the road. There's a nice little clearing nearby, likely used as a camp by some bandits before. Trees surround us on all sides. I circle around them and stop in front of an old, crooked birch tree.

At a height just above mine, the tree looks like it was struck by lightning. It continued to grow bent almost in half, but the lower part of the trunk is covered in strange bumps and growths, and the upper part is hanging by a thin piece of wood, ready to break off at any moment.

"Sibi, we don't have a hatchet among our loot, do we?" I ask.

Thanks to her high stamina, Sibyl can carry almost as much loot as Simba. She pulls out a small hatchet from her inventory. The blade is too narrow, but we're in no position to be picky.

In a few strikes, I lop off the weak splinter tethering the broken treetop to the trunk. We don't need it, so I drag it away. Now, in front of me stands a tall wooden post, slightly taller than a person, and I desperately try to recall what ancient idols looked like and which one to use as my model.

What I need is some kind of a patron of warriors, maybe Hachiman in a samurai helm or a defiant Mars or a one-eyed Odin... I tentatively chip away with the hatchet, trying to impart at least a rough resemblance to one of these deities on the wood.

"Can I give it a try?" Sibyl asks.

I hand her the hatchet with relief but not much hope. Sibyl scrutinizes the post, circling it. She starts chipping at it haphazardly, stepping back from time to time to admire her work. Gradually, the wooden trunk begins to take on human features.

"You're doing great," I compliment her.

"I went to art school," Sibyl proudly announces, "though I've never... carved with an axe before."

The birch is old, its trunk bent and covered with dark growths that, upon closer inspection, resemble...

"Sibi, what have you carved? It's a woman!"

"You wanted me to make a man out of such a curvy figure?" Sibyl responds unfazed. "The wood itself suggested this form. And what kind of man would demand a vow of celibacy from his followers? A goddess, on the other hand, easily. Women are jealous..."

I noted that she said this about women in the third person, as if trying to show she was above such female prejudices.

"AngelCake, could you turn a little?" Sibi asks. "Just like that, so I can... yes, that's perfect!"

"What's perfect?" Stacy asked puzzled.

"Just stand there, don't move!" Sibyl pleads.

Damn! I just realized who the wooden statue reminds me of. With its ample bust, slim waist, and full hips, the wooden goddess crudely but surprisingly resembles AngelCake.

"Done!" Sibi finishes the goddess's pouty face with a few strokes. "Meet the goddess... An... An...," she glances at AngelCake, "Anima! Accept our humble offerings, oh goddess!"

She kneels dramatically and places the hatchet at the base of the post. I drag Simba over to the idol and force him to kneel before it.

"Simba! Look... look up! This is your goddess!"

"Gaaargh!" Simba ogles the idol, drooling.

"Goddess," I intone, "forgive this foolish... clueless man. He meant well, but his forgetful nature got the best of him. Restore the remnants of sense to his brain. He needs every little bit he has."

I grab the intransigent Simba by the scruff and force his head down to the ground, while I look at the goddess's chubby-cheeked face, shadowed as if by a passing cloud...

"Andryusha… damn, what the hell?! What did you guys tie me up for?"

At this point, I'm just glad to hear coherent words coming out of him.

"Stay put, you lousy paladin!" I start untying the knot at my friend's wrists. "Don't you remember anything?"

"Nope… I was walking down the path and then everything went dark."

"Don't you know that you have to pray daily?" I scold Simba. "I mean, I'm sorry I forgot to remind you, but you should've gotten a notification."

"I thought it was spam…"

"Well, that 'spam' got you running around the woods pantsless, scaring AngelCake!"

"Staceeey?" Simba guiltily cranes his head. "Is this true?"

"Just listen to Targe more closely next time, you chatterbox!" Stacy absolves him, examining her wooden alter-ego.

The idol really turned out well. Sibi even captured Stacy's facial expression — naive, slightly petulant, and very pleased with herself. I suspect this goddess will have quite the personality. Thank God it's just a hunk of wood.

"Thank your friends. We even made you a goddess," I stand up, patting Simba on the shoulder. "Now pray, and let's go. I'll wait for you on the path."

"How do I pray, though?" Simba blinks.

"You don't know how to talk to girls?" Sibyl asks. "First, tell her how awesome she is, then ask for something."

"But that's a girl, and this is a goddess..."

"Same thing," the healer waves her hand, "just on a different scale."

"I can do that!" the newest convert to our newly-founded cult said cheerfully. "Anima, you're fierce, mighty, unbeatable, and super sexy! All other goddesses are nothing compared to you! Grant me strength, power, and something else useful, and I'll exalt your name!"

Leaving Simba to his theological experiments, I walked back to the path. Finding a good spot where I could see the path without being easily spotted, I sat down, enjoying the summer sun. It'd be nice just to sit here and not move. No running, no fighting. It's nice here. There's a blizzard swirling outside the walls of the MosTech office tower, but here in VR land it's warm. Who needs a resort when in this place, the sunshine's eternal? Maybe there's a river nearby. A beach with white sand. Dive in, splash the girls with water... listen to them squeal...

"Enjoying the view?" Stacy stated the obvious and sat down next to me.

Her chains clinked provocatively, and I suddenly realized she was practically naked. Her chest was definitely in full view. After that one time in the locker room, nothing had happened between us. She had quietly taken a backseat, willingly becoming my battle buddy — and now I realized it wasn't out of spite, but rather a sacrifice she had made.

All for me. She might grumble or throw tantrums, but she'd go anywhere with me, and even tolerate Marina, Yumi, and others if more showed up. For my sake, she would endure, understand, and bake me pies.

On a whim, I hugged Stacy — and she, as if waiting exactly for this, snuggled up to me, resting her head on my shoulder.

"How many people did we take down today?" Stacy mused. "Will they all be kicked out of the beta? Who'll be left then?"

"Oh they won't be kicked out." We heard Sibyl's voice behind us. She had come up silently. "Didn't you guys check the quests?"

Stacy jerked as if she wanted to straighten up, but I held her. Why be embarrassed or hide anything? Sibi wasn't bothered by our intimacy; she sat down on the other side of me. Here I am in a garden of flowers, while Simba's up there chatting with his wooden lady.

"We checked," I opened the interface. "'Guardians have discovered five wyvern nests outside the city. You must...'"

"No, higher up!" Sibyl interrupted. "The one that begins with 'Create a party...'"

"'Create a party or join an existing one...' Is that all?!" I laughed. "Then why all these crowds and battles?!"

"It's a tutorial, right!?" Sibyl's eyes widened in surprise. "Otherwise, after today's quest, there would only be one player left..."

She had such long and fluffy eyelashes that

when she batted them, it seemed like there should be a gust of wind. I mean, it's not nice to stare at one girl while hugging another but...

And she was right about the single remaining player bit. Well, not player, but single party. Today's King of the Hill quest suggested precisely that. It wasn't about defeating wyverns; it was about gathering all the eggs in one basket. And that basket would inevitably be carried by the strongest — or the luckiest.

I already knew most of the favorites. Of course, Anna was first. I wonder how she'll handle the party requirement. Will she take someone and then kick them out once it's done? As far as I understand, she's a born loner, but even loners have to follow the game's rules.

Can't count out Lance's squad either. We played a dirty trick on them last time, stopping them from leveling up, but champions are made, not born. Now he'll be fighting tooth and nail for any advantage. Honestly, I'd be more wary of Lance's team than the rest of the low-level rabble.

I mean, I just don't get how anyone could still be Level 2 after five rounds of this beta. I guess for some people, there's nothing odd in it as long as the money's coming in and the quests are being completed. If it weren't for the Purge, there would be Level 0s still running around. Noobishness is ineradicable.

"And how do you know so much?" I turned to Sibyl.

"Marcus told me..."

"Who's Marcus?" The mention of some unknown guy unnerved me. Was I jealous? That'd be funny.

"The knight who had me on a rope."

"What's his problem anyway?" Stacy became outraged on behalf of our new friend.

"He was afraid I'd run away. And I did run away from him three times," Sibyl laughed as if escaping from in-game abuse was some joke. "He kept threatening to tie me up and finally that's what he did. He also threatened to kill me. I told him, 'if you kill me, I'll fail the quest and won't come back.' That's when he explained what would really happen."

"What a creep!" Stacy jumped up. "I'll tie him up myself if I meet him again!"

And leaning over me, they started plotting revenge against this unknown Marcus bloke. My inevitable arousal and the ensuing bout with my satyriasis was only prevented by Simba's appearance.

"Guess what? I got a new quest!" he boasted. "A divine one!"

"What kind?" I untangled myself from the female bodies.

"I need to create four more altars for my goddess and then I'll not just be a paladin, but a chaplain, and I'll be able to grant blessings in her name!" Simba struck a proud pose. "That's right, oh children of Anima, hear now our deity's word and rejoice!"

Wow! What initially seemed like an annoying

hindrance now shaped up to be a very interesting opportunity. But that's for later; now it's time to go — run even! Time was slipping away. We had spent over an hour on one egg, and there were five total!

We raced along the trail back to town, I checked the map, turned onto another path, and we dashed to the next boss. We moved along as a tight party now with no time for small fry like gankers or griefers. And yet, it turned out that we were still too late.

The next wyvern was in a valley to the northeast of town, but it was already dead and three knights stood pensively over its nest. The piles of loot lying around suggested that the wyvern had sold its life dearly. The few survivors were either about to draw straws or figure out who was stronger. We relieved them of this difficult choice by offering to exchange their lives and gear for the egg.

One didn't accept our extremely flattering offer and died, while the other two proved wiser. I even left them some of the loot the monster dropped. Our inventories were full anyway, though we tried to take only the most valuable items.

On the path to the third wyvern nest, a bad feeling began to nag at me. No mysticism in it, though. We'd been lucky so far, but sooner or later, we were bound to run into one of the top parties.

We had covered about half the distance when my premonitions began to prove true. First, we heard stomping and shouting, then a funny fat guy burst onto the road in front of us. He was desperately moving his short chubby legs and seemed out of his mind because he didn't even think to stop and ran smack-dab into Simba.

"What's up with you?" asked the peaceful servant of warlike and awesome Anima.

"Back there... Back there!" the fat man pointed behind him. "Certain death befalls anyone who goes there."

He squeezed between the girls and managed to run another five meters before catching a crossbow bolt in the back. Stacy turned around, met my gaze, and shrugged. I trained her well — XP doesn't grow on trees. You have to knock it down with well-aimed shots.

Then we started encountering piles of loot. Singles and small groups. Curious as ever, Sibyl examined them, holding up any good weapons and expensive gear for my review. Sometimes she even threw something out of her stash to take something new.

Whoever was there ahead of us didn't bother with trinkets.

"What do you think? Who's this certain death we're headed for?" the healer asked me.

I didn't have to think because I knew. So when we reached another convenient spot, I turned off the road and began to lead my party. The trail here skirted a small hill, overgrown with bushes. The climb wasn't very steep, but it would give us a few extra seconds. Even if our opponent wanted to drop in on us, it would be hard for her to *Dash* in without seeing exactly where we were.

All these little details add up to victory. Absolutely every factor must work for you — and against your opponent. Sun, wind, position, time... There's no "second place" in battle. It's either you or her: Kill or Die.

There, on the hill, I unloaded my loot, completely emptying my inventory so that I could move light on my feet. Then I issued orders to my party.

"Sibyl, lie low and don't breathe. Heal me only when my health drops into the red. You're the ace up our sleeve. No one can know about you until the moment comes. Simba — her life is in your hands. The enemy can only get to her over your dead body. Stacy, when I lower my hand, use your most powerful attack, your *Air Ram.* You'll probably only have time for one shot, so aim well."

After leaving the rest on the hill, I went down to the path, sat on the grass, and leaned my back against a big pine tree.

I didn't have to wait long. Soon enough, I spotted a white figure flickering amid the distant trees. Like a poisonous insect, she didn't hide her presence but rather flaunted it.

The red droplets of blood on her white satin corset looked like designer embroidery. When I stood up to meet her, she froze, demonstratively spreading the fingers of her right hand. I stood in front of her in a similarly dramatic pose, like two samurais in a showdown where the victor is the one who draws his sword faster.

Level 20! Daaamn! How does she do it?! To me, this Level 20 seemed far more dangerous than a predictably dumb wyvern.

"Hello!" I cheerfully raised my hand and waved at her. "What a meeting. You're probably wondering about the surprise I have in store for you."

Anna stayed silent. Her lips were pressed together; her eyes were squinting. After my words, she quickly scanned the treeline on both sides of the path. Smart girl. Her prey is acting strangely. It's not afraid, not running away, not launching a desperate attack. So Anna bides her time.

"Do you have the eggs?" she asks.

"Yeah, two of them," I say with a grin. "Or do you doubt my manhood?"

"Idiot!" Anna snorts. "We're supposed to be fighting to the death. How am I supposed to kill you now?"

"I have a proposal," I reply. "We can make a deal. You're stronger, but I can still surprise you. I'd rate your chances as seventy-thirty. Are you willing to risk those odds?"

"What are you proposing?" Anna can't help but ask.

"I'll let you win this quest," I pause for effect, "on one condition."

"I hate conditions," Anna says. "I'd rather just kill you."

"As you wish," I smile and lower my hand.

Chapter 14

WITH A BURST OF DUST Anna's figure explodes into sudden motion! I knew she had a skill for surprise attacks, a passive skill that's always available to her. I kept meaning to pick up one for me too, but there were tastier options. Our builds are very similar, except she's seven levels stronger.

Anna scans the treeline. She's used her *Dash*... Well, I wasn't wrong when I said AngelCake would only have one shot. This bitch calculated where the bolt would come from. A second later, I hear loud cursing from inside the woods and I *Dash* in after her with a smirk.

AngelCake's trap skill was called *Windfall*, a funny name for a first-level trap. Stacy wasn't just an archer, but a jack-of-all-trades. Right now, her trade could be admired from a lower angle in all its glory. Simba and I had spent a good five minutes getting Stacy up onto the branch of a pine, accompanied by Sibyl's snide remarks and Stacy's complaints. She ended up not too high, yet just over where Anna had dashed to in order to ambush the archer she expected to find there — and set off the trap that AngelCake had set under the tree.

"Gah! Damn you! You fuckin' freaks!" Anna hacked at the clingy dry branches that firmly held her in place.

Rapid Fire! Stacy lets fly almost point-blank and most of the bolts hit their mark. Anna jerks in pain and that's when I join in. *Precise Strike*, *Two-Handed Cleave* and even *Whirlwind.* I unload all my special skills into Anna in a few seconds. In a rage, Anna, begins to thrash and holler:

"Bastard! I'll tear you apart! I'll wipe all of you out!"

At last she shatters the fragile trap, rolls away and comes up in a combat stance. She looks roughed up: covered in cuts, her stockings are torn, even her cheeky corset has slipped, exposing a dark nipple. Her demeanor reminds me of a Siamese cat, unsure whether to fight or flee. The start of battle clearly hasn't gone in her favor. She hasn't even scratched us.

AngelCake keeps her in her sights. As for me, I re-sheathe my katana once more and hold out my hand...

"Now the odds are fifty-fifty, right?" I say with a smirk, "Or sixty-forty in our favor? I just want you to know that you won't get your fancy corset back if we win... I'll give it to AngelCake... And you'll be all sad and jealous 'cause she's got bigger boobs than you..."

"Enough chatter! Let's fight!" Anna barks.

"My offer still stands," I say. "You get two wyvern eggs and leave peacefully. We could even escort you back to town, in case someone tries to mess with you."

"Go to hell," Anna responds, but without her earlier malice. "What do you want from me anyway? A night of passion?!"

AngelCake snorts indignantly from the branch above.

"You think too highly of yourself," I smile. "Or is a night with you so great that it's worth failing a quest over?"

"Who knows with you. You're the militant fuckboi here, after all," Anna fires back. "So, what do you value more... me or your eggs?"

She lowers her sword and strikes a pose. It looks stunning, like it's made for a foldout. But more, importantly my charm roll worked! She's not fighting; she's talking, ready to bargain.

"You're worth much more than those two pathetic eggs," I lay on with a convoluted compliment. "But in the future, I'll surely find something worth paying you back with."

"So, what do you want?" Anna asks seriously now, no longer joking.

"Tell me everything you know about the AI, the neural network. No riddles, no half-truths. We meet up out in meatspace and you spill the beans about everything."

Anna looks at me thoughtfully, weighing her options, then nods slowly.

* * *

"My disappointment knows no bounds," says the mayor.

His facial expression — the down-turned corners of his mouth, the slightly closed eyelids, the very tip of his nose drooping in dejection — all demonstrate the depth of his disappointment. He's trying his hardest to show that he doesn't understand how we dared to bother him if we failed so badly.

"Fortune wasn't on our side, Your Honor," I shrug indifferently, not going into any details. "But we got lucky in another way. Look what we managed to obtain! An artifact of divine power!"

With a magician's gesture, quite easy in the virtual world, I pull out a hefty club and, holding it in both hands like a ceremonial weapon, present it to the mayor.

He tenses up at first — it even seems like he's about to call the guards — but then relents and relaxes. I'm acting peacefully, and for a sudden assassination attempt, this isn't the likely weapon.

The club really was a miraculous find. After parting with Anna, who declined the honor of an escort, I spent another ten minutes explaining to my party the difference between strategic advantage and tactical victories, then lost my patience and yelled, "Anyone who's not happy with my decision can go to hell!" Then I spent some more time accepting apologies, tearful ones from AngelCake, and grumbling ones from Simba.

The only one who initially supported me was Sibyl. Although I think she just didn't care. Yet her "the raid leader is always right, guys" and "don't listen to those fools" still warmed my heart.

After some team-building and team spirit exercises, I turned my attention to Simba's divine quest. I've had a strange intuition for such coincidences lately. Maybe I always had it and merely dismissed it: In my crappy everyday life, a coincidence seemed more of a threat that could make an already bad situation worse.

Here, however, I began looking around with curiosity and anticipation. Life gives us signs, especially in a world where every blade of grass is created with a purpose and serves a greater design.

Sure, there were other paladins in the game. It's a popular class that's even OP in some games. Tanking... dealing damage... blessing... healing... An entire party in one character. There are many ways to nerf this class, one being the complex and tedious questing for skills. It's a class for role-players who enjoy playing the "holy warrior" role. For casual gamers, it tends to be a hellish nightmare.

I have no idea who the others prayed to. Maybe they also invented a deity and mumbled something to it without extra pomp, or maybe they just succumbed to their first fit of "holy madness."

Not everyone would be fussed over like Simba and I were. The main thing is, we were lucky to be at the beginning of something new. And as everybody knows, the early bird gets the worm.

There were five wyvern nests, so I figured there could be five altars too. The country roads radiated out from the town like the rays of a big star. We'd already done one, so there were four to go. We could make it if we didn't dawdle. There was only an hour left till the end of the round.

The AI seemed to be on our side too. Every path we tried, we'd find a cozy glade with the right kind of tree for hewing into an idol. And if we didn't, Simba would whip out his two-handed battleaxe and turn the "wrong" tree into the two-meter pole we needed.

Sibyl sculpted, AngelCake posed, Simba prayed, and I oversaw these holy works — that is, I stood aside, ate strawberries, and yelled at my party members to hurry up. Fittingly, each glade looked like it would have wild strawberries growing in it — and there always were.

By the final idol, Sibyl had gotten so good at her art that the goddess looked as good as living: Any moment now, she'd pull her wooden legs out of the ground and start smacking some sinner. And when Simba finished his prayer to "Awesome Anima, before whom other gods are nothing," a club fell on his head, hitting him squarely on his pate.

Touching it granted the "Blessing of Anima" buff, boosting all stats by 10% for half an hour. As a servant of the goddess, Simba could also bestow this blessing, but only five times per hour, whereas the club worked continuously. This plunged my buddy into a state of gloom and envy, but I decided to hold onto the weapon anyway.

As I hoped, Simba's divine quest was the first in a series. Now the goddess wanted her own altar within the town limits. And so here I was, presenting the divine gift to the mayor, who was very disappointed... but I've mentioned that already.

"Touch this wondrous item, Your Honor," I offer the club to the mayor. He looks at it warily, then picks up a silver bell from the table.

Ding-A-Ling! The sound fills the room. Out of nowhere, a Level 5 guard pops out. Just a regular soldier, not an officer. It looks like the town guard is growing in strength — good thing that we're still ahead of them.

"Touch this club," commands the mayor.

The guard obediently reaches out and touches the club. A golden glow runs over it, transfers to his hand, runs up his arm, and disappears before the soldier can take fright.

"How do you feel?" the town head looks on with interest. The goddess didn't skimp on special effects.

"Great, Your Honor!" the guard clenches his fist emotionally. "I feel...woooah, so good!!! Ready for battle. If I had a chance now, I'd really stick it to those eight-legged freaks!"

"Then go stick it to them..." the mayor

approves graciously. "No time to waste... Go on now..."

"Happy to serve, Your Honor!" The guard grabs his spear and rushes off to do his military duty.

The NPC's expression changes. Now it's thoughtful, even a bit dreamy. He's probably imagining his army, blessed with the sacred club, enthusiastically smashing the spiderlings that have infested his town.

"And what do you want for this marvelous item, oh mighty TargetAi?" the mayor tries to feign indifference, but the twinkle in his eyes betrays him.

"Nothing," I reply. "I offer this sacred weapon to the town for free... Though, under one condition..."

"Speak," the mayor stands up impatiently.

"I request a suitable place to house this artifact..." I go all in. "The denizens of this fine town should know who to thank for this grace... An altar in testament to the Goddess Anima and... their wise town leader."

The mayor lifts his head proudly. In his dreams, he's probably already cutting the ribbon to the new temple.

"Let it be so!" he declares. "You've surprised me twice today, TargetAi. The doors of my residence shall now always remain open to you. Come see me any time you like, no invitation required."

+2 REPUTATION WITH THE MAYOR.

CURRENT REPUTATION: 2/10 (INTEREST).

"Thank you, Your Honor, you won't regret it," I say quickly, "but now we must take our leave."

The timer counts down the last seconds of the quest. Just before leaving, I manage to say:

"Don't disappear, Sibyl. Let's meet at the building's entrance!"

Then I feel the floor drop under my feet, leaving me midair for a second before I begin falling and falling...

* * *

This time I changed into my street clothes without any further adventures. No one needed me — not affectionate battle companions, not cunning careerists, not vengeful competitors, not even the deceitful company execs.

I went downstairs to find Simba and AngelCake waiting for me, dancing from the cold.

"Have you seen Sibyl?" I asked.

"Nah..." Simba replied, "Maybe she's shy? Or it takes longer to change in the main VR hall?"

Honk! I heard from the parking lot.

I saw Marina, already sitting behind the wheel of her red Mazda. *Honk honk!*

"Damn, I gotta go. Simon, wait to see if she shows up... If anything, at least get her phone number... Tell her we need to meet up to discuss team strategy."

"We'll wait, don't worry," my friend waved me on.

I couldn't explain why I was so insistent on seeing Sibyl in real life. I just wanted to. I needed to see what she was like in the real world, as if that could explain something important to me.

Marina didn't nag me for making her wait, or for a dozen other reasons girls usually nag guys. She just asked, "Home?" made a sharp turn, and, flinging snow with her wide tires, drove onto the road.

"Uh-huh," I nodded. "Home."

We ran three traffic lights before I noticed something was off.

"Whose home are we going to?"

"To mine, of course," Marina didn't hesitate for a second.

Just like that, she had already settled me in her place. Quite fast — but more importantly, I didn't have any objections to it. Her place was cozy, clean, spacious... Why not? Especially since it came equipped with Marina herself.

"I was hoping I could see my mom first."

Without another word, Marina made a U-turn, and we headed in the opposite direction.

"Oh, won't my little Marina come up?" said my mom with some disappointment. "At least for some tea."

Mom definitely saw Marina's car from the window and now dreamed of luring its driver inside. But you can't argue with a mother's intuition. At our first meeting, I couldn't have imagined this turn of events, but it seemed now like my mom's intuition had been accurate.

I quickly changed in my room and sat down in the kitchen with mom, handing her another part of my payment for the beta. The TV blared so loudly in my parents' room that mom had to restart her count of the cash for the third time.

"What's with the noise?"

"Dad's watching the news," mom replied indifferently.

My parents' room was dark, noisy, and reeked of alcohol. The TV was cranked up to the max. Dad didn't care. He slept, sprawled on the sagging sofa, still in his winter coat.

I found the remote, turned off the TV, and stood in silence for a bit, staring at his completely unrecognizable, bloated face. Dad snored loudly, twitching in his sleep. A strip of drool hung from his open mouth. His cheek was scraped, the skin from a sore dried into a red scab on his unshaven stubble.

I'm about to walk out the door, get into a beautiful, expensive car, go to a beautiful, expensive apartment, and sleep with a beautiful, expensive girl. And they'll stay here.

"Mom..." I asked, returning to the kitchen, "should we put dad in a clinic? We have the money. Let them treat him..."

"It won't help," mom said wearily. "I've tried so many times to persuade him. I've bought pills and special teas. He doesn't want to sober up. He says it's shameful to look people in the eye when he's sober. He used to be a role model, an upstanding citizen... Now he's a bum."

"I've to go, mom..." I didn't feel like continuing the conversation, stood up, and awkwardly kissed mom on the head.

"Go... be happy, son..." she said softly, then remembered: "Say hi to my sweet little Marina. Let me pack some food to take with you... Wait here, I'll be quick..."

"I'm in a hurry, mom!" I quickly dashed into the hallway and slammed the door.

"You're wearing that rag again..." Marina frowned disapprovingly. "Why did you change?"

"It was clean..." I tried to explain.

"Fine." Marina stepped on the accelerator so hard the car bounced over a snowbank and screeched out of the yard. "In that case, we're going shopping! And no arguing, I have big plans for you tonight!"

We parked in the deck of a large shopping center. Marina led me through the crowd of shoppers unerringly, like a salmon heading upstream. For reasons known only to her, she wrinkled her nose at some stores and dashed headlong into others. Finally, we chose a boutique where the prices scared me, but the clothes were easy on the eyes.

"Hello... welcome..." a girl in a pantsuit rushed to meet my companion.

"Hello," Marina nodded regally. "We need to pick out some clothes, a jacket... pants... basically a full..."

"Mari!" a loud, smarmy voice interrupted Marina. "What brings you to our neck of the woods? Shopping for new outfits?"

We turned around in unison. A guy with slick black hair, in tight pants and a blue silk shirt, stood looking at us. Practically glowing with joy, he hurried towards us with open arms, as if expecting a hug. What am I saying, "us?" Nah — he was aiming for Marina, breezing past me as if I were just part of the scenery.

"Ollie! Hello!" Marina chirped cheerfully, smiling.

I was already irritated by having to go to a mall during rush hour and everything related to the process of trying on and buying apparel in general — and now this stooge's sudden appearance unnerved and infuriated me completely. As I stood there feeling invisible, I felt torn between wanting to tell "Mari" to get lost and throwing a stiff uppercut at this guy's gut and watching him double over and gasp for air.

"What the heck, Ollie? Where did you come from?!"

CHAPTER 15

"FANCY A CUP OF COFFEE to catch up?" lilted the prig like a nightingale. "These rags aren't going anywhere... You could tell me all about where you've been all this time while we're at it."

"Oleg, I... I can't right now," Marina shuffled in place, then took a step to the side. Away from me. "The coffee will have to wait..."

Is she embarrassed by me or something?! She seems to be trying to come up with an excuse to this Oleg character for why on earth she came into this fancy store with a dummy like me.

In the past, I'd probably just walk out or flip out and tell Marina to get lost. I already knew she wasn't from my social sphere and had rich guys like him circling around her.

Who does he think he is anyway? The king of the hill? Standing there in just a shirt and polished shoes. So then he's not a shopper like us, but an employee here. It's freezing outside. No one's going to go stomping through the snow in such dainty shoes. Even if he changed in the cloakroom, I doubt he'd swap shoes. The salesgirl stepped aside, not interfering, so he must be with this store. Could he be the owner of this place?

No, he's too polished for that. But I believe in the saying that men in coats and ties work for men in jeans and T-shirts. Anyway, might as well check!

"Hey! Are you Marina's beau?" I blurt out stupidly, wedging myself between them. "I'm her relative, just in from the countryside."

Marina blinks dumbly, while Oleg wrinkles his nose in disgust.

"Hello..." he manages. "No, we're just acquaintances..."

"Oh come on, don't be shy," I whistle, looking around. "'Just acquaintances?' Is this your store? Living the high life, aren't you?"

"No, I'm the senior sales manager here," he replies awkwardly. "It's an expensive store."

He looks at Marina as if to ask, "Who's this clown?" But she just stares at us blankly, holding her breath. Girls love to watch guys butt heads over them. Sometimes they even engineer the confrontation to get a good show.

"Well, I'm loaded. A real slayer, uh-huh," I raise my fist, showing it to little Oleg. "I slaughter bulls... at the meatpacking plant, uh-huh."

"What are you talking about, Andrew?!" Marina finally snaps out of it.

"So, you work here then." I unclench my fist and give Oleg a "friendly" but stiff smack on the shoulder. "Good for you! I'd like to buy some slippers... You do sell shoes, don't you?"

"We do," says Oleg the sales manager, rubbing his shoulder in pain.

"Bring me something stylish. Your choice." Then I clap loudly and bark, "In a jiffy, Ollie, in a jiffy! We're busy people!"

Oleg dashes off to the shoe racks.

"What are you doing?!" Marina hisses at me. "What did he do to you?"

"If he *had* done something, I'd have killed him," I joke.

Oleg comes back, carrying some shoes.

"Got any Gucci, Ollie?" I ask on a whim.

"Loafers, clogs or derbies?" he asks.

"Really, you have all those?!" I'm surprised, hearing unfamiliar words. "Something for the season..."

"You're acting like a thug," Marina snorts.

"A thug would have already smashed his face, darling," I laugh. "I'm just having fun."

Marina can't help but smile. Then she looks at how Oleg is bustling about and giggles into her fist. And then I understand what the Master told me about women. They really are testing us constantly.

It's an eternal battle in which as soon as a woman wins by finding a weakness and breaking the man — bending him to her will — she loses respect for and interest in him, thereby losing the war at the very moment of her triumph.

And it's no different if things go vice versa: Getting rejected and yielding time and time again, she realizes that her chosen one is the best. However, that doesn't stop her from testing him further.

Oleg brings over some sneakers that look comfy even at first glance. I thought Gucci was all about incredible showing-off, but these look like any ordinary shoes.

"That will be 1,232 Euros," Oleg says, looking at Marina for some reason.

She nods, confirming I'm good for it and spreads her hands as if to say, "What can I do? My relative is a little odd."

"Size 42," I declare a bit belatedly.

The salesgirl gets involved, almost escorting me by the arm to a low, plush bench next to the standing mirrors.

"Oleg, I thought you were better than this," I finish off the dandy vengefully. "Will I really have to change all by myself?"

* * *

"You don't have to go alpha at every turn," Marina grumbles.

"What, should I have run off to get you guys coffee?" I respond.

"No. You should've kept quiet... We were just talking... And you blew up like some brute..."

"It doesn't work that way, Marina," I explain.

"You can't just switch from cutting throats in one place and sucking up in another, especially when your girl is hiking up her tail in front of every loser. It's your fault alone I humiliated your friend. He had no idea who I was. But you knew."

"He's not my friend," Marina admits to my surprise. "He just gave me good discounts and let me know about what was coming out... I won't get that from him anymore."

I stop and spread my hands.

"I'm not holding you back, go apologize... Treat him to coffee. Maybe you'll wrangle a discount out of him."

Marina falls silent and just fumes angrily for a while. We end up passing by a couple of boutiques she seemed interested in earlier.

We spent three hours shopping. The Gucci sneakers were the most extravagant purchase, but we seriously splurged on other items too and barely managed to squeeze the bags in the trunk of Marina's car.

Her plan was to drag me to a nightclub that night. "You don't relax enough," she declared. "It's time you let loose a bit."

I suspected there was another reason, and I wasn't wrong. Marina wanted to present me to her girlfriends. Whether it was to show off or seek their approval, I don't know, but she went about preparing for this event meticulously.

There were two friends. A tall, long-haired, model-like blonde named Alla who worked as a lawyer, and a tanned and fit yoga instructor named Yana who owned her own studio.

Alla dreamed of getting married so that she'd never have to work again, and Yana was crazy about esports athletes. Or maybe it was the other way around. It was hard to keep track in the flood of information they dumped on me, especially since I could barely make out half of what they said amid the din of the nightclub.

We went to The Underground, one of the new, trendier clubs in Moscow. Marina had connections here too, so instead of a long line, we were ushered through a side entrance and escorted to a table. Marina chose a spot downstairs, close to the dance floor, a small oval table semicircled by a soft couch. The other side faced the stage and dance floor, giving us a view as if we were in the box of an opera theater.

Two levels of balconies were suspended over the center of the large dance hall. On the first, people leaned over the railings looking down, while above, where the techno beat and crowd noise were much more tolerable, sat an older crowd — ladies in evening dresses and men in suits.

Groups of girls swirled around us, as colorful as tropical fish, with multi-colored braids, false eyelashes, rhinestones, piercings, their body parts covered in bold and suggestive tattoos, and dressed in short skirts, shorts, tops, or practically nothing at all. They laughed, drank, chatted with each other, flirted, danced on the dance floor, in the aisles, and right by the tables, never pausing their chatter and laughter.

There were about four times fewer guys, completely dissolving into this colorful, cheerful mass of women. Marina wore tight pink shorts and a loose T-shirt that slipped coquettishly off one shoulder. At first, I thought her outfit seemed too provocative, but now I realized she was actually being modest.

Yana's silver dress reminded me of the chain mail that AngelCake dreamed of in the town treasury. It hugged her perfect figure like a glove and ended where decent dresses are supposed to begin. She didn't even need to bend over for people to catch a glimpse of her underwear. It was silver too. Maybe it was a full set, intentionally designed that way?

Alla's lace top was more modest, but it shone like a light bulb in the club's neon light and was almost completely see-through.

The girlfriends chatted non-stop. I mostly stayed quiet. Not because I was shy, but because I couldn't get a word in. Marina sat to my right, Yana to my left, and Alla ended up next to Marina, which seemed to upset her.

"What do you do, Andrew?" Alla leaned over the table, all but pushing Marina aside.

"He's an esports athlete," Marina chimed in. "One of the best! A champion! Top-tier!"

"But you said Lance was top-tier!" Yana interjected. "You even showed us pictures."

"It's Alla who's crazy about Lance!" Marina defended herself from the crossfire. "I took those photos for her."

So, Alla's into esports. That's why Marina seated her further away.

"And are you better than Lance?" Alla's eyes grew wide. "What's your game name?"

"TargetAi," I managed to say over the music.

As Alla pondered, a wrinkle crossed her flawless, porcelain face. It crossed her smooth forehead and disappeared as quickly as a cloud on a sunny day.

"I've never heard it before," she confessed at last.

"He's beaten your Lance several times!" Marina declared triumphantly. "They're competing even now. Only in the closed beta!"

"Oh, how interesting," Yana joined in, pressing her warm thigh against mine. "Do they really kill people there, for real?"

She snuggled up to me. Marina twitched as if she regretted not being able to sit on both sides to shield me from her friends.

"Uh-huh," I replied. "For real."

Marina and Yana squeezed me from both sides as if in a sandwich, even though there was relatively plenty of space on the couch.

"You have such big muscles!" Yana casually ran her fingers over my arm. "And they say esports athletes are frail. You should come to my yoga studio... Flexibility is very important in sports... You should see how well I can do a split..."

"What do you say, girls? Shall we dance?" Marina suddenly stood up.

"TargetAiiii... Come dance with uuus..." Alla

whined. "It'll be fuuun!"

Either she liked my handle or she thought it was a good way to get my attention.

"I'm not going," I shrugged. "Guys don't dance! Besides, I don't know how."

"Nonsense," Yana declared. "Have a cocktail, and you'll catch the groove!"

"Four sambucas!" Marina yelled at the waiter.

"I'll have a whiskey..." I stammered.

"No whiskey here," Alla protested. "We're initiating you into club life!"

A genteel guy in a bow tie, too normal for this carnival, brought four strange contraptions to our table: wine glasses with a clear liquid that were arranged on top of ordinary snifters, and in front of them plates covered with napkins from which cocktail straws protruded like periscopes.

While I was trying to figure out how to drink this, the bartender skillfully ignited the alcohol in the wine glasses, let it burn while twirling them by the stems, then suddenly, in four swift motions, poured the flaming liquid into the snifters, covered them with the wine glasses to extinguish the fire inside, and then one by one started moving the snifters onto the plates, inserting the straws.

One! Alla downs her drink in three gulps, squints her eyes, and leaning towards the straw, comically sucks in the hot vapors with puckered cheeks.

Two! Marina is already waiting, she drinks in small sips like milk, without stopping until she swallows the last drop, and leans down to the table repeating the strange ritual.

Three!

"Come on!" Yana nudges me.

I down the alcohol boldly, like vodka, nearly gagging from the sharp, spicy smell. A lump of warmth rises in my throat, then sinks down, spreading like liquid fire through my veins. I inhale, and a hot wave hits my head, making it as light as a balloon.

Four! Yana drinks and loudly sets her glass on the table. She drinks standing, and when she leans over the table, she arches her back and hikes her butt. I involuntarily glance at her and get an elbow in the ribs from Marina.

"Let's go already!" Alla jumps up and starts dancing, twirling her hands above her head. The light rays flash and reflect off her shiny dress. "Come with us, TargetAi!"

Marina pulls me along. I don't resist; I'm having fun too. Colorful outfits, faces, glances — all blend together like in a kaleidoscope. I'm turning my head, curious about everything around me. It's like I've found my way into a carnival — I'm nineteen, I'm rich and I'm surrounded by beautiful girls who think I'm awesome.

My gaze drifts upward to the balconies, to the bored-looking spectators seated up there. Why are they sitting up there? Why aren't they here, down below? A woman on the top tier, at a table right at the edge, seems familiar. She's dressed in a bright red cocktail dress. I probably wouldn't have noticed her if not for its color. I think it's Dr.

Skuratova, the psychologist from MosTech, but I could be mistaken. She's too far and too hard to make out.

We push through the closely standing crowd, but no one minds, everyone's having fun, everyone's smiling at us. The crowd absorbs us like a living organism. The beat rocks the hall. We move with it, grooving to the rhythm. I no longer care whether I can dance or not. We just move together, dissolving into the beat and the bass.

How long has it been? Half an hour or an hour-and-a-half...? I completely lose track of time. We step aside to rest, just standing by the wall. Marina kisses me, the girls laugh. "Lucky you," they say, and I don't fully understand — lucky me or lucky Marina?

Yana brings more cocktails. This time it's B-52s. I blow out the flames and drink, leaving the glass right on the floor by the wall. This is how it's done here: Someone will pick them up later.

We dance again and the strobes and bright light tire my eyes. Turns out, you don't have to keep them open to dance. Someone presses against me from behind, rubbing against me. A firm, agile, strong body. I turn around, but Marina isn't there — it's Yana who's next to me. She laughs and winks.

I smile back and start pushing my way to the table. I bump into Marina in a narrow passage by the bar. She pounces on me, yelling:

"Got your eyes on Yanka?! I saw how you were touching her! You bastard!"

Marina's drunk, I've never seen her like this. I push her aside.

"I'll cut your balls off!" she yells after me.

I need some fresh air. The buzz in my head is no longer amusing, but annoying. What the hell did I come here for? All I accomplished was getting caught up in these dumb chicks' drama.

In the coatroom, they hand me my jacket and a security guard escorts me to the door, which leads to an alley.

"Going for a smoke?"

"Just need some fresh air."

"Potato–potatto," he quips, laughing.

Outside, I understand why he was laughing. No fresh air to be found here. Groups of smokers have taken over the porch. I have to move on further if I want to get a bit of oxygen.

The cold clears the alcoholic fog from my head. It's snowing very lightly. Tiny snowflakes bite my face in fleeting flashes of cold. The snow muffles all sound. Just a few steps from the porch and it's quiet. Completely quiet.

And in this silence, I distinctly hear a car door slam and a woman scream.

"Let go! I won't go with you! Let me go, you freak!"

If I had stayed by the porch, I wouldn't have heard anything. And I could pretend now that I don't hear anything too. It's not my business, I'm just relaxing at the club. I'll take another breath of the frosty air, let the cold into my lungs and go back inside. I'll make up with Marina, drive her home, bang her and fall asleep. And if we don't make up, then I'll sleep with Yana... or Alla... or someone else from among all these ostentatious and beautiful girls. But I definitely won't go to the corner of the alley to see what's going on there.

"Let me go, it hurts! Please let go!"

A large dark car. An SUV. I can't see the make, but the back door is open. A man is pulling a woman by the wrist, she's resisting. Another jumps out from the driver's seat, pushes from behind. They pull her over to the car and the interior light illuminates them. That's when I see the bright red dress.

Chapter 16

FOUR STEPS AND I'M THERE. The guys are all the same, in black jackets and dark pants. "*Like a uniform*," flashes through my mind. I grab the collar of the one pushing the woman from behind. Not expecting this, he gives in easily and loses his balance. I push him forward and slam his head against the car. He falls on all fours and crawls away. That's one down.

The second guy turns to face me and stares at me point-blank, trying to figure out where the hell I came from. I headbutt him abruptly — forehead to nose. My dad used to say he could break bricks with his forehead. The frontal bone is really strong, especially if you know how to hit with it. The man's nose crumples and he slumps like a sack. If for whatever reason the cops get involved, my knuckles aren't bruised. It probably won't make much of a difference, but it is something.

"Let's go," I take the woman by the waist, but her legs give out.

Automatically, I pick her up in my arms and carry her, just like in a romantic movie. As we round the corner and step into the bright light, the security guards rush over to us.

"The lady feels unwell," I shout. "Got any sedatives?!"

No need to mention the brawl. Who knows, they might call the police, and we don't need publicity. I doubt those idiots would even show up.

"I'm better now, thank you," says the woman. "I think I can walk."

Hearing her voice, I realize that it's Dr. Skuratova for sure. She looks pitiful — hair disheveled, tears in her eyes, the strap of her dress torn. It's slipping off and she has to hold it up with her hand, but still, the edge of her lace underwear is visible.

I let her go and she stands on her own. I take off my jacket and drape it over her shoulders. People make way as a security guard brings a glass of water and some pills.

She looks up and seems to recognize me at last.

"Andrew?! Is that you?! My God, how embarrassing..." She lowers her head and hides her eyes, as if she's about to cry.

"Here, take this," I offer the pill, not immediately remembering her first name. "Dr. Skuratova, it's all right now. You're safe. Let's go inside, you'll freeze."

"No, Andrew..." she suddenly clings to me, and I feel her shivering. "Please, take me away from here... Please! Do you have a car?!"

"What about your clothes?"

Dr. Skuratova is only in a dress and shoes, and my jacket over her shoulders. Clearly, she didn't arrive here like this.

"It doesn't matter," she waves. "I'll see to them later. I'm begging you, please take me... I need to go home..."

It seemed like she was on the verge of a breakdown. There was a line of taxis already waiting outside the entrance. I waved at one, and it pulled up. The driver grumbled that he didn't pick up people without an official call or app request but after receiving a hundred-euro bill, he brightened up and hopped out to open the door for us.

I helped her into the car. She looked at me so pleadingly that I ended up sitting beside her in the back seat.

"2B Garden Lane," she told the driver her address.

She still had my jacket on, and suddenly my phone in the pocket began to vibrate. She flinched, then fished it out from inside the inner pocket and handed it to me. "Marina" flashed on the screen. She was looking for me, no doubt swept up in a tempest of jealous suspicions. I didn't feel like dealing with drunk and irrational Marina, so I muted the phone and put it in my pocket.

"Did I ruin your evening?" Dr. Skuratova

asked.

Her voice was low and slightly husky, the kind that resonates deep within you. It felt like even the most mundane words spoken in that voice had a sultry undertone.

"It's fine," I lied to her. "I was about to leave anyway, Dr. Skuratova."

Even in the backseat of a well-worn Solaris, the psychologist looked like she was riding in a limousine.

"Irina... Just call me Irina," she corrected me. "It seems silly to be so formal after what happened... I'm so grateful to you..."

Tears welled up in her eyes again and she clasped my hand in hers. She didn't look her age at all, though I had no idea how old she was. Probably not younger than my mom, but that was just a guess based on the age of MosTech's male executives. They treated her as an equal, so she must have been on their project for a while.

In the flickering streetlight, she could be anywhere from just over thirty to well into her forties. All I could see was that she was very beautiful, with polished, aristocratic features. By comparison, high-maintenance Marina seemed like an ordinary stray.

We were an odd pair, with the taxi driver peeking at us in the mirror, while we sat in silence the entire ride, her hand gripping mine as if even here she was afraid to be alone.

The car stopped in front of a high fence with wrought-iron gates. Irina rolled down the window and spoke a code into a microphone on a post, just like at a drive-through. The gates opened, and we drove among snow-covered private cottages.

"Here!" Irina announced next to a two-story house with large panoramic windows.

We got out. I was about to say goodbye and leave in the same car, but Irina didn't let go of my hand.

"Please, come in... just for half an hour," she pleaded. "I gave the staff the night off. I'm scared to be alone."

The house was luxurious inside. I had thought Marina's apartment was fancy, but this place was on another level. Irina entered a combination on a wall panel and the lights came on, some soft music started playing, and a fireplace flared to life in the living room.

Paintings hung on the walls and it wouldn't surprise me if they were originals. Some statues stood on small cubic pediments, one a figure of a dancing nude woman of dark bronze, another an abstract steel structure of twisted metal sheets, resembling either a frozen gust of wind or a bird ready to take flight.

"Come in, Andrew..." Irina hung up my jacket, kicked off her shoes in the entryway and continued on barefoot. "You've got blood on your forehead. Have a seat. I'll clean you up."

I took off my Guccis and followed her into the living room. The soft carpet swallowed my feet, and the furniture looked so white I was afraid to sit down lest I leave a mark.

After her invitations, I anticipated some kind of seduction in the back of my mind. I imagined Irina might come out in lingerie or a nightgown, a scenario straight out of *Delivery Driver and Rich Milf.* Little old me, the MC of a fantasy of my own!

But instead, Irina reappeared in a modest silk robe, covering far more than her previous dress, and silly slippers with pompoms. She had cotton balls, antiseptic and a bandage in her hands.

I bravely endured as she disinfected my forehead. If there was a scratch there, I couldn't feel it. But Irina played the role of a merciful nurse, applying a bandage and examining her work with satisfaction.

"Now for coffee," she declared, "I haven't cooked in a while, but I think I could manage some coffee."

Along with the coffee came brandy from a bulbous bottle, unfamiliar to me. I asked for just a little for myself, but she didn't skimp serving herself, which was understandable given the stress she'd endured.

"I got very lucky that you happened to be there." She settled into an armchair, pulled up her legs and sipped the brandy. "I've never felt so helpless."

"Who was that?" I asked.

"An acquaintance," Dr. Skuratova frowned. "Well, obviously, an ex-acquaintance now."

I didn't mention that MosTech's head psychologist happened to be at The Underground at the same time as Marina and me. There was something else I was more curious about.

"Aren't you a psychologist, Dr. Skuratova?" I inquired a bit naively. "Can't you see right through people?"

"It's a bit like cobbler without shoes," Irina laughed. "Where your personal emotions are involved, no psychological analysis works. And didn't I tell you to call me Irina?"

"Let's drink to friendship then!" I suggested, curious how she'd react to my offer.

Irina moved closer, intertwined her arm with mine, and we both drank from the glass. Not wanting to look foolish, I also downed my brandy.

Her lips are tangy, burning, and very soft — scented with expensive alcohol and chocolate. Irina pulls back slightly, laughter in her eyes.

"Am I still Dr. Skuratova in your mind?" she asks.

"Needs testing," I say and kiss her again.

Drinking brandy, kissing, and feeding each other chocolates is pleasant. Funny enough, I've never done anything like this with girls before. It was always either sappy romance or straight to sex. But this was... cozy... and fun...

"Ira... Irisha... Irén... Irusik... Irushka..." I listed.

"What's wrong with just 'Irina?'" Dr. Skuratova snorted.

"Irina... Marina... too similar," I declared, "I might mix you two up..."

"Oh, you... scoundrel!" Irina threw a pillow at me, which I caught mid-air. "I wouldn't even hire that Marina as a maid... little wretch... He says he'll mix us up... you won't forget me till your dying day... I'm the best fling in your pathetic life..."

"I'll hold you to that," I said.

After that further conversation ceased to matter.

Irina wasn't lying. She knew my body better than I did myself. With her hands, fingers, tongue, even her hair and tense nipples, she drove me wild, at first not allowing me inside her, then giving herself completely, wrapping her legs around my hips and pressing me into her.

I came almost immediately the first time I entered her, but she aroused me again and again, rallying me to battle. We started in the living room, continued in the kitchen where we went for a second bottle of brandy, and ended in the bedroom just before dawn, completely spent.

"I hope you paid those guys well."

"Which ones?!"

"The ones trying to drag you into the car. I definitely broke one's nose, so I think he earned a bonus."

Irina nearly jumped out of bed, staring at me.

"What are you talking about?!"

"If I didn't know that that was a set-up, I'd never have gotten involved. You know my dad ended up going to prison for two years over a similar situation? If you knew, you would've come up with something more original."

"Wow," Irina didn't even try to deny it, "so we

blew it..."

"Yep," I could tell someone was going to get it in the morning.

"Then why *did* you get involved?!" she continued.

"I was curious to see where it would lead," I admitted shamelessly. "And look how far we've come."

"We wouldn't have come this far if I didn't liked you," Irina stated. "I mixed business with pleasure. And you're still lying... you're smart, alright... but you realized later... you jumped into that fight sincerely."

"How can you tell?"

"Otherwise, you wouldn't have carried me in your arms."

Recalling that moment, I realized Irina was right. Then we both fell asleep.

* * *

I woke up at 5:30 a.m. — a new habit I've picked up lately. Surprisingly, my head felt fresh after such a wild night. Irina was still asleep. I slipped out from under her arm, took one last look at her flawless body and wandered around the house gathering my clothes.

The code lock clicked behind me, leaving Dr. Irina Vladimirovna Skuratova, chief psychologist of the MosTech Board of Directors, to sleep in her luxurious, empty mansion. With each step, the night felt more surreal, and I knew I'd never come back here. Yet, alongside this realization another feeling gradually grew within me.

It was an extraordinary sense of calm. Suddenly, I felt incredibly strong, almost invincible. Every step I took was right, every decision turned out to be correct. The world seemed to bend to my will and I couldn't help but feel like this was just the beginning.

The guard at the entrance gave me a friendly wave, and the taxi I had called was already waiting beyond the gates. Where else would I go this early but to MosTech?

Once settled in, I checked my phone again. Twenty-six missed calls from Marina, 15 text messages, and 142 unread messages on WhatsApp. I selected them all and deleted them without reading. She'll tell me everything herself if she wants to.

* * *

As soon as Andrew closed the door behind himself, Dr. Skuratova opened her eyes, fully awake. She reached for her phone and dialed a number.

"Hello Eli... Yes, he's gone... Just now... I bet he's heading your way... Did he pass the test? The tests are your department. This was therapy, like I explained to you." The psychologist began to speak slowly, as if quoting herself: "He was hindered by an old psychological trauma. An episode with his father that led to a family tragedy. Now, he subconsciously puts himself in his father's place whenever he is challenged. He's afraid of conflict and avoids blind corners. To rid himself of the inhibiting factor, he needed to relive the situation again, but with a different, just, and maximally pleasant outcome... The hero must accomplish the feat and get a reward... Yes, Eli... the reward was pleasant indeed... Okay, see you soon."

Irina stretched, looked at the clock with a satisfied smile, and shut her eyes again. She had worked hard today and she had earned her rest.

* * *

The city was waking up. Solitary windows were lighting up in the dark high-rises. On one of the avenues we passed a convoy of snowplows with yellow flashing lights, pushing the remnants of the night's snowfall to the sides. Early-morning commuters huddled at bus stops.

The MosTech campus, however, gleamed with lights on in all its windows as if it operated around the clock. Busy janitors were clearing snow from the stairs and walkways. Guards, as uniform as clones, patrolled near the front entrance. It seemed to me like there were even more of them now.

After my sleepless night, all sorts of nonsense was creeping into my head. None of those around me — neither the driver who dropped me off in the parking lot, nor the guards, nor the cleaners briskly moving through the corridors now — knew that inside this drab office building lies a doorway to another universe. A small, imperfect, but constantly evolving world.

I wonder which building, which server rack, holds our VR solar system, our VR galaxy? Who was the technician who looks on — yawning as he unwraps his sandwich — as on his monitors, we "immortals" are born, die and are reborn again.

The guards recognized me and nodded in greeting without asking any questions. I entered the empty lobby, turned right as usual and took a seat in one of the visitor's chairs. If I'm lucky, I could even catch a few hours of sleep here.

"*Pam-pam... Pa-ram-pa-pam...*" hummed a familiar voice in the lobby.

Who does he remind me of? Why, the Soviet version of Winnie-the-Pooh, who else? He mutters to himself, talks nonsense and never feels embarrassed.

"Andrew," the Master notices me too. "Were you kicked out of your house or what?"

"Why would I be kicked out?" I joke. "I left on my own."

"Come on, I'll make you some tea."

"Why do they call you the Master anyway?" I ask as we ride the elevator.

I'm surprised at my own audacity. In my mind I'm as calm as the surface of a lake. No turmoil. Not the slightest ripple.

"Do you know the Russian expression that 'the work fears its master?'" He pauses and waits for me to nod before continuing. "Well, I am that

Master. Not only does the work fear me, but everyone else does too."

"I'm not afraid," I say unexpectedly.

"Because you're foolish," the Master chuckles approvingly. "But that's probably for the best. Intelligence only causes problems."

He taps his forehead with his finger, producing a hollow sound as if it's an empty barrel. I burst out laughing and he joins in.

In his office, we both take off our shoes, sit down at the low table, and wait for the impassive secretary to bring us tea. Judging by the secretary's appearance, he probably spent the night in the office.

The door opens, and another person joins us. Despite the early hour, Dr. Dmitry "Doc" Kotov is impeccably shaved and fresh — dressed in his usual business suit and smelling of expensive cologne. He takes off his shoes, nods at us and the Master, and sits down with us, as if performing some ritual. We nod back at him without breaking the silence.

The tea is delicious. I hadn't noticed it before. My head was always filled with all sorts of doubts and worries, questions such as "What do they want from me?" or "Who's this odd grizzled fellow?" It was like sitting through an endless exam, listening to voices in my head whispering hints, arguing with each other, interrupting...

But now, there's just silence... It feels so good. And the tea is delicious. Especially when paired with dried apricots, just wonderful.

"May I have some more?" I raise my cup.

The Master silently pours me more tea from the porcelain teapot. Is it etiquette not to interrupt at such moments, or is he waiting for me to start talking? Everything's fine with me, they pay me by the hour, my party is leveling up, I'm meeting all their requirements. They're the ones who need something from me, so I'll wait for them to do the talking.

"Aren't you going to rescue your girlfriend?" Doc asks suddenly.

The Master grimaces slightly at his impatience.

"Did something happen to Marina?" I raise my eyebrows in polite surprise.

"You've mixed up your women," Doc shakes his head disapprovingly. "I'm talking about Yumi."

"What is she to me?" I knew this conversation was coming, and now I'm ready for it. "Just... a fellow traveler."

"Don't you feel responsible for your party members?" Doc presses on.

"Is she one of my party members?" I respond in kind. "It's not my fault what happened, but yours."

"Mine?!" Doc's eyes go wide.

Seems I've managed to catch him off guard. He and the Master exchange glances.

"Because you orchestrated the massacre in the game, right? Not you personally, but everyone in charge of the test. It wasn't the AI that started a bloodbath, but you lot."

CHAPTER 17

"WHY DO YOU THINK that?" the Master interjected.

His face wrinkled into a smile, like a baked apple. It felt like he was pleased with my question. It was like this every time. As soon as I figured something out, uncovered the cunning machinations of MosTech's senior executives, the Master would look at me like a school teacher who's finally coaxed a correct answer from a struggling student.

"Because the system assigns different quests, but they're all basically a simple tutorial. It suggests completing obvious, elementary steps. Farming, choosing a class, forming a party... And it doesn't eliminate ANYONE." The truth was finally dawning on me as I spoke. "You're the ones in charge of elimination. Otherwise, why is it that when the first round was voided, everyone who was eliminated was allowed to return?"

"It took a year before the first neural network started killing players," the Master said. "They spent a whole year running around the countryside, leveling up and bragging about their gear. To this day, no one knows how it all started..."

The office door opened again. Now, Benjamin Zvyagin joined us, disheveled and wrinkled as if he had slept at his desk. What a well-attended meeting at 6:30 in the morning! It would be funny if Dr. Skuratova showed up too. Though I wouldn't dare wake Irina today. Ira... Irisha... Irén...

"Happy to see me?" Zvyagin asked.

"Huh? Why?" His question forced me back to reality.

"You're smiling as if I'm Santa Claus with a sack of gifts," Benjamin adjusted his pants, sitting cross-legged at the table. "Could I get some coffee, Uncle Eli?"

"Have some tea. It has more caffeine than those silly paper cups of yours," the Master grumbled. "You kids nowadays. This isn't a restaurant."

Just a family scene. Three men, each capable of buying this entire damn city, having tea with a nineteen-year-old kid. Maybe Benny will pull out a spoon and say "Andrew, you're The Chosen One" And the Master will put on Morpheus's glasses and offer me two pills.

I recalled Marina's words: When people like this treat you as their equal, it means they want to drag you into something very nasty. My sense of danger began screeching inside me like a siren, flashing red lights and all. These guys only speak this sincerely and affectionately to a potential dead man. I'm expendable to them. A rat that runs their maze better than the other rats.

And yet, there's already another one like me... Anna. Do they also talk to her? Maybe they already have... Why not? I'm a dark horse, but she's a known favorite. They've been grooming her for a while and they must know her tastes and preferred MO. Well, why did you think you were the only one, Andrew? Mere promises don't add up to marriage. And all these corporate rituals and dances around you are only a show to boost your self-esteem. Though... if you factor my night with Irina into this scheme, then this whole situation is completely messed up. Isn't that a bit much even for a promising candidate in a rat race?

"What are you thinking about?" the Master asked. "Do you want some coffee after all?"

"No, I wanted to ask you for a phone number..."

"Mine?!"

"No, of a niece of yours who likes blackberry cascara."

The Master's face expressed mere curiosity. But Benjamin's twitched unexpectedly. Why? What does he care about Anna?

"What do you need it for?"

"I want to ask her out to the movies."

"Well, well..." the Master puffed up his cheeks thoughtfully. "Young love, eh? Remind me later.

But for now... Benny, what was I talking about before you interrupted me?"

Surprised, Benjamin stared at the Master in puzzlement.

"About how this mess started," Doc chipped in, frowning with irritation.

"You see, Andrew," the Master tossed a handful of nuts into his mouth, chewed, and continued. "Everything was going swimmingly. Nothing, as they say, foretold a catastrophe. And, well, it all began with magic..."

* * *

It all began with magic, and in *Lutetia* — a new role-playing game with full VR immersion — there was plenty of it. Magic could heal and resurrect players, buff them in battle or summon magical creatures to fight beside them. It could burn, crush, and tear apart enemies, or, on the flip side, weave protective auras strong enough to withstand any physical attack.

Players loved magic. I mean, you can bash someone's head in with a battle axe in the real world too, right? Though that tends to come with its own set of problems. But it was only here that you could incinerate your opponent, turning them into a living torch, drop a meteor on them, or summon a hellhound to rip them to shreds, all the while feeling like you were doing it in real life.

The players were ecstatic and happy to spend their days and nights in the game. The only thing that held them back was the four-hour playtime limit. That's alpha restrictions for you. And to ensure compliance, MosTech didn't let just anyone in. They filled the VR pods with their own employees, their relatives and especially their children, as long as they were over 18 of course. Another three thousand pods were set up in boarding schools for disabled orphans.

Corporate lobbying easily sold this to the public as a "rehabilitation program." The media even ran a few stories about MosTech's "charitable initiative." And people who were forever bound to their beds or wheelchairs would have signed anything for a chance to take a stroll through the woods again.

The spell was called *Soul Snatch.* Mana-intensive and nearly useless in combat, at first it was treated as a joke, an Easter egg, *snatching* someone transferred a player's consciousness into any game item, living or not. For two minutes, you could experience being a rat, a stone, a bucket in a well, or a raid boss. You could experience it, yet you had no control over it. Once you were *snatched*, the game interface disappeared, and for the spell's duration, virtual reality became your only reality.

However, some crafty players discovered an unusual side effect. Soul snatching reset the game timer. It was as if the connection to the VR pod would break momentarily, then reset. Within the confines of MosTech, the attending technicians kept a strict watch on the time players spent in-game, but the technicians at the orphanages were more lax. Disabled players were willing to trade their meager government benefits for extra time in the game, corruption flourished, and soul snatching became extremely popular.

Perhaps that's also why the first cases went unnoticed. Who cares about some miserable orphans? What does it matter how long they spend in their VR pods? By the time corporate realized what was happening, it was already too late. Several people were trapped in the game, their pods resetting over and over with each cycle. Attempts to extract the players and disconnect the pods ended tragically — in comas, cerebral hemorrhages and even death.

After that, they left the other snatched souls alone. They tried to find them in the game, but even that was futile. The renegades refused to communicate, they tried to hide, and responded with hostility and aggression to any attempts to "rescue" them.

Dr. Skuratova was hired to deal with the problem. She in turn recruited a whole department of psychologists to MosTech — but their conclusion was that the alpha testers had made a conscious choice. They wanted so badly to feel whole that they literally rejected meatspace, wishing only to stay in the game. And the game's neural network facilitated this.

Then it was decided to scrap the "charitable initiative," but even that decision was too late. The in-game Kingdom of Tellaria declared all players outlaws. The kingdom sealed its borders and unleashed a horrific massacre across its domains. Those who were lucky enough to pop out of their VR pods recounted horrid tales of gruesome slaughter.

Royal guards... mages... merchants... ordinary NPCs on the streets... even the prostitutes in the capital's infamous Forget-Me-Not brothel killed any player they came across. One player recounted how his friend was strangled with a silk stocking. He himself managed to jump out of a window and logged out mid-fall. Another was beaten to death on the street with a basket of pastries, a third was torn apart by the roots of suddenly sentient orchids in the royal greenhouse to the soundtrack of a maniacally laughing gardener.

No one who died emerged alive in reality. The technicians managed to establish that the NPCs were using *Soul Snatch*, albeit in a different, altered form. It was not for nothing that Tellaria's mages were considered the strongest in the game. After this purge, a "fog of war" descended over the kingdom.

This was why in the current beta test, the game featured no magic whatsoever. None. I didn't bother telling them that they were wrong, that there was at least one healer in there. After all, any healing would count as a kind of magic.

"We made a mistake back then," said Benjamin. "We should have shut down the test and the project for good."

He and the Master took turns speaking, while Doc just frowned in silence, clearly reliving those dark days.

"You're probably thinking, 'Why the hell are they crying about it in front of me for?' and 'Why are these rich dinosaurs pretending to be my friends?'"

"Are you reading my mind?" I replied.

"Well, I suppose I'm not old enough to be a dinosaur yet," Benjamin disagreed.

"It's not so hard to read your thoughts," the Master said cheerfully, crunching on nuts and ignoring him. "I'd think the same in your place. Back then, we really screwed up. See, I can even admit it. But why did we screw up? Our team had scientists, donors, programmers, and psychologists. Even military and counterintelligence folks. And gamers. Regular ones, not from esports."

"And what did your gamers advise?" I asked.

"To launch a scenario. To put a bounty on the crown bitch Queen Dautery's head. Start a holy war, give experience for each Tellarian head, even more for each forest cut down, and a whole heap of it for every city burned." The Master made a chopping gesture, showing the grim fate that awaited Tellaria.

"We even had fun then," Doc suddenly laughed. "We assembled a task force of five thousand players who were supposed to crush the rebellious NPCs. Bets were made on how long the AI forces would last."

"And in the end?"

"The next day, the Steppes rose up," Benny took over. "According to the lore, the nomads were Tellaria's irreconcilable enemies since time immemorial, but here suddenly they became allies. Those boys quickly cleared their ranks — all business, no theatrics. Tellarians sent their mages as military specialists, and the steppe tribes quickly picked up new spellcasting techniques. It was either swear fealty to the Great Khan or have your consciousness transferred to a stone idol. Permanently. The AI had creatively reinterpreted soul snatching, so to speak, and a silly joke turned into real-life abduction... from real life. As you can imagine, most gave in to the Khan's demands. Even the girls... The generals really did replenished their harems back then."

"They formed separate combat brigades of converted players who slaughtered their own with a ferocity NPCs couldn't dream of. It was a convenient deal. The 'locals' die once and for all, but the players respawn."

"The game world was too vast. Three kingdoms: Tellaria, Lutetia, Olvia, the Steppe, and the island kingdom of Bregen, home to merchants and pirates. Other locations were planned for future expansions. The game server could support a hundred thousand players. Just under five thousand testers dissolved there like grains of salt in a barrel of water. Less than three hours passed before it was all over."

"After that, *Lutetia* simply cut off any means

of monitoring what was going inside of it. A fog of war descended on all the kingdoms. And all the players, except for those first ones we disconnected ourselves, are alive. Their condition resembles an induced coma. All organs are fine. But something keeps them inside and won't let them wake up. A spell... Sounds crazy, right? But as long as they're alive, there's a chance to bring them back."

"There you go," the Master added, playfully puckering his lips. "Now you know almost everything. But even that's a lot. Nobody knows everything."

"Why would the AI do all this?" I couldn't help asking. "Why does the game need to keep the players trapped?"

"That's your homework. If you figure it out, you can call me anytime, day or night. Call any one of us in fact, because that, my friend, is the million-dollar question. And it's the primary reason why we created the current sandbox. Perhaps you've already guessed the secondary reason too. We need a champion, someone who can take on the AI. You can train in the sandbox we set up and then... *Tru-tu-tu-tu...*" The Master waved his hand, mimicking fanfares. "Ever heard of Yuri Gagarin?"

"The astronaut?" I asked, puzzled about what he had to do with anything.

"The very one," the Master declared with such flair, as if he had known him personally. "A senior lieutenant. All of the Soviet top brass shook his hand, because if he managed to return, he'd get fame, honors, medals, and the rank of major. And if he didn't return, he would've just died a lieutenant. Back in the day, they sent guys into space, and not into some unknown simulated crapola that's sitting in our basement. But the gist is the same. No one has any idea what's out there. And only the best candidate will go in there. In Gagarin's day there were another twenty or so candidates in the astronaut corps, yet the top brass figured that Gagarin was the only one good enough. The methodology doesn't change, you know. Because it works... the methodology. You're not the only one... that's true. But as of today, you're the best. The most promising. You're our Yuri Gagarin, damn it. That's why we're coddling you here. Sorry for the bluntness," he spread his hands. "I wouldn't go into that thing myself... I don't trust anyone else. It's up to you."

The Master's plain and dreadful words sent a chill down my spine. I thought testing was dangerous, but if you're careful, avoid charging in a la Leroy and follow the rules, then nothing bad will happen. The AI is only just learning, taking its first steps. But to dive into the maw of a neural network that's been evolving for years?! That's just another elaborate way to commit suicide. It's definitely not worth any amount of money they could offer me: The dead have no use for that.

"Thanks for the tea, it was really tasty," I stood up, politely nodding to each of the executives. "That was an interesting conversation.

I'll be sure to keep mum as per the NDA. All the best to you."

"Wait!" I was already leaving, but the Master's exclamation made me stop. "You think this isn't worth the money? Well, you're right. But there are other things you'd sign up for!"

"Like what?"

The Master also stood up and walked past me. He paced around his office in his soft slippers: a relaxed and insolent SOB. What could he possibly offer me? A position? An apartment? Marina for life? What does he have to offer me that I couldn't just tell him to get lost with a clear conscience?

The Master sat down at his desk, put on his glasses, and stared at the screen. He was dragging out the pause like this was a play, and it was becoming increasingly unbearable.

"'Oleg Dmitrievich Severyanov, born in 1970,'" he began in a deliberately indifferent, officious voice. "'Charged under Article 111, item D of the Criminal Code of the Russian Federation for aggravated battery and affray. Sentenced to five years in a high-security prison.' Are you familiar with this case, Andrew?"

"That's my father." I didn't understand what the Master was getting at. Was he trying to get a rise out of me?

"You must realize our capabilities, Andrew," Dr. Kotov's voice made me turn around. "We have lawyers and connections. And most importantly — money. We can do practically anything. We can have your dad's case reviewed. The lowlife that he beat up will end up behind bars. His daddy, who got him off the hook and destroyed your father, will lose his position and won't recover his reputation for the rest of his life. Your father will receive all the official apologies... all his honors will be restored... 'wrongfully accused'... articles... television... And you'll be the one to do it for him. Here's your chance."

"What do you want from me?" I asked.

"Get smart... Don't hang around in bars... Think..." Kotov started counting on his fingers. "Aim to win."

"And then? Come back victorious?"

"Even just getting off the launchpad is enough. If you make it through this beta test and enter the old VR world, we will take care of all of your father's problems. I promise. But for that, you'll first need to come out victorious in the current test."

"And what do you want from me now? To get Yumi out of there?"

"What?! No way!" Doc even sounded frightened. "Don't you even think about doing that!"

CHAPTER 18

FROM EARLIEST CHILDHOOD, Anton Richter didn't know how to lose and hated losing more than anything else in the world. When his mom and dad would sit down to play board games with him — a Richter family tradition on Tuesday and Thursday evenings — they always made sure to let him win. Otherwise, little Tony would throw a tantrum, hurling cards and pieces around. When he got older, he'd just go silent, sulk, and storm off to his room, slamming the door behind him.

Anton had his own bedroom from birth. He was born into an academic family; his grandfather was a dean with a doctorate, his dad was a lecturer with a PhD, and his mom played the cello in the symphony orchestra. They adored their laterborn child and did everything to shield him from the harsh realities of the world. He didn't go to daycare — what if someone bullied him? He rarely played outside, to avoid bad influences. And he didn't spend summers in the countryside with grandma — what respectable family had a grandmother in a village? That would have been in poor taste after all.

Thus, before he started school, Anton thought the world was full of adults who were polite, kind-hearted and somewhat dimwitted at that, since he regularly outsmarted even his grandfather, the academic.

The "wonderful school years" initially turned out to be a nightmare for Anton. No one wanted to follow him, treat him as the leader he was, or even listen to him. His noisy and crude classmates knew a fraction of what Anton did, yet they mocked every idea and suggestion he had.

They only respected brute strength and Richter was seen as weak and sickly. At least, that's how his parents viewed him: running was bad for his feet, gymnastics for his joints, and boxing could break his nose, they reasoned. So, Anton never even got a chance to test whether he was truly frail or not.

Moreover, through some strange herd instinct, the crowd sensed that Anton was an outsider. With light blonde hair, milky-white skin and oddly transparent eyes, he was the odd one out from day one. Even his last name, "Richter," set him apart from the Sidorovs and Kuznetsovs. Germanic, it sounded hostile and frightening to his classmates, like the creak of knight's armor or the clangor of tank tracks.

Anton wasn't physically bullied, though at times he almost wished he was. Such interactions would imply some sort of emotional connection. Richter ended up isolated, as if in an invisible bubble. His classmates blatantly ignored him. He sat alone at his desk with no neighbors.

Also the adults at school weren't as kind or gentle as those at home. They didn't like being argued with, they refused to give in, and they detected no signs of genius in Anton.

So Anton Richter became a bookish child. Fantasy replaced the real world for him. Discovering his grandfather's library, Anton immersed himself in a world of knights, valor, and nobility. The house was full of books, considered luxury items in Soviet times, and the Richters had entire walls filled with hefty collections of works.

One of Anton's first heroes was Lancelot. The ideal knight, a lone hero. An outcast among his own, condemned for his forbidden affair with King Arthur's wife. Learning about women through books, young Richter understood even then that they were nothing but trouble.

By age ten, Anton could distinguish an estoc from a flamberge, and a saber from an epee. He knew heraldry and noble titles inside out. When his schoolteacher, breathless with excitement, told them about the Battle on the Ice, Anton felt desperately sorry for the splendid Teutonic knights, overcome by the more numerous Slavic rabble.

Only online games competed with books for a

place in Anton's heart. "Lancelot" became his gaming handle of choice. But since most gamers were unfamiliar with classic literature, it soon got shortened to "Lancer" (as in a mounted spearman), and then just to "Lance."

At first, Anton didn't care for multiplayer RPGs. Just like in real life, no one listened to him or wanted to follow his lead there. Guilds and clans ruled, and loners weren't welcomed. Lance preferred FPS games, ideally involving melee weapons.

He didn't need to negotiate there, build relationships, or form alliances. Strike, block, feint, counterattack... And always combos... lots of combos. Here, he was unmatched. Here, at last, he lived out his childhood dream. He always won.

Then came esports, the first competition his cautious parents approved of. Their little boy was safe in a VR pod, under specialist supervision. The reflexes honed over thousands of hours of online gaming and a lifelong will to win quickly made him a rising star.

Lance would spend days in the VR pod, slicing through hundreds of training bots. His parents generously paid for extra time and personal trainers for their son's only hobby. And he conquered one competitive league after another. From juniors to the adult league and then to the pros.

With victories, Anton Richter also found friends. Suddenly, everyone wanted to hang out with him, share his desk, mock dumb teachers or flirt with cute classmates during lunch breaks. His classmates competed for his attention; they fawned over him and adored him.

Girls would bring their friends over to take selfies with the class celebrity, arguing about whom he smiled at and whom he liked. They giggled, they flirted and brushed up against him casually.

But Lance couldn't care less. Lance, not Anton Richter. Now, he insisted on being called that in real life too. Even by classmates, even by parents. And no wonder: Anton was introverted and lonely, while Lance was popular and successful.

He crafted his image meticulously, planning every detail. Black-and-white Kevlar armor with a winking lynx on his back. A pair of Katzbalgers — the signature blade of German Landsknechts — his weapons of choice. And for his hair, a short, bleached fringe instead of his natural, pale albino color.

A circle of friends always buzzed around him. Those who would admire his achievements, meet him for coffee or booze, suggest a new movie, bring girls over, just to create a nice atmosphere. Lance never admitted it, but he was afraid of being alone. He made friends in lieu of keeping pets. His previous alienation had scared him so much in childhood that he now constantly surrounded himself with people.

There were also girls. Any kind. Lance quickly moved beyond the level of schoolgirl crushes, appetizing neighbors and adoring fans. The virtual reality industry was booming. Lance started getting invites to appear in ads. He became the face of companies producing gaming hardware, teenage cosmetics, clothes, electric scooters, mobile services... Suddenly, he had a ton of money on his hands.

The young champion was invited to photoshoots and TV shoots, parties, and fashionable gatherings. He struck up affairs with models, aspiring actresses and singers, journalists, and bloggers. Plenty of girls wanted to be seen with the gaming celebrity. Lance got used to changing them even faster than he changed his "friends."

At eighteen, he moved out, buying himself a two-story loft in an upscale new building for his birthday. With his kind of money, being drafted into the Russian army wasn't a danger. His military ID was delivered to his home in an envelope, tied with a red gift ribbon. That's how he requested it, on a bet with friends.

But all that was just tinsel, the external trappings of success. The only thing that truly captivated Lance was winning. He tore through one tournament after another, training furiously and constantly improving.

It was his drug, his only real thrill. His luxurious apartment was filled with hangers-on and glamorous chicks tired of trying to get his attention. Managers and agents handled his schedule, but he only felt alive in the Gladiator

Games.

One day, Lance's manager suggested he try out a new multiplayer game. The pay was modest, but participating in the launch of a revolutionary new project would be good for his reputation. Besides, his manager had an old connection at MosTech — Marina Skvortsova, the head of PR, who was happy to help out by bringing another star into her company's project. You scratch my back, I scratch yours — one of those kinds of deals.

Strutting around in his patented armor, chopping up those slow, ridiculous spiders to mincemeat, posing for virtual cameras — what could be easier? Lance was happy to put on a full show.

But things didn't go as planned. By the second day, his team of pros had been stripped of their flashy gear. T-Rex and Xavier threw tantrums, but Lance found their newfound predicament intriguing, and the others quieted down. Sure, the cash prizes were laughable. But surrounded by ordinary beta testers, Lance felt like a predator among sheep. He was thrust into a world straight out of his childhood books. A world where the strong could do anything. If it weren't for that bitch...

"That damn bitch!" T-Rex slammed his shot glass onto the bar and grabbed a slice of lime from the dish, biting into it after his tequila and squirting lime juice in two directions. "How long are we going to be scared of that damn bitch?! We need to trap her and gank her. And before that, screw her in every hole. So that next time that slut will know better than to mess with us!"

T-Rex was the most experienced of Lance's buddies. A fighter, a champion too, though on a smaller scale. Not a lackey... more like a junior partner. Sometimes Lance would even listen to his advice, though not in this case.

"Have you ever faced her in the Gladiator Games?!" Lance asked with a frown. He couldn't stand sloppiness, especially not in his own apartment. "I did. Three years ago at the European Cup, I made it to the semifinals but she won the overall championship. In the exhibition match, she went out alone to face eight of us. No armor and barefoot. Wearing nothing but a bikini. At first, we were drooling all over the floor, then she wiped that drool with us." Lance paused. "That girl may as well have been born in cyberspace. A meatspace human just can't move that fast."

"And here? Didn't you recognize her? Why didn't you say she was in the beta too?"

The three of them practically lived in Lance's loft. They ate here, drank here and even slept here from time to time. None of the others had an apartment like it. For a long time, Lance didn't care; there was plenty of space for everyone. He had three guest bedrooms and a housekeeper who did the cleaning. But now they were whining and it was starting to piss him off.

"I didn't recognize her," Lance shrugged. "It's been ages. That tournament was held in Germany, and she played under a different game handle."

"So, what, we're supposed to run from her now?!" T-Rex's voice cracked, verging on a scream. "Hide in corners and farm quietly?! *US?!*"

"It's all because of that slut… that whore…" Xavier babbled from his corner. "We have to catch her… I'll show that bitch… it's all her fault."

Xavier was already pretty drunk. Lately, he'd get drunk quickly and start ranting about his plans for revenge against Yumi. Yesterday, he spent all day lurking at the MosTech entrance, waiting for her to appear, without any luck however.

"That bitch is hiding… and the executives are in on it." Xavier grabbed Lance's arm. "You've got connections… Hit up that chick from the ads department… You always have these horny chicks drooling over you… Talk to that Marina… Have her tell us where they're hiding her!"

"And what will you do with her?" Lance curled his lip in disdain. "You want to get slapped with a charge? Or you think you can bribe your way out? You don't have that kind of money."

Xavier was a mediocre esports player but a pretty good actor. He looked great in commercials, and Lance's manager asked him to train the guy so he'd appear not just on screen but in the rankings too. A party animal and club regular, Xavier introduced Lance to the nightlife of the capital and was an irreplaceable guide in that sense.

But lately, Xavier had become obsessed with

this Yumi girl. Getting killed twice in-game had turned him into a real psycho. All he talked about was betrayal and revenge. He was completely losing his marbles.

The funniest thing was that initially Lance had genuinely liked Yumi, the ebullient and restless fangirl. Compared to the cold and calculating women who saw Lance merely as a career opportunity or a potential ATM, Yumi seemed genuinely thrilled to be with him. She admired him and lit up any time he approached.

Cold and calculating with women himself, Lance, who had been dubbed "the reptile" by socialite predators, even felt something akin to feelings for her. A fleeting sympathy, nothing more, but for him, even this was extraordinary.

But then Xavier and T-Rex vividly described to Lance how the newbie had gotten tipsy and proposed a threesome. "Just another gold-digging whore," Xavier remarked at the time. "I'll play with her and toss her aside." Lance was a bit letdown but not surprised; he'd encountered this type of gold-digger too.

What Yumi did next didn't fit that role, however. Gold-diggers don't kill their meal tickets, nor do they seek revenge. Lance felt annoyed that he had believed Xavier back then. And that's where all the trouble started.

They had gotten too comfortable. At first, during the Purge, they acted like daring Landsknechts in a conquered city, indulging in executions, looting and pillage. Then they allowed themselves to get killed twice in a row, losing all their gear in the process. They flunked the beginning of the test, losing precious time and the chance to gain XP. First, they were leaders, then middlings, and now they were trailing.

When the game assigned the quest for the wyvern eggs, Lance decided that his party would not take part in it. He crushed any dissent in his squad and instead led the four of them to farm spiders at the other end of town. What followed was three hours of tedious and methodical grinding. The town was almost empty of players. Everyone was seeking their fortune on the forest paths.

He may have been bored out of his mind, but Lance did level up twice. Now he was at Level 9. Xavier and T-Rex had reached Level 8. Only Shugga had slipped up a bit and fallen short, languishing at Level 7.

Lance understood that Anna, TargetAi's party, and even other players who had outleveled the rest of them would steamroll his squad like a bulldozer. In this predicament, he told himself, retreating wasn't cowardly. Fade into the background, level up, and then re-enter the race for first place.

But these idiots he was working with just didn't get it. For four straight hours, they drank, sulked, and threw accusations around. Only Shugga, as usual, silently tapped on his controller.

"If we can't catch her here, we need to nail that bitch in the game," Xavier persisted.

"You won't catch her in there!" T-Rex interrupted. "The town guards nabbed her. She's probably stuck in some dungeon."

"But that's perfect!" Xavier lit up. "That means those freaks, TargetAi and the others, aren't around her now. And the NPCs will be no obstacle for us."

"What do you mean?!" Lance asked with surprise.

"We'll just kill them all!" Xavier hopped in place, thrilled by his new idea. "Did you see their levels?! No one's above Level 6! We'll level up on them... and become the top dogs! Then this town will be ours! They're NPCs after all! They can't respawn."

"Seriously, listen!" T-Rex cracked open another bottle of tequila and started pouring generous shots all around while sloshing alcohol over the countertop. "We'll rename the dump 'Lanceburg!' Unlock the treasury, raise a militia. You'll be the local duke. That's how all aristocrats were made! We'll take this town by sword and fire... Then we'll exploit and plunder it all!"

"And send those other bitches straight to the dungeon!" laughed Xavier. "Both of them. The busty one from TargetAi's gang too. Let them pay in blood, the whores. And then to the brothel! Let them work off their debt to their new lord! Hear that, Shugga? Are you with us or what? What do you think?"

"Yah, kill them all, I say," Shugga responded without looking up from his screen.

"Are you serious?!" Lance couldn't believe his ears.

"To Duke Lance!" Xavier shouted, raising his shot. "Hooray for the duke! HOORAY!"

"Long live Duke Lance!" T-Rex clinked glasses, supporting him. "Come on, Shugga, you're either with us or against us!"

"Dummies!" Lance laughed. "What am I going to do with you dummies?"

"Charge! Burn! Kill!" Shugga jumped up on T-Rex's shoulders, spilling tequila.

"It's decided then," Lance raised his shot, and the other voices fell silent. "Tomorrow we storm the mayor's residence and show these NPCs who their true masters are!"

Chapter 19

"BACK OFF," I SAID calmly. "Just leave me alone and let me pass!"

"You ditched me! You left me there all alone! How could you?!" Marina's voice trailed off into dramatic sobbing. "Did you leave with some chick? Is that why you didn't answer my calls?!"

"Nice try, Marina," I grabbed her wrists, which she had raised either to hug me or to claw out my eyes, and just to be safe, I forced them down. "Nice, but it doesn't count. You were the one who dragged me into that snake pit and left me to be devoured by your viper friends. Deal with them yourself."

Marina had ambushed me on the way to the locker room. I had let my guard down and totally didn't expect an attack in this part of the building. My head was still buzzing from the revelations of the local executives. I was clutching Anna's phone number, old-school penciled onto a colored sticky note. On top of that, I was occupied with my plans for today's raid.

The last thing I needed was Marina and her dramatic accusations.

Actually, looking at her, you wouldn't have guessed that she'd spent the night at the club and had vodka up to her eyeballs by midnight. Marina was now wearing an immaculate light-colored pantsuit, a striking cream blouse and sharp-heeled pumps. The very picture of wronged innocence, as you can imagine.

I looked at her and couldn't understand how just a week ago, her presence had made me so speechless I babbled nonsense. She had seemed like a creature from another world. And now here she was, dabbing her tears with a tissue, careful not to smudge her mascara.

I once heard that our real age isn't counted by the number of years we've lived but by what we've lived through. Over the last week, I had more extraordinary things happen to me than my entire life up till then. And essentially, I had few options: give up and fade away, go back to my crappy little two-room flat with my perpetually drunk dad and eternally crying mom — to poverty and despair — or to "weather the storm," as the Americans like to say.

And to do that, it turns out, it's not enough to know how to fight in meatspace or in cyberspace. You need to know how to talk to people, especially those wealthier and more powerful than you.

Those who want to bend you to their will and use you. Women especially.

Just recently, Marina seemed like a goddess to me, as distant as Delta Cassiopeiae. Now, however, I saw her with completely sober eyes.

She's not too bright, I had already figured that out. It's true that she had attained a junior executive position, but she still did incredibly stupid things all the time. She wasn't that beautiful either. She was well-groomed, attractive and she took good care of herself, yet Yana, her friend at the club, a fitness fanatic, eclipsed her by a mile. And Yana wasn't opposed to getting to know me better. Right there, on the dance floor...

Actually, every other girl in that club wasn't opposed to it either. And it wasn't about money. No one had peeked into my pockets or checked my account. It came down to confidence. Women sense it with some kind of primal instinct. Whether you're worthy of their time or not. And it's got nothing to do with how you approach them, or how you show them attention, your rizz or what pickup lines you use. They might not even notice any of that. Either they bite or they don't. And it's not even the goal. It's just an indicator. One of the markers of what you're really worth.

Probably like any experience, it's built up over time. Not the number of "victories," but the potential interest you spark in women, and when there's a bunch around you, the XP just falls on your head, and your skill levels up... Much gratitude for this to Marina, for taking me out to mingle.

"What's this?!" The blonde noticed the sticky note in my hand, snatched it, and started reading, "Who's this bitch that gave you her number?! Did you spend the night with her?!"

I once heard that if a girl is not into you, even the sweetest word could upset her. It's pointless to kneel, beg for forgiveness, degrade yourself...

And conversely, if she is into you, it absolutely doesn't matter what you actually say. You could tell her to get lost, and she would listen and smile as if you were showering her with compliments. It's like a filter switches on in their heads. They always hear only what they want to hear.

Great opportunity to test it out.

"Tell me, are you stupid, Marina?"

"Why?" She suddenly stopped and stared at me, puzzled.

"I don't know, you're acting like a complete idiot."

And just like that her tantrum abated. She just blinked and even her tears dried up. I had stumped her.

"Let's go into the locker room and talk." I opened the door and practically shoved this nutcase inside. "Let's not make a scene here in front of everyone."

Marina stood in the middle of the tiny room, silently clenching her fists and waiting for an explanation. I sat down on the couch, curiously watching her. Inside, I felt nothing... no stirrings of emotion... no jitters... If she walks out now, so be it... That's where she belongs.

"Tell me, Ms. Skvortsova," I inadvertently mimicked Dr. Kotov's manner of speaking with devastating effect. "What use are you to me?"

"What?!" Marina expected apologies or explanations — anything but such composure from me.

"We're partners, right?" I continued. "Not just in terms of fooling around, but in business too. So, what have you done for me, partner? Set me up to fail? Pumped me full of some nonsense so I'd cover your pretty ass? You almost got yourself kicked out of the project... And I was the one who had to save you... I put my own reputation on the line... Now, when I need to be *completely* focused, damn it!" I made a dramatic pause. "And here you are, getting on my nerves... Turns out, you're of no use to me, just trouble."

Marina looked like she'd been doused with a bucket of cold water. That meeting with the three executives "over a cup of tea" had given me not just a goal worth dying for and Anna's coveted phone number. More than that — I had listened to them and I had learned from them. And I began applying what I'd learned almost immediately.

"But Andrew, I... I do help..." Judging by the wrinkle on her smooth forehead, she was digging through her memory and could come up with nothing but taking me to buy Gucci slippers, offering me sexual favors and teaching me how to down Sambuca.

“Have you find out anything about Anna Falk?”

“No, Andrew, when could I?!” Her eyes widened in astonishment as if she was swamped with work.

“You have there in your hand her phone number,” I said calmly. “Judging by the country code, it’s Russian... I want you to trace it and find out everything you can... Who it’s registered to... Where she lives... Marina, come on, you’re smart...” I jumped off the couch. “Prove to me that you’re not just great at sucking dick. Prove to me that you can do something else!”

“You asshole!” Marina blurted out.

“That’s it, get to work, I’m busy...” I turned Marina towards the exit, gave her a slap on the butt, and as she yelped “*Ow!*” pushed her out of my locker room.

* * *

“Targe, where the hell have you been?!” Simba stalked up to me as soon as we met in the game. “Your phone’s off, your mom says you’re with ‘the fiancée!’ I mean, what the fuck? A fiancée?! Where did she come from?!”

AngelCake frowned silently, displeased at hearing about the fiancée. Weird how she didn’t seem to mind about Marina or even Yumi. Probably thought if it was all fair game, yet “fiancée” implied some preference on my part, I guess.

"Simba, why the hell would you call my house?!" I grew irritated. "You've probably got my mom all worried. I told her I'm staying at your place."

"And I'm not worried?!" Simba bellowed like a wounded bear. "One day you're getting hit on the head, the next some doctors are locking you up in their hospital ward — and who has to save you? Me!"

"I'd like you to explain 'the fiancée' bit to me," AngelCake added sternly.

"That's just my mom. To her every girl in my proximity is 'the fiancée,'" I found myself explaining. "And if she tries your pastries, I'll never hear the end of it."

AngelCake smiled. It's amazing how little it takes to make someone happy, sometimes a compliment and a bit of hope is enough.

"Did you find Sibyl?" I changed topic.

"Nope!" Simba shook his head for emphasis. "We froze our asses off for an hour out there. She never showed up."

"Well, here's our chance to ask her directly." Stacy put her hands on her hips and glared down the street.

Sibyl was approaching us. Along the way, she managed to smile at every player she passed and look around as if she was admiring every shack and every fence. In her simple yet very sexy dress, she looked like a forest fairy lost in the city.

"Hey Sibi!" Fighting the strange urge to just stand and grin at her like an idiot, I immediately started asking questions. "Remember I asked you to wait at the MosTech entrance? Why didn't you come?"

"Sorry, I forgot my purse... then the locker room was locked... then the guards hassled me... asking what was inside my purse and wouldn't give it back..." She blushed and got so flustered that my desire to keep pressing her or scold her just vanished. "Oh, you were waiting, right?! Was it very cold?! Oh, I'm so sorry... Please forgive me..."

"Ahem, well, it's nothing. These things happen..." Simba said understandingly and even made a clumsy attempt to hug our healer.

"Don't forget about your vow of celibacy now, you oaf," I snapped at him sternly. "We don't need to chase after you as you run rabid all over town again."

"Wha...? I'm cool!" Simba puffed up, but I was already trying to figure out what just happened. Why did I snap at him like that? Jealousy? Seriously?! And yet there was no denying that the thought of someone touching Sibyl somehow really pissed me off. I wanted to look at her constantly, see her smile, see her move, see her talk...

It was a strange obsession, barely noticeable last time, but much stronger now. And I still had the odd feeling like I had seen her before. Like an actress in a movie who you've seen somewhere else and really liked, but you can't remember her name or the film's title. Even her name was attractive, its very sound as bright and resonant as a bell...

Sibyl… Sibi… Sibyl…

"Sibi…" I said out loud.

"What?" She immediately turned around and smiled.

"Wait for us today…"

All at once, the icons in my interface began lighting up and flashing. A quest! Finally! I noticed how the other players in the town square around us zoned out for a minute and then began looking around confused. What's going on?

I quickly selected the icon with the flashing exclamation mark to open my quest log:

LIFE WILL BE EASIER WITH DIVINE PROTECTION! EARN THE BLESSING OF A DEITY OR ITS FOLLOWER.

My first thought was that we'd struck paydirt! We have Simba, a real ace up our sleeve. Are there even any other gods here but his Anima?

"Bless us, Simba!"

MAY THE POWER OF THE AWESOME ANIMA BE WITH YOU!

I felt a wave of coolness wash over me, tingling pleasantly on my skin.

THE GODDESS SPEAKS TO YOU! (+10% TO ALL STATS.)

Simba quickly reached out and touched every one of us. I looked on as a cloud of silvery sparks enveloped AngelCake and then Sibyl.

"Is she always going to be 'Awesome?'"

"She likes it…" Simba shrugged.

How can she like anything, damn it?! We made her up. Carved her from a log. Simba's losing it, seriously. Paladins are a dangerous class. I've already seen one episode of him losing his mind, and now I had to keep an even closer eye on him.

"I've got a new quest... a divine one!" Simba was absorbed, reading his interface. "I have to bless a hundred players. Then I'll be given the title of Magister!"

"And what do you get for becoming a Magister?!" Sibyl joined the conversation.

"A stronger blessing. I can consecrate items and appoint new chaplains of Awesome Anima!"

"Let's go!" I decided.

The others hurried after me, even before they understood where we were heading. Finally, I'd instilled some team spirit into my little party. It wasn't far to the town square, but my jaw dropped when we reached it.

"Awesome!" Simba gasped.

"Oh," AngelCake squeaked.

"Not bad," Sibyl mused thoughtfully.

On a massive cubic pedestal of dark marble stood a golden statue of Anima the Awesome. In one hand, she held her heavy sacred club, resting it's business end on the ground; she held her other hand raised high, as if greeting the crowd. Tight curls scattered over her shoulders, cascading down over her ample chest, barely covered by the thin chains of her outfit. Anima's eyes squinted haughtily and her plump lips were twisted in a capricious smile.

I looked back and forth between the statue and the original, finding more and more similarities. In fact, the more I looked, the less differences I could spot. A statue of AngelCake towered over the town square.

"It works!" a player yelled, touching the sacred club.

The crowd buzzed, pressing in. The pedestal was surrounded by a dense mass of players trying to reach the holy weapon. There used to be a guard around the statue and I could still see the pointed helmets of the guards among the crowd. They were attempting to restore order but with no success. The zealous mass, craving divine grace, simply pushed them aside.

One after another, players jumped onto the pedestal, grabbed the club, and fell back.

"Bastards… What are they doing!" I groaned through clenched teeth.

"What?!" Simba didn't understand.

"They're getting blessed for free!" I explained to him. "Bypassing their own chaplain. What the hell do they need you for, holy servant?! They have a magic… ugh… sacred club!"

"Those bastards!" the paladin understood. "Make way! Make way for the servant of the Awesome Anima! Now then, line up, you sorry sons of bitches! Get in line!"

"Where do you think you're going?!" someone in the crowd objected. "Look at him! Are we not all equals before the goddess?"

The beta testers closed ranks, refusing to let Simba through.

"Turn around, you idiots," yelled the paladin.

"I can bless youse too."

"We don't believe you!" they shot back. "Piss off, you conman, you false prophet!"

"Just bless them!" I couldn't take it anymore. "Why are you arguing with them?! Bless them and end this!"

"I can't!" Simba said desperately, stretching and then clenching his fist. "They need to ask for the blessing, like you did before. I can't just bless people without their consent."

"Move, you bastards!" I roared, pushing one of the players aside.

"Who the hell do you think you are, pushing people around?" In an instant, I found a dozen swords, knives, spears, and other pointy objects pointed at me. "Think you're a tough guy, eh? We'll give you a stomping."

It looked like Anima's followers were up for a fight! They may have been a bit dull, but they were fighters. I could have shredded them like cabbage all by myself, but that wouldn't bring me any closer to my goal. A fistfight in this situation would be the height of idiocy. Sure, you could scatter the crowd, but how long would that take? And would our opponents want to be blessed by their attackers afterward? A complete deadlock.

Our presence should have pleased this crowd, but they didn't know who we were. A common problem for prophets, I guess.

"Make way for the incarnation of the Awesome Anima!" Sibyl suddenly cried in a clear, resonant voice. Then she fell to her knees and intoned, "May the Goddess bless and bestow her mercy on my poor soul! Make way!"

"Put on your chain mail, quick!" I hissed.

"What?" Stacy didn't understand. "Why?"

"Your moment of glory has arrived!" said Simba. "The people clamor for your love!" He laughed, having figured out what Sibyl had in mind, and he turned around and bellowed at the crowd, "MAKE WAY FOR THE AWESOME ANIMA!"

"No way!" Someone turned around. "Look, it's really the goddess!"

"Look at that, she's alive!"

"A perfect match!!!"

"Look at those boobs! I've never seen knockers like that on a mortal chick!"

"Well, she's a real goddess. Her knockers are divine!"

"They are divine mysteries!"

"Goddess, bless us!"

Naturally, no one actually fell to their knees. But at least they noticed us, and began turning towards us, reaching out... Simba and I held off the crowd like movie bodyguards. AngelCake was initially hesitant, then caught the vibe, lifted her chin and strutted forward proudly.

"The Goddess does not issue blessings directly!" yelled Simba. "To receive Anima's blessing, please see her appointed chaplain — me that is."

"Bless me... Bless me!" the players begged all around us.

MAY THE POWER OF THE AWESOME ANIMA

BE WITH YOU!

Simba punched one guy in the chest and a cloud of sparks showered over the player.

"Anima has blessed me," he cried in raptures. "She has blessed me! Praise be to Anima!"

"Make way…" we yelled. "Make way!"

The crowd parted like the sea. A path opened straight to the pedestal. Stacy walked down it like a runway model, hips swaying, her eyes fixed straight ahead. Simba marched alongside her, grandly, touching one fortunate player after another.

MAY THE POWER…

…OF THE AWESOME ANIMA…

…BE WITH YOU!

Simba was ecstatic. Together, they finally reached the statue. The golden Anima — or her living copy — and her humble servant, the triumphant paladin.

"Line up!" he yelled. "EVERYONE will be blessed!"

If someone in this world ever decides to write the local chronicles, this day will be remembered as the "Awesome Coming of Anima the Awesome." Sibyl will go down as a prophetess, and the chroniclers will invent an even cooler role for Simba. The event will be embellished with details that never happened and some moral lessons that will be invented later. That's how lore is made, after all.

"They look good, don't they?" Sibyl nudged me with her elbow to get my attention. "And what about us? Are we just going to stand here like extras?"

"No, of course not," I replied. "But I have other plans."

"Can I take a guess?" she looked at me slyly.

"You can try," I was curious to see what she'd come up with.

She couldn't possibly guess my real goal, especially since it wasn't assigned in the game, and none of the outsiders knew about it.

"I would go..." She wrinkled her nose cutely in thought. "...to the mayor's residence!"

"How did you...?!" I said with a start.

"That's where the juiciest quests are!" Sibyl was clearly pleased with her guess. "And you only want the best!"

She grabbed my arm decisively and added, "Let's hurry. There's no time to waste!"

* * *

The mayor came out to meet us personally. Either my growing reputation with him had had its effect, or he was eager to burden me with some chore.

"TargetAi," he said, barely nodding in my direction and turning to Sibyl, "Lady Sibyl." He bowed deeply, gallantly. "'Tis a delight to welcome you to my humble halls. What brings you to my residence?"

"I've come to know that my... umm..." I was searching for the right words. In dealing with this NPC you have to articulate your thoughts very precisely. Reputation is far easier to lose than earn... "My uh compatriot is languishing in your custody. May we be allowed to see her?"

Sibyl stared at me in surprise, apparently not expecting such a request. On a side note, I'm curious why I'm referred to as "esteemed" and she's a "lady?" How did she earn that title? Or is this fucker trying to flirt with her?!

"Your information is somewhat outdated," the mayor smirked, twirling his mustache. "One of the immortals was indeed apprehended by the town guard for her crimes. She underwent punishment, acknowledged her guilt, and has cleared her reputation. She is now completely free!"

"Free?!" I couldn't believe my ears, "But why haven't I seen her since then?"

"That can be arranged." The mayor clapped his hands sharply a few times. "Lieutenant," he addressed one of his guards, "please have Lady Yumina deign to pay us a visit!"

CHAPTER 20

“FUCK THE GODS!” Xavier declared. “When the town is ours, their priests will come running. ‘Duke Lance... May we bless you?’” he aped. “They’ll be falling over themselves, just to have their religion favored.”

“We need to pick some chick,” said T-Rex.

“What chick?” Lance asked, surprised.

He was preoccupied today and had already missed a good part of the conversation.

“There are always chick goddesses,” T-Rex explained. “The patron deities of lechery. Like Aphrodite, for instance. Their priestesses are always hot and easy.”

“We need a god of war,” Shugga, who was typically silent, spoke up unexpectedly, “to beat the crap out of everyone.”

“Exactly,” Xavier echoed him. “With a proper deity of our own, we can take on any priestesses...

ours or others..."

"Alright, enough leering over unbedded priestesses," Lance commanded. "Business first, pleasure second."

They were circling the mayor's residence, delaying the inevitable with their chatter. An assault! They all understood that once they killed the first guard, there would be no turning back for them. It would either be victory or a shameful exit from the beta test. Lance was under no illusions about this. If their plan failed today, they wouldn't be allowed to play peacefully. They'd be hunted like animals every time they logged into the game.

Flee the town and regroup out in the forests? But then how would they complete the quests, half of which were tied to the town? How would they even get to the shop, for that matter? No, their plan had only two outcomes: either they would take over the town and set their own rules, or...

Or it wasn't worth worrying about yet. Simply put, whatever they started now, they'd have to see it through to the end and not screw it up along the way.

By this point, you could pretty much call the mayor's residence a palace. The main entrance had been expanded into a porch with columns and a wide staircase. Ornamental molding adorned the walls and the building itself seemed to have stretched out and widened. In the first days of the beta, this was just an ordinary little house, and just yesterday, there wasn't even a hint of a second floor.

Now, the building boasted carved balconies and even something like a greenhouse or an enclosed veranda. The entire complex took up at least half a city block, and was extended by a further facility — a barracks or an arsenal — of massive gray blocks painted in dark ocher.

A separate back entrance was located there and full of constant, frenetic movement with small squads and individual guards constantly going in and out, carrying crates and baskets and even pushing wheelbarrows.

Unexpectedly, Xavier bee-lined for this entrance. He had chosen the assassin class mainly for its stealth powers, but later on he discovered that this class had other effective skills. One of those was *Life Insight* which allowed him to determine an enemy's level from a distance, including stats such as stamina or HP.

"There are elites at the main entrance," he announced. "Level 8s with stronger builds... Tanks. We could kill them, but we'd end up stuck in a tough fight. However, there are noobie Level 3s guarding the rear entrance."

Lance nodded reluctantly. He liked this idea less and less. Under the influence of tequila and his friends' drunken banter, everything had seemed somewhat easier yesterday. On the other hand, they really needed to take a leap of faith to catch up with the current leaders, or else they'd be doomed to trailing behind and picking up their scraps.

There was no such thing as a "balanced

party" in Lance's squad. Not for a moment did he consider that the world around him was a multiplayer RPG. It reminded him too much of esports, and even more of the true, historical Middle Ages that he had read about so voraciously at an early age. As a result, all of his gang had chosen exclusively combat classes.

Xavier chose to be an assassin, mainly for the stealth, but then discovered other effective skills in this class. *Acupuncture*, a passive skill that granted +5% to critical hit chance, was noteworthy. If you leveled up the skill to level twenty, Xavier calculated, every hit would become a crit. *Life Insight* allowed him to assess an enemy before combat and *Long Reach* allowed him to throw any weapon without a damage penalty.

Shugga had chosen to be a thief. Or rather, Lance chose this class for him, and Shugga had to comply, as usual, without anyone really knowing what Shugga himself thought about it. A thief could also go into stealth, but this didn't give him damage bonuses like it would for an assassin. In exchange, detecting a thief in stealth was much harder. Plus, a thief could pick any lock and chest, which, in the squad leader's opinion, would come in handy for looting.

T-Rex chose to be an adventurer, a classic two-handed melee fighter.

Initially, Lance also intended to choose this class. An excellent duelist with a multitude of purely combat skills. But the adventurer had one critical flaw. This class had no leadership skills.

Such an important role couldn't be entrusted to someone else. There had to be one leader, and it was unthinkable for it to be anyone but Lance.

Thus, after much consideration, Lance found what he needed: Captain — a class similar to German Landsknechts, Swiss Guards, and Italian Condottieri. Most importantly, a captain could could form a party and endow it with buffs.

Ignoring the stupid jokes about Captain Obvious and the "Aye, cap'n" remarks, Lance appreciated the strengths of this powerful and well-balanced class. He was perhaps the "heaviest" among the classes in the team, although not quite as resilient as a light tank. Especially pleasing were the captain's abilities to disarm or break an enemy's weapon. Something Lance was known for even in his bouts in the Gladiator Games.

Back in that other game, Lance never tried to end a fight quickly. He liked to toy with his opponent like a cat with a mouse. Wearing them down, drawing blood with minor cuts, draining their stamina to zero, breaking their weapons. It was only when the victim was doomed that he'd deliver a powerful, flashy fatality. Lance was loved not just because he won a lot, but because he knew how to turn every each fight into a spectacle that really got the crowd going.

Another passive skill, *Agile*, reduced armor penalties, so unlike the others, Lance now sported a breastplate and a light helmet. He didn't want to die again due to some silly accident or a sneaky assassin in stealth mode. No, no — Lance told himself that he was truly one of a kind and approached the issue of his own safety very seriously.

The rest of the squad showed up to work in simple leather armors, barely managing to scrounge up the coins to buy them after a whole day of farming. Spider venom and fangs were dirt cheap. T-Rex and Xavier complained together that there were whole flocks of sheep in good gear just outside the city, waiting to be shorn. But Lance quelled the rebellion with an iron fist. He wasn't willing to risk another day of leveling for the slim chance of profiting from PKing.

Thus, from the start, Lance's party managed to hit both the training camp and the shop. They wanted to swing by the town square for a blessing from the new goddess Anima the Awesome, but T-Rex noticed something was off just in time.

"That's the chick hanging around with TargetAi," he said, stopping short as soon as he caught sight of the statue.

"Screw them then," Xavier chimed in. "Waste of time."

In truth, both realized they wouldn't get anything out of it, and given the crowd's adoration for their old enemies, going there could even end badly for them. In the end, Lance's squad skirted the town square without receiving the blessing, turning their faces away just in case.

"*Pssst... Pssst...*" came from one of the alleys, either a hiss or a clumsy whistle.

"Who's there?!" Xavier jumped, drawing his

daggers. Two sudden deaths had made him jumpy.

The gloomy, hooded figure making the strange noises didn't even flinch. It was a player, however, not an NPC. A Level 4. His face wasn't visible and his entire body was covered by a shapeless cloak. He seemed to just be standing there, waiting for something.

"Wait up," T-Rex spoke up. "Whatcha got for us?"

"Need a 'blessing?'" the figure perked up.

"How much?" T-Rex continued, clearly on the same wavelength as the hooded figure.

"Five coins each."

"We don't have that much!" Lance protested.

They had really stocked up at the shop and were now broke, though the opportunity of quickly completing the day's quest and getting a buff before their assault was tempting.

"What if we find some middle ground...," the hooded figure paused, checking their levels. "How much do you have?"

"Twelve coins between the four of us," Lance figured.

"Let's go," nodded the hooded figure, and dashed into the maze of alleys as quickly as a giant gray mouse.

The fighters followed, their weapons at the ready.

"Is he leading us into an ambush?" mused T-Rex.

"The worse for him if he is," Xavier said

dismissively. "We'd cut them to ribbons."

Lance didn't share his team's optimism and cautiously fell behind. But everything turned out better than expected. After a couple of minutes of snaking through the city's alleys, our faceless guide led them to what seemed to be the town garbage dump. The place was full of the skeletons of broken carts, construction debris, shattered baskets and even rotten fishing nets.

If Lance's companions had any idea about how neural networks worked, they might have wondered whose mind had spawned this revolting place. But they were simple bros and didn't fuss about such details. Here and there, small fires smoldered around the dump, with gray figures in identical cloaks huddled around them. Despite the lack of heat, they pretended to warm themselves by the fire.

The dump had its own unique vibe — it looked so damp and chilly that Lance shivered reflexively. The gray folk seemed to strip him with their stares, appraising the value of every piece of gear he had.

"I've brought four more, Shiloh," mumbled their hooded guide as they approached the brightest campfire at the foot of the largest heap of trash.

"Sit down and warm yourself, Shnir," said the gray figure called Shiloh, gesturing magnanimously. He was so fat that his cloak bulged over his belly. He pulled off his hood, revealing chubby pink cheeks and small, puffy eyes.

"Wanna join our humble society?" Shiloh winked mischievously.

"We're here to get a blessing," Lance stepped forward. "The rest doesn't concern us."

"As you wish," the chubby man's mood seemed to deflate. "Throw your share into the pot, and the Whispering God will aid you."

"Who?" Lance asked with surprise.

"The Whispering God," the fat man said more confidently. "The patron deity of those who honor secret and daring deeds. You, especially, seem like one of us," he pointed a sausage-thick finger at Shugga. "These guys you're with... their path is not the path for you. You should be working with the thieves, advancing the brotherhood, contributing to the common pot..."

"Listen here, fatso, don't go filling my fighter's head with nonsense," Lance briskly took Shugga by the shoulder and moved him away. "Just bless us and be done with it. We're in a hurry."

"As you like," the chubby man nodded again. He looked at a large glass jar labeled "COMMON POT" demonstratively. Lance took out twelve coins from his inventory and placed them in the jar. The chubby man watched each coin with sad eyes, but said nothing once they were all in. Apparently, the price of the blessing was negotiable.

The circle of gray figures closed around them, but their levels were so low that Lance wasn't too worried.

"FROM THE HEART TO THE SOUL... A GIFT

FROM THE WHISPERER TO YOU... LISTEN..."

"YOU ARE NOT LIKE THE REST... YOU ARE THE BEST..."

THE WHISPERER IS WITH YOU... HIS GIFT TO YOUR EARS..."

Suddenly, the fatty started scatting some weird lines, lightly punched everyone in the shoulder, and hopped back. The gray figures thoughtfully nodded their hooded heads to the rhythm.

THE WHISPERING GOD WHISPERS TO YOU! (+10% TO ALL STATS.)

A dark fog enveloped each figure in turn, then seemed to absorb into them. Lance felt a pleasant buzz, as if he'd taken a shot of whiskey.

"Let's go," he turned abruptly, pushing through the gray figures. "We've wasted enough time in this... dump."

His party followed, giggling cheerfully. Despite the buff, they were eager to leave the dump and its unpleasant inhabitants behind.

"Arrogant scum," the fat man called Shiloh spat after them. "It's all good though. We'll see each other again. The Whispering God doesn't let anyone off the hook so easily."

* * *

The rebels were blessed and equipped as they approached the mayor's residence. It was at this point that Xavier, scanning the guards, decided to attack from behind — as true heroes do.

They waited for the moment when the gates opened again to let a cart full of straw through and rushed inside before the gates could close again.

"Halt! Where do you think you're going!" yelled one of the guards, blocking their way with a pike. "You can't just..."

Xavier rushed him and with a grin and drove his blade right into the guard's stomach. The stiletto glowed red, piercing the armor as if it were cardboard, and the assassin twisted it, increasing the damage. The Level 3 guard died before he could finish his sentence.

T-Rex chopped off the coachman's head, simply to keep him from getting underfoot, and pounced on the second guard. A feint... a quick dagger thrust to the throat, and the second guard dissolved into a handful of dust. The way was clear!

However, the attackers immediately regretted breaking through the gate. The entryway narrowed into a corridor, without any cover, and the walls on the second floor had embrasures which allowed the sentries posted up there to pepper them with bolts from their crossbows.

One of Lance's passive skills — *Fore!* — triggered, reflecting an incoming bolt. Without even thinking about it, his hand turned his sword, making a crossbow bolt deflect off to the side.

"Move it, Shugga! Forward!" ordered the captain. "The rest of you... cover him!"

The corridor wasn't very wide and only about five meters long. The mayor's residence hadn't yet grown to the size of a royal palace, so all the traps here were still rather limited in size and scale. It terminated in a gate that looked much like the ones out on the street.

Shugga bent over the lock, pulling out his lockpicks. Lance once again congratulated himself on his foresight. Not only had he ensured that his squad had a thief, but he had made sure to buy lockpicks just for this occasion. Lance really liked to pat himself on the back and now was as good a time as ever.

Thankfully and possibly even due to the Whispering God's blessing, the gates were massive but their lock was as ordinary as that of any door you could find in the city.

"Hurry up, Shugga!" yelled T-Rex. "What are you fishing in there for?!"

All three fighters covering the thief were desperately swinging their blades around themselves, deflecting incoming projectiles. But T-Rex was the weakest so he occasionally got hit by bolts in various parts of his body, causing him to yelp in pain.

The injuries were unpleasant but not fatal, confirming that the crossbowmen's level was probably not high. And this meant Xavier was right and they had a chance. If only Shugga would stop fiddling around!

Click! Barely audible, the long awaited release of the lock's catch sounded louder than a gunshot. The gates swung open and the rebels rushed inside.

"T-Rex, take the right. Xavier, you take the left!" Lance commanded.

Right next to the entrance, two staircases on either side led up to galleries from which the crossbowmen had been peppering Lance's party. Now it was time to clear them. Lance heard agonized screams and the clash of steel from both sides. These ranged guards weren't so hot when it came to close combat, Lance thought vindictively.

The corridor was a trap they had almost gotten caught in. So, upon breaking out of there, Lance felt that playful anger that fuels every athlete. The next moment a rush of exhilaration swept over him so forcefully that he had to take a knee.

Level up! He was at Level 10 now and the assault had only just begun. For the first time today, Lance believed they had a chance of success.

"We're under attack!"

"Cut them down!"

"No... Take them alive!"

"How are you going to do that, you fool?! Cut them down to the last man!"

"In the mayor's name, surrender your weapons!"

As Lance was making his way down the corridor, a scrum of guards came rushing towards him. Their numbers quickly grew from five to eight to ten. Lance was so busy that he couldn't keep count and as the reinforcements kept coming, counting became the least of his worries.

He was spinning like a dancer, fending off five pikes at once — blocking, parrying, and retreating. Always preferring the cunning route, Shugga immediately went into stealth mode, leaving Lance to face the entire mob alone. Step by step, Lance retreated, unable to reach his enemies with his short swords, yet also managing to hold off the guards from getting too close to him.

Lance thought things would get dicier in the passage ahead. It was wider there, meaning more enemies could attack at once. But on the other hand, if his party members did their jobs right...

Feeling the space open up, the guards pressed harder. Lance was now fighting against seven pike-tips at once. He didn't have enough strength to launch counterattacks. All he could do was dodge and delay the inevitable.

"Crush him... Push him towards the doors!"

"Go for the legs, sweep the legs!"

"We got this!"

"Caught you!" The guards babbled excitedly among themselves. They seemed all too real to Lance suddenly — lively and... foolish.

Then, with a loud bang, the gates behind the guards shut closed, and Shugga, emerging from stealth, quickly locked them from the inside.

Whomp! Whomp! The sound of crossbows firing came from the galleries above.

Neither Xavier nor T-Rex had been trained in shooting, but there was no missing at point-blank range either. The passage was so crowded that every bolt found its target without any chance of hitting the ground.

As the guards began falling, Lance once again felt the thrill of the fight. Judging by their shouts of excitement, T-Rex and Xavier had each gained two levels as well. In less than five minutes, it was all over. The gates swung open again, revealing Xavier's face with a satisfied expression.

"Your Highness, Duke Lance," he curtsied foolishly. "The city begs your lordship's mercy at your feet!"

CHAPTER 21

THEY FOUGHT FOR EVERY CORRIDOR and every room, winning time and time again. Guards popped up everywhere, but they couldn't put up any serious resistance. It seemed like their defensive strategy had ended with the fortifications at the entrance. Beyond that, they were just like bots, weak and clumsy.

The level difference also played a role. Lance's team hadn't encountered anyone above Level 7. Now at Level 9, T-Rex and Xavier were effortlessly slaughtering the NPCs while trading banter.

"That makes eight!"

"I've got fourteen!"

"Doesn't count with a crossbow!"

"Why not?! Did they just die on their own?"

Shugga trailed behind, finishing off the low-level enemies that the others didn't bother with, stunning or disarming them. Lance advanced majestically amid this fray, barking orders without bothering to draw his sword. His companions, eager for easy prey, took care of everything.

The guards only put up a real fight in one corridor, where four dozen of them, armed with short swords, fought desperately, using skills like actual players for the first time.

"Damn!" T-Rex cried out when his rapier blade snapped at the base. "Crush them!"

Xavier dashed to get behind the guards, but they skillfully maneuvered back-to-back to meet the threat. Even so, it was four against two.

The assassin held them off, gradually retreating. His daggers were not the best weapon against their long swords.

"Move aside," said Lance, nudging T-Rex with his shoulder. He positioned himself in front of the four guards in a high combat stance, crossing his blades in front of him and ready for their attack. That's when the superiority of the esports athlete over the high-level but AI-generated bots became apparent.

The first guard delivered a powerful blow, obviously enhanced by some skill, hoping to break through Lance's guard, but Lance simply stepped aside. Then he turned his body, as if dancing a tango with his attacker, but instead of catching his partner, he hit the guard on the head with the hilt of his sword, adding extra momentum. The guard collapsed at T-Rex's feet.

"Finish him," Lance commanded curtly. He had no interest in a defeated enemy. That's one down.

The second guard didn't repeat the first one's mistake and merely assumed a defensive posture. Lance immediately switched to attack mode, forcing the enemy back with powerful strikes. With both swords he attacked from above, below, left, and right, pressuring the guard, wearing down his stamina, and forcing him to retreat until he was back-to-back with those fighting Xavier.

Leg Sweep — a sneaky move, a favorite of that Ratmir, who now went by TargetAi. Lance didn't think it beneath him to learn from his enemies. The guard's knee buckled, and he fell backward.

"Finish him!" That's two down.

The two idiots didn't even think to turn around. The dumb bots failed to react to the threat in time. Lance performed a showy somersault, delivering a dramatic fatality to one of them with a dropkick. The guard's helmet flew off, clattering across the stone floor, and he slumped down lifelessly.

"Finish him!" he called to Xavier. That's three down.

While the assassin bent over the stunned guard, Lance grappled with the last one. *Disarm!* With a clever feint, Lance's sword flicked the enemy's weapon out of his grip, causing it to slip from the guard's hand as if it suddenly had a mind of its own.

Stripped of his weapon, the guard helplessly lowered his arms, and at that moment, T-Rex stabbed him several times in the neck with a stiletto. Four down!

Yes! Another wave of pleasure washed over Lance. Level 11. The levels came so easily that it was hard to argue with the plan they had settled on.

The elite guards were supposed to protect the Arsenal. It sounded impressive, but in reality, it was just a large room filled with armor and weapons. The invaders found no special treasures there, just standard guard gear, though some items were better than others.

"Look at this!" Shugga held up a dark gray cuirass, which looked like it was made of smoky silver with engravings, over his head — a nice piece of gear for the captain.

Lance, who normally didn't bother with loot, showed interest this time, trying on the new gear. The "Parade Officer's Cuirass" offered +10 to Armor and +5 to Dexterity, and reduced damage from projectile weapons by 20%. All in all, a worthy piece of gear. Lance put it on and signaled to his fighters to plunder the Arsenal more thoroughly and carefully.

In the end, the raiders looked mismatched but effective, like typical marauders.

"Should we take some with us?" the ever-prudent Shugga suggested.

"Why bother! It's all ours anyway!" Xavier kicked a helmet lying on the floor. "Soon, all of this will be ours."

"Don't count your chickens before they hatch," T-Rex shook his head. "The hardest part is yet to come."

"What's so hard about it?" Xavier laughed. "They're just *bots*. I've cut through crowds of them at the training camp. And so have you. They can *never* beat a human player. They're just too dumb."

Lance didn't take part in their conversation, quietly searching through the Arsenal. He had already picked out a full officer's set for himself and was now looking for new swords. He settled on straight, short sabers — heavy, powerful, and reminiscent of his beloved Katzbalgers.

He was surprised that they had heard no alarm, or even an in-game notification or quest announcing that his party had been declared outlaws. The instant that Yumi had broken the rules, the game had literally howled, declaring a manhunt after her. But nothing of the kind had happened here yet.

It felt like they were just clearing out a typical raid location. Could that idiot Xavier really have been right? Would the AI really just let them seize power like this? And what then?! His dumb bros could delude themselves with reveries of raiding the treasury and suchlike debauchery. For Lance, only victory mattered.

And that meant crushing the competition. Lance understood the advantages being in charge of this place would give him. He'd set everyone against Anna: Let that bitch be killed and stripped every time she showed her face. Let her be handed over to the authorities and then Lance would personally lock her in the deepest dungeon. If necessary, he'd build one himself. Let her give up and quit the beta with her tail between her legs.

The same with TargetAi. Hound him like an animal. Declare venerating that silly goddess of his — whose statue he had glimpsed in the town square — a heresy. Eliminate the competition. Then his victory would be absolute. It was the only kind of victory he could accept.

Or maybe none of this would be necessary?! Just killing the mayor might be enough. Corner the king and checkmate. Beta test over and Grandmaster Lance earns his well-deserved reward!

As the goofy grizzled man from the MosTech board of directors had told him himself: "There will be only one winner." Back on the first day of the beta, Lance went to his office after that first round's results were annulled and the esports players had their custom competitive armors taken away. Lance was ready to throw a fit. Waving his contract in front of the MosTech's representative's face, he was prepared to spit on it all and make his exit. It's not like there wouldn't be other beta tests for him to take part in.

However, the MosTech representative didn't argue with him. Instead, she immediately took him to see one of the executives. He greeted Lance politely, offered him pu-erh tea with macadamia nuts and cashews, nodded understandingly while the champion aired his grievances, and then asked a simple question.

"Tell me, Anton," he said, "what do you want from life?"

Lance was taken aback but answered anyway:

"Please call me Lance." He stubbornly pursed his lips.

"Of course," the grizzled man laughed. "Don't like your name? I don't like mine much either. Everyone calls me the Master. But my question stands, do you know what you want?"

Lance thought about it. The setting wasn't conducive to throwing tantrums and his irritation faded by and by. The artificial waterfall hummed quietly. Music played somewhere within earshot… a light, gentle jingling of bells. He inhaled the aroma of the pu-erh tea, well aware of how much such a cup could cost. Lance had bought the same for his mother as it was said to be good for the stomach.

At last he confidently answered: "To win."

"The response of a warrior," the Master said with approval. "But you do realize you can't win forever, right?"

This question touched a sore spot for Lance. An athlete's career is short-lived. There are no physical injuries in esports, yet the competition is fierce. Younger, stronger competitors are always ready to take your place, devouring those who slip up — even if the "old-timers" are only 23 or 25. Like it or not, reflexes dull over time. It's just physiology, an aspect of nature you can't fight against.

How many contracts, endorsements, sponsorships, and prizes could he rake in before he was past his prime? Lance wasn't dumb, and he was set on milking his success for everything he could get.

"As long as I can," he replied.

"Do you know there's only one way to always beat the casino?" the Master asked slyly.

"Buy my own casino?" Lance laughed. "You're overestimating me. I don't have that kind of money."

"But I do." The grizzled man slapped his hand on the table as if he was putting down an invisible domino. "I have the money and the casino. Well, it's more of a game, really. One you can win again and again. You see..." the Master lowered his voice as if confiding a secret to Lance, "our developers have created an awesome game, but we have no clue how to play it. We need someone who can figure that out. An executive position — Head of Gaming — with a chance of promotion to the board. You could be our equal, and that would come with its own money, fame, and power. More than you've ever dreamed of in fact."

"So you're just testing us," Lance immediately began thinking. "Putting us through a 'rat race' to find the best candidate for your role."

"Ugh, how crude..." the Master rolled his eyes. "Think of it as an interview... A test of professional suitability. To be honest, I'd offer you the position right away. But it's not up to me alone... There's also the matter of accountability...

transparency... you know how it is."

"I understand," Anton Richter nodded.

Opportunities like this came once in a lifetime, and he was not about to let this one slip through his fingers.

"Wake up, my Duke! Great deeds await us!" Xavier touched his shoulder, snapping him out of his reverie.

"Let's go," Lance agreed.

After leaving the Arsenal, the rebels found the corridors empty. They ran until they reached a fork in the path. Straight ahead, an archway clearly led to the official part of the compound, where the bare stone walls gave way to luxurious tapestries. To the right, a staircase led down to a subfloor, emanating cold and damp air.

"Down!" Xavier shouted. "Let's get that bitch!"

"What in the hell for?!" T-Rex disagreed. "She won't get away!"

"First the dungeon," Lance unexpectedly supported Xavier. "But only for a short bit."

In the last conversation they had, the Master had asked him many questions about Yumi. That pest had stayed in Lance's apartment for days, yet Lance knew nothing about her.

The dungeon was dark and gloomy, living up to all his expectations for such a place. A wide corridor lit by torches ran down the middle, with cells on either side — all empty. At the corridor's end was a long bench, presumably for the guards.

"The bastards have fled!" Xavier exclaimed.

"From here too?" Lance asked, entering one of

the cells.

Hand and foot shackles were attached to the wall. Lance deliberately placed his hand next to them. The cuffs were clearly designed for much thinner wrists — female, he figured. On the floor was a pile of straw with many rusty stains. Lance had never seen dried blood before, but it looked similar.

"Hey! What are you doing?!" T-Rex suddenly yelled.

Bang! The door leading to the dungeon slammed shut loudly. Voices and the sound of a bolt sliding into place could be heard from the other side.

* * *

The grand hall of the mayor's residence was so quiet at the moment that if there were flies in the game, we would have surely heard them. In this silence, the sound of footsteps was especially loud. *Click-click* came the merry clicking of the bright red high heels.

If I hadn't been sure it was Yumi, I might not have recognized her. She appeared like a blazing torch, in a brightly red dress of shimmering silk, somewhat resembling a kimono, with a high waist or wide sleeves that didn't restrict her movement. Her shoulders were bare, and there were slits on both sides of her skirt going up to the thigh. She could well manage a kick in a dress like that, even in heels.

Previously, Yumi had resembled a cute,

slightly clumsy kitten. Now, there was something lithe and serpentine about the way she carried herself. She walked, casually clicking her heels on the floorboards, yet she also seemed ready to shift into a combat stance at any moment. The plump lips of this new Yumi curved in a polite, but insincere smile, and her slightly snub nose was turned up haughtily.

Her usual braids had been refashioned into a complex, high Oriental hairstyle, adorned with two pins that stuck out ornately. I wouldn't be surprised if these also turned out to be weapons, with pretty good stats. The label above her head read Level 12. Had she even managed to level up?!

"Yumi, hi, how are you?!" I rushed towards her.

"My lord!" She jumped back, like a prim lady recoiling from a drunkard. "I am pleased to meet you, but let's refrain from taking liberties! I am not Yumi, but Lady Yumina. And I request that you address me accordingly."

The mayor watched us with amused curiosity.

"How interesting..." whispered Sibyl.

While I was blinking in surprise, she stepped forward.

"Lady Yumina, I am pleased to meet you."

"Hello, Lady Sibyl," Yumi... I mean Yumina, smiled. It was like she was the same person, yet completely unrecognizable at the same time.

"May I examine you?" Sibyl took her hand unceremoniously.

"Of course," to my surprise, Yumina agreed quite calmly. "You are a doctor after all."

"No debuffs... stats are normal..." mumbled Sibyl, "You are an assassin?"

"Milady," Yumina blushed. "Is it appropriate to mention that in polite society? I am a lady of the court..."

"Since when?" Sibyl asked sharply, looking Yumina straight in the eyes.

"As long as I can remember..."

"And how long is that?"

"Not long... but I was told I had been ill for a long time... It happens."

"So, you don't know this man?" Sibyl pointed at me.

"First time I've seen him," Yumina carefully looked me over and shook her head.

"Come here," Sibyl waved me over.

"Yumi... Lady Yumina..." I was more cautious this time, "do you remember me? I'm TargetAi. Also known as Andrew. In another world..."

"In what other world?" Yumina laughed unexpectedly. "I've never left this city in my whole life. Is this how you proposition ladies that strike your fancy, Tar-get-Ai?" She pronounced my name syllable by syllable and smiled flirtatiously.

In that smile, I recognized the old Yumi. The one I met as I was waiting for the first round of the beta to begin. The one whose belly I promised to sign if I won the beta.

What the hell did the AI do to her?! Brainwash her?! Or is this not even Yumi, but her digital copy? Just an NPC. I'm flirting with an ordinary NPC right now. So then where's the real Yumi? Lying in a coma somewhere, her consciousness wiped out?

So many questions and not a single answer. Who to ask? The mayor, who stands there smirking into his fancy mustache? Sibyl, who, it turns out is a doctor to the NPCs?!

I didn't get the chance to ask either one of them.

* * *

"It's useless!" Shugga backed away from the door, "We need more lockpicks. And I'll need to level up my lockpicking skill."

"Man, what the hell kind of level is this!" Xavier spat. "They shut the bolt on us. We're screwed! We're *fucked*, my bros!"

He squatted down, cradling his head in his hands, quietly sobbing.

"Why are you giving up?!" Lance kicked him in the ribs. "You're not defeated until you give up! A bolt, you say?! There's a drill for every bolt!"

He quickly looked around. A bench. Heavy, even for the four of them, even despite their newly leveled Strength stats. Was it made of iron or what?! Even better if it was!

"Let's go for it... One... Two!!" The heavy bench slammed into the door. "Three... Four... All together, my bros!"

"It's giving, bro!" cried T-Rex. "It's giving!"

There were shouts from the other side of the

door too. Shrill cries, full of fear.

"Hit it!"

After the fourth hit, the door flew off its hinges, knocking the guards off their feet. Shugga wisely finished them off quickly so they wouldn't be a problem later.

Someone was running upstairs, but the rebels were unstoppable now. They sprinted over the bodies of the guards as they turned to dust, past the bundles of fallen loot, and burst into a large, brightly lit hall.

"There she is! There's that bitch!" Xavier stopped, pointing ahead. "I've got you now, you slut!"

CHAPTER 22

YUMINA STOPS MID-SENTENCE, turns around and instantly vanishes into stealth with a barely audible pop. I catch a glimpse of Xavier before he follows after her, vanishing a second later. Then, the rest of Lance's gang barges into the room. T-Rex is Level 11, Shugga is Level 10, and Lance is Level 12. He's almost caught up to me now. How the hell did he do that?! And where did these idiots even come from?!

The katana appears in my hand on its own, but Sibi latches onto me:

"No, wait!" She points in the other direction. "Look!"

Pikemen come pouring into the hall from both side entrances. There are about twenty of them. They are all Level 15+. This must be the mayor's elite guard… the Praetorians… Call them what you like, it's clear no one stands a chance against them, neither Lance nor, most likely, even me.

The mayor smirks and raises his hand, and the pikemen point their pikes at the intruders. Crossbowmen stream in behind the pikemen. They ready their crossbows, take aim, and wait for the order, but the mayor hesitates.

T-Rex and Shugga freeze in confusion. Only Lance seems unsurprised. He even smiles like someone who knew how everything would play out from the start and is now pleased to see his expectations met.

Hack! Lance's cleaver comes down on the back of Shugga's neck. A powerful blow, enhanced by some skill of his, adding on multiple damage multipliers. The little thief doubles over and dies from the next hit. Lance is seized by an almost instant spasm of pleasure — he's just leveled up to Level 13. All the XP from the kill goes to him, meaning he has left his own party.

"Are you out of your mind, Lance?!" T-Rex turns around, his rapier en guard. "What the hell are you doing, you bastard!"

He looks pathetic... his posture ridiculous. He's bewildered and already defeated. *Cling!* His blade breaks off at the base with the sound of shattering glass. He takes one hit... then another... then a third... He falls and Lance finishes him off. T-Rex was almost Lance's equal, so Lance needs very little XP for his next level.

The invisible duel between the two assassins is interrupted. Xavier emerges from stealth, disheveled, followed by a triumphant Yumina. She delivers several strikes from her stilettos, which is what her hairpins have transformed into. Xavier backs up, backs up — and impales himself on Lance's carefully positioned blade.

"Ahhh... That's good." Lance stretches like a cat that's had its fill.

Level 14 blazes over his head. He's surpassed me now.

Lance kneels and offers one of his cleavers to the mayor, ceremoniously sustaining it with his palm under the blade, as if presenting a gift.

"Your Honor... My Lady," he bows his head, "the rebels have been dealt with. My name is Lance and my blade is at your service."

"Interesting..." the mayor gestures with his hand and the guards let him pass.

He approaches Lance closely. Lance is still kneeling, eyes downcast, his whole demeanor showing submission. The mayor extends his hand and places it on Lance's head, as if he's about to bless him.

"You have not spilled the blood of my soldiers." The mayor chuckles in surprise. "But why then did you help the rebels? Why did you barge in here with them?"

Lance replies slowly and deliberately as if he prepared his speech in advance.

"I did indeed come with them, your Highness, because I learned of their conspiracy. But how could I stop them? Tie them all up as they slept and bring them to you?" Lance smirks crookedly. "There were three of them and only one of me. I could only have killed them, but not restrained them."

"And what stopped you from killing them earlier?" the mayor asks with interest.

"The law!" Lance lifts his eyes. "The law did not declare them outlaws, even as they killed your men. Only when they attacked a player, did I realize that I had to stop them."

"Lies!" I burst out. "Complete lies! He led them here himself, and when he realized he was losing, he killed them to worm his way out of his predicament! He's their leader!"

The mayor turns around and his gaze glitters like steel.

"Do you dare interrupt, TargetAi, as I am conducting an investigation?"

-1 REPUTATION WITH THE MAYOR.

CURRENT REPUTATION: 1/10 (PASSING INTEREST).

Wow! And there goes my reputation! What a touchy NPC! We gave him a holy relic, laid the foundation for the first temple, and only got a +2 to Reputation. And now, over a mere word, a -1. And after all, reputation with this guy matters. All the interesting stuff happens here, in his residence. And that's where Yumina is too... whoever she is now. So, I bite my tongue and watch this circus.

"You made one mistake," the mayor tells Lance. "Lady Yumina is not an immortal. She's one of us."

I see Lance's face slump. I'm shocked myself.

What does "not an immortal" mean? Is she a digital clone? Or is the damn AI now turning human players into NPCs, stripping them of their memory... their will...? How does that even work? Clearly, I'm not allowed to talk to Yumina, so maybe I could send Sibyl to ask her? After all, she's a "doctor" to these clowns.

"I knew her formerly as an immortal," Lance insists stubbornly.

No wonder! His whole rotten plan was built on this. I think I'm starting to understand his scheme for getting into the top ranks: level up using his own people while gaining reputation with the mayor. I bet if the system had sounded the alarm earlier, he would have taken them out at the gates. "Canned goods," that's what it's called, I think. A fellow traveler who becomes fodder.

"I don't remember him," Yumina says with surprise. "I don't remember any of them." She turns to the mayor. "How do they all seem to know me?!"

"They're mistaking you for someone else, Lady Yumina. That's all!" Sibi interjects.

To my surprise, they listen to her. The mayor nods in agreement, and Yumina smiles.

"Lady Sibyl," the mayor smiles at her fondly, "would you like to examine the criminals? You are a doctor, after all."

In my opinion, they don't need a doctor, but a gravedigger. It's strange that these bodies haven't disappeared yet. But maybe there's a reason for that. Maybe they plan on beheading them posthumously and then displaying them in the square as a warning to others. Medieval, barbaric customs. The bodies of players killed by the spiders didn't disappear right away either. They were turned into cocoons and dragged into spider nests. So, I'm not seeing anything surprising here, I guess.

Sibi nods and walks over while the guards start dragging the bodies to one spot. They lay the three bodies side by side. Shugga's head has to be held up; it's dangling precariously as if it's about to fall off. Sibyl bends over him, holding her hand a few inches above the thief's body, slowly moving it from head to feet. Then back again. Her eyes are closed, her face tense. Although her movements are smooth, it's clear they're difficult for her.

The space between the body and her palm seems distorted, straight lines bend and spiral as if the air itself has grown dense and viscous.

The body twitches, then moves. Shugga sits up, looks around in amazement, blinking as if he's just woken up. There's not a trace of wounds on him, not even scars. Of course, dammit, we're in a game! An incredibly realistic game, but still a game. How could there be scars? The player has just been resurrected from the dead.

Good thing Sibi isn't a necromancer, a ridiculous thought crosses my mind, eliciting an inappropriate chuckle. Otherwise, she'd be raising zombies right now — and that's the last thing this place needs.

Shugga tries to stand up, but a guard points

a pike at his face and the thief freezes. Sibyl doesn't pay him any attention; she repeats the procedure on T-Rex and then on Xavier. Only after ensuring that all three are alive does the healer shake her hands tiredly, like a surgeon after an operation.

"I'm tired," she informs me as she returns to my side. "Doing this drains a lot of energy. My stamina is down to zero."

"Why the heck did you do that?!" I flare up again. "Do you realize what's going to happen to them now?!"

"Shhh..." she presses her finger to my lips. "Do you want to get us thrown out? We'll talk later."

I know these "laters." Later is when everything has already blown over and discussing it makes no sense. But I see the mayor watching us, so I clam up again.

"Take them away," the mayor orders, and the guards pick up Lance's fighters under their arms and begin dragging them away. "Lady Sibyl, we are once again in your debt," he turns to us. "How can I repay you for your... ahem... invaluable services?"

"Your Highness, my companion and I..." Sibyl bows her head and nudges me to do the same, "are happy to serve you for the city's benefit. May we be of further use in some way?"

A quest, of course. We really need a quest to boost our reputation. This damned NPC is gaining more power. We have to befriend him if we want to stay on top. And then there's Yumi... or Yumina. The new name suits her. How do we get closer to her? How do we find out if she remembers anything from her previous life? Is her new personality like the old one, or is it just the shell that's been copied? And once again, all roads lead to the mayor. And also to my mysterious companion, who's all too well-known around here.

The NPC scans the room and his gaze alights on Lance.

"What am I going to do with you?" the mayor muses. "You took part in the rebellion and deserve punishment. At the same time, you protected Lady Yumina and punished the rebels, which are undoubtedly actions worthy of reward. I am wise and fair," he declares humbly, "so I will neither reward you nor punish you. Your life is your reward. You are free to go!"

Damn it! He levels up at the expense of his own men and gets off scot-free. I can feel the rage building inside me. But Lance doesn't seem to be leaving; instead, he kneels again, again offering his sword.

"Your Highness, I am not a mere warrior, but a leader too. This attack demonstrated that your ranks lack leadership. We..." he stumbles and corrects himself, "...the rebels made it through without facing significant resistance. Allow me to lead the guard, and your residence will become a fortress, while your city will be completely safe."

"Hmm... That's a bold statement, *Captain* Lance," the mayor ponders. "It is however worth discussing further. Lady Yumina, you too are a warrior. Surely, you have something to say."

I'm waiting for an invitation too. After all, I'm *also* a warrior. And I have something to say about this freak's proposal. He wants into the guard...

But the mayor turns to us with a joyful smile.

"I have a task for you! Tomorrow, my palace will host a ball. The first in the city's history, isn't that lovely? A feast in honor of the new gods. I ask you to meet with each of the high priests and personally deliver my invitations!"

DELIVER INVITATIONS TO THE MAYOR'S BALL TO THE HIGH PRIESTS OF ALL THE DEITIES.

REWARD: +3 REPUTATION WITH THE MAYOR AND +10,000 XP.

PENALTY FOR FAILURE: -3 REPUTATION WITH THE MAYOR.

INVITATIONS DELIVERED: 0/5.

"What, am I your errand boy or something?" I snap.

"Quiet," Sibyl hisses in my ear. "Do you want to ruin everything?"

"You refuse my quest?" The mayor arches an eyebrow.

"No," I grit my teeth, "but meeting with unknown cult leaders could be dangerous. Who knows what crazed ideas could occur to those religious fanatics? And if they do attack me, how will I be able to defend myself? Or am I supposed to take solace in them being declared outlaws once they've already killed me? Should I just stand there and hope someone avenges me?"

"You are executing my will!" the mayor declares. "Anyone who attacks you puts themselves outside the law and is subject to retaliation. But remember, your blow must always fall second."

"Thank you, Your Highness!" Sibyl grabs me by the arm and pulls me towards the exit. "We must make haste!"

So, there are five gods total? Besides our Anima, there are four more cults? It's an interesting quest and the reward is substantial indeed: 10,000 XP is an entire level for me at the moment. Plus, I'll get the chance to meet all the gods at once. I would have been thrilled with such a quest not long ago. Yet why do I feel like I've just been sent on a fool's errand?

* * *

"Don't you get it?!" Sibyl is practically skipping with joy. "He just gave you a license to kill! You're practically James Bond!"

As soon as we step out of the mayor's house, all her societal polish fades, and she's back to being her direct, girlish self.

"I can only use it in self-defense though," I object.

But it does sound cool, I guess. Especially since I could easily exercise my new powers. There aren't many warriors in the city who could stand up to me, basically only Anna, and that jerk Lance.

Not only did he surpass me in levels, but he also wormed his way into a position of trust somehow. It's uncertain what that will mean for the future, but he definitely won't leave a rival like me alone. By the way...

"Why didn't you tell me you could revive players?" I ask Sibyl.

"You never asked," she replies with a silly, childish excuse.

"When did you pick up that skill? Haven't we been together all this time?"

"I took it right away," she answers, looking me in the eye honestly. "I got my class at Level 2 and I chose *Heal* and *Revive* as my skills. I just couldn't use *Revive* earlier because I didn't have enough stamina. Now I can."

"Do you even realize that you've basically handed those players over to these NPCs?!" I practically yelled at her. "Death was a mercy for them, and you've sent them to prison. And who knows what will happen next. Did you see Yumina?!"

"She's something else, huh?" There wasn't a hint of remorse on Sibi's expression, only curiosity. "I didn't know her before... Tell me, is she very different now?"

"I don't know," I replied, frustrated. "We didn't really get a chance to talk. Anyway, don't change the subject, why the heck did you revive them?!"

Sibyl looked around worriedly, as if someone might be eavesdropping on us.

"I told you that I'll tell you later!"

"When is later?"

"In real life." She sighed as if making a difficult decision. "Let's meet up in real life and talk. Right after this round ends."

"Fine," I didn't get an answer, but the prospect of finally seeing her in real life was more intriguing. "It's a date."

"Let's not get sidetracked," Sibi seemed eager to drop the topic. "We have an hour and a half left, and five invitations to deliver."

The map flashed with five quest markers, two of which were outside the city. One was Simba and AngelCake. I decided to leave them for last. In the worst case, they could come to us if we ran out of time. Another waypoint was glowing somewhere on the city's outskirts, near the training camp. And the location of the third, I knew all too well — it was right next to the spider nest.

We chose to go there first and set off right away. Sibyl deftly hooked her arm with mine, acting as if we taking a stroll. As we walked, she craned her head left and right, commenting to me about everything she saw.

"Wow, look at that chunky fella! His chain mail looks like it's about to burst..."

"Oh, what a tunic, I wonder where she got it? Miss... where did you buy that piece of cloth?.. How rude... I didn't really want it anyway..."

"Look! Are they planning to open a store?! There's nothing in the city but a single shop..."

Indeed, two NPCs were busy hanging up a sign on one of the buildings. Potions... Crucibles...

some kind of distillation nonsense. It looked like an alchemist's lab. Is the AI introducing crafting? Or maybe the NPCs will start selling potions themselves? I began to pay closer attention to the ever-evolving world around us.

There were more NPCs now and they seemed more confident. They went about their business busily, paying little attention to the players. Carts passed by. A patrol of four guards marched somewhere purposefully. Here and there, hammers banged and saws whined, but I knew these were just decorative effects. This place was growing by itself. Two-story buildings now stood where ramshackle huts had once been. Moreover, their first floors were often designed to be workshops or stores, not mere living spaces.

The area in front of the spider nest was relatively calm. And I do mean "relatively." The low-level spiderlings continued to attack the guards' fortifications in waves, and there were some newbie players here fending them off, grinding their way up. The game was leisurely leveling up its new warriors.

The houses to the right and left of the spider nest remained empty, but there weren't any mobs nearby. It seems that we had stopped the spiders' expansion by killing their queens and now they were probably regrouping, regenerating their broods. The quest location glowed in one of these abandoned places. What idiot would place their temple or altar, or whatever else they have, in such a sorry spot?

I boldly pulled open the door to the gothic mansion I knew all too well. This was where we had our epic battle with the spider queen and hid Yumi from the guards. The hall on the first floor was empty now. No furniture, no debris — nothing. The walls were cleared of webs and painted with strange symbols — mostly resembling childish drawings of spiders crawling and digging...

"Watch out! TargetAi!" Sibi suddenly cried. "Something's not right here!"

Smoke. A barely noticeable greenish smoke. It was streaming in thin wisps from the cellar. I rushed to the exit, but my legs went weak midstride, I stumbled, fell, and lost consciousness.

* * *

It's cold. Not freezing, but there's a chill that creeps along your skin, seeping into places it shouldn't reach. I'm completely naked, my arms and legs bound so tightly with ropes that I can't even wiggle. Turning my head, I see Sibyl next to me, naked. She looks pretty good without clothes. We're lying on the floor, tied to some hooks hammered into the boards. A stone ceiling is overhead. This looks like the mansion's cellar, although I can't be sure because I didn't get such a good look last time, and the view isn't great now either. My inventory's disabled and so is the party chat. The whole interface is covered in a pale-green haze. When I try to open something, a UI notification pops up:

INTOXICATION.

YOU HAVE BEEN DRUGGED WITH AN UNKNOWN SUBSTANCE.

DURATION OF DEBUFF: 27:33... 27:32...

A dark figure looms over me. A girl. Skinny with dirty black hair hanging like icicles. Completely naked, her body painted with black patterns and symbols. A huge spider is painted on her chest, its abdomen pressing against her neck, and its head resting between her small, perky breasts.

"Your life was empty and worthless," she chants, "but now you will become a sacrifice to our Goddess! Come unto us now oh children of Lolf, come and claim your feast!"

I hear the screeching of a hatch being moved aside somewhere near me. Then, a quiet, insidious rustling fills my ears. I know this sound all too well. It's the sound of spiders. Lots of spiders.

Chapter 23

I DIDN'T TAKE OUR PREDICAMENT very seriously at first. Mostly I just lay there staring at Sibyl's boobs, waiting for this farce to end. The debuff wasn't part of my plans, sure, but there was still plenty of time left until the round ended. And afterwards, I planned on giving this skinny, tattooed witch a piece of my mind for every wasted minute.

The rustling of spider legs, however, made me go alert. These maniacs were about to feed us to the mobs and they wouldn't even be punished for it. It sounded like they thought they were back in the Forgotten Realms, roleplaying drow. Like the spiders here give a damn about their prayers! Pray all you want, the mobs wouldn't be any less dangerous, especially when you're tied up and naked as the day you were born.

"Lolf... Mother with many limbs... accept our

sacrifice..." the witch chanted. "Embrace these insignificant humans... bestow upon them your love... feed your children with our offering..."

"High Priestess," another squeaky, ingratiating voice chimed in, "I thought we only offer men as sacrifices. Maybe we should make this other one our sister?"

"Fool," another invisible voice spoke up, "what the hell do we need this chick for? So our warriors and servants drool over her? Let the spiders eat her. Uh, I mean, let the glorious children of the great mother feast on her flesh."

"Hey, spider nuns!" I called out. "I'm actually here on a quest from the mayor."

"He's awake... Look, he's awake..." the voices whispered. "He's so strong... Maybe we should make him a temple servant? Let him serve our many-limbed mother and us, her priestesses..."

The last sentence was uttered with a dreamy sigh. I guess, the priestesses were short on servants.

"Are you ready to swear loyalty to Lolf and serve the council of priestesses?" asked the skinny witch, leaning over me.

This time I got a better look at her. I'd think she was cute if it weren't for all the spiders and cobwebs scrawled all over her body. She was slim with a narrow waist and firm breasts. Probably on a diet, that's why she's so cranky. The evident glint of crazy in her eyes, however, negated all her outward attractiveness.

"What's in it for me?" I inquired.

"Look... Look... He's agreeing..." whispered the invisible voices. "High Priestess Theophilia can persuade anyone!"

In reality, swearing loyalty to some Theophilia was the last thing on my mind. Even as a tactical move. The AI could take such an oath literally, and I'd end up running errands for a bunch of maniacs. I was just buying time, waiting for Sibyl to wake up and figure out how to deal with our debuff.

I wasn't totally sure she could pull it off, but I didn't see any other way out. Unless the spiders suddenly developed some sense of brotherly love for me and decided to gnaw through my ropes. At least Sibyl had said something nice about them, something about liking their furry backs...

By the way, the sound of spider legs wasn't getting any louder. Seems like some kind of grate was separating us from their lair. I guess, the priestesses had merely wanted to scare me to make me more talkative. And, well, it worked.

"It's not your place to make demands, you nobody," Theophilia declared. "But I can give you a glimpse of your future. You'll have the honor of becoming our servant, to protect us and fulfill our whims. And you might even pleasure the priestesses, when we feel like it."

"I got dibs..." whispered one of the voices.

"As if! Theophilia's going to take him all for herself again..."

"No way... He's Level 13."

"Ladies, there's enough of him to go around."

Finally, I noticed Sibyl coming to. The party chat didn't work, but she figured out what had to be done. However, after a bit of struggle and straining, the healer frowned and shook her head in disappointment. Her healing wasn't working.

How do we get out? The debuff wasn't a long one, but its timer kept resetting. So, whatever gas was intoxicating us was still being released. Why doesn't it affect these ladies then? If it's divine influence, I know only one way to get it.

"Why you'll fuck me to death!" I smirked boldly. "I'd rather die right away!"

"Your choice," the priestess replied with a hint of regret. "Receive the blessing of our many-limbed mother before you die. It'll make your sacrifice easier for you."

I don't know about easier, but hey, you get a bonus for every believer. It works the same with all gods, shouldn't be different here.

"Let's do it," I agreed.

"Embrace the Spider Mother within your heart!" The high priestess leaned over and kissed me on the lips.

Sweet ritual. After that, she did the same with Sibyl. I felt several curious female hands exploring my body. Part of the ritual, or just freelancing, but it was oddly arousing, which was totally inappropriate given my situation.

THE GODDESS LOLF FAVORS YOU! (+10 TO ALL STATS.)

DEBUFF REMOVED: "LOLF'S DREAMS"

The inventory. First thing is to the inventory,

ya bitches! I must have twitched with impatience because Theophilia burst out laughing.

"Stupid men! How I love watching this! Ready to kiss feet and beg for mercy, but as soon as the divine fog lifts, they all reach for their gadgets. Tough luck! Our Bella is a thief. While you were drooling and sprawled out, she cleaned out your inventory! You're a MURDERER!" She dramatically raised her hands. "You killed the Spider Mother's younger sister! We saw her remains in your inventory. A sacrifice like you is especially pleasing to our goddess!"

Cleaned out? As if! Some items can't be stolen. My daishō — the twin swords I got from the mayor's treasury for killing Lolf's kid sister — were right where I left them. Coincidence or fate? With one move, I cut the ropes and sprung free. Naked and very, very angry.

"Eeeeek!!!" the priestesses shrieked in unison.

The only dude among them, a big boy decked out in tight leather shorts, charged at me with his axe. Level 5. Laughable. With one strike, I drove a short sword into his chest, enough to turn him into a pile of dust. The axe clattered to the ground. It was so quiet in the cellar, the sound reverberated in my ears.

The priestesses seemed to have forgotten how to breathe. There were eight of them. All completely naked. Their bodies smeared with either ash or dust, making their skin look gray. Just like the drow, damn it. And over this layer of grime, their bodies were covered in all kinds of scribbles: lines, symbols, and spiders. Lots of spiders... big... small... crawling or weaving webs. On their thighs... bellies... breasts. Three of them, including the high priestess, were actually pretty hot. But the scribbled spiders totally killed the vibe. With every movement, it seemed like the spiders were moving their legs, shifting from one place to another on their bodies... Yuck....

The high priestess turned out to be the smartest of the bunch. Seeing the blade's tip pointed at her nose, she dropped to her knees — and the others quickly followed her lead.

"I can't stand spiders," I explained. "I've hated creepy crawlies since I was a toddler. I really, really, *hate* them!"

The ladies flinched as if I'd slapped them. I leaned closer to Theophilia, pressing my katana's edge pointedly against her neck. I had just killed a player in her presence, and no thunder or lightning had struck me down. So, she figured if I killed once, I could kill again, and she trembled with fear. Sure, death here is temporary. But if she gets booted from the beta, there will be a scramble for her spot as the high priestess.

"Give me one good reason why I shouldn't end your totalitarian cult right now?!"

"You've proven your strength, hero!" Theophilia coyly licked her lips. "Each of us is ready to share her bed with you... We'd all be delighted to lie with you..."

"Only if you wash up first," I cut her off. "Not

good enough. What else?"

If I had more time, maybe I'd entertain Theophilia and a couple of her friends. Who knows what perks you might get from sleeping with a priestess. And the decor here is... exotic. You definitely won't find anything like it in reality. But I don't have time to explore my kinks at the moment.

"We have some belongings of other players... those who... um..." The chubby brunette next to Theophilia got flustered and trailed off.

As if looting temples was on my to-do list. Even nasty ones like this. I'm sure I'd end up catching some curse and then have to do extra chores to get rid of it.

"I want one of whatever that is." I pointed at one of the half-spherical bowls which was billowing with pale green smoke.

"A capsule of Lolf's Dreams?" the priestess guessed. "If we give it to you, oh hero, will you spare us?"

"Live and let live." I waved her off. "Just don't forget to free my friend."

After all, it would be pretty silly if none of the Lolf's priests showed up to the mayor's ball because I'd wiped them all out. That could make things awkward with the mayor.

The priestesses jumped up happily and began untying Sibyl. Next to their gray bodies, she looked especially alluring, which my body instantly reacted to, so I started dressing quickly.

Theophilia handed me several yellow

capsules, each the size of a chicken egg.

"Once crushed, they will release their gas for about half an hour," she explained.

"Where did you get these?" I was curious.

"The Spawn of Lolf leave them for us when they take our sacrifices. Right here." Theophilia gestured to the floor between some stakes that had been driven into it. "Mock us all you like, but the Spider Mother really does hear me. She gives us special gifts, and I feel she's pleased with us. Her children don't bother us." The priestess casually stroked my chest. "Stay with us a while, hero! Why do you need that pale weakling? You can have as many women as you want, even all of us at once! And with Lolf's magic, you'll be invincible!"

"Who are you calling a weakling?!" Sibyl stood up across from Theophilia, proudly thrusting out her chest. "Look at yourself, flatty!"

"Both of you, be quiet!" I had to shout at them, "Sibi, if you keep interrupting, I'll leave you here. For reeducation."

"Leave her, leave her!" Theophilia seemed pleased at the idea. "We'll bring her back to you wrapped in silk."

Sibyl pouted but stayed silent, just standing there glaring with outrage.

"I'm here on business," I remembered. "I hereby officially invite you, Theophilia, high priestess of the goddess Lolf, to a reception at the mayor's residence..." I glanced at the priestess and added, "I recommend appearing in clothes, as there's sure to be a dress code for admission."

"Wow," said the high priestess. "I almost sacrificed the messenger."

"Yeah, be more careful from now on," I agreed.

"We shall always happy to see you... Come back any time, oh hero... The spiders here are so cute... You'll get along..." The pack of priestesses escorted me to their cellar's stairs. "We'll decorate the upstairs too eventually. It'll be beautiful, just you wait!"

"Tell me, why do you call her Lolf and not Lolth?" I asked one last question. "Isn't that what her name's supposed to be?"

"We tried that at first, but our prayers wouldn't go through," the high priestess shrugged. "We kept getting a copyright infringement error from the AI, so we chose a different name."

* * *

"Were you really going to leave me there?" As soon as we emerged from the temple of Lolf, Sibyl started to pester me.

She did it gently, almost jokingly, but she was watching my reaction closely. Ever since I saw the resurrection of T-Rex, Shugga, and Xavier, my opinion of Sibyl had changed significantly.

I got the feeling that there was a lot that she wasn't telling me. Whereas formerly I had considered her an indispensable team member, now she seemed more of a ticking time bomb to me. That's why I tried not to part ways with her.

Keep your friends close and your enemies closer. And I mean, Sibyl wasn't an enemy, but she was definitely playing a game of her own.

Still, I enjoyed her company. She was even amusing when she got mad. In general, it was a weird situation. My brain was screaming about danger, while my heart was desperately trying to convince me everything was okay.

Here she was, buzzing around me, blaming me for all sorts of transgressions, and I just wanted to scoop her up, throw her over my shoulder, and carry her off to the nearest secluded spot.

"Would it have been better for me to stay? I wouldn't mind," I said, slowing down.

"Those spider women would have loved you to death!" Sibyl declared.

"So you were worried about me?"

"I was worried about them!"

We delved deeper into the maze of city streets. Occasionally, gloomy figures in hooded cloaks popped up and shadowed us — then vanished, deciding that we were out of their league. Eventually, the map waypoint led us to a dubious-looking garbage dump.

There were plenty of the shadowy figures here. They scurried about their business, all the while closing in on Sibyl and me. Circling like sharks, tightening the noose.

Sibyl even took my arm and pressed herself to me. The hoods scrutinized her with ill intent.

"Got a smoke?" One of the cloaked figures

approached me tentatively.

"Beat it," I replied curtly.

"Why so rude?!" the hooded figure protested. "Are you real tough or what?"

"I'll cut you up," I warned tersely.

The hooded figure turned away, as if bumping into us was a complete accident.

The quest location was in the very center of a square cluttered with junk. Four men were sitting on crates, playing a card game with homemade cards. One of them was obese. His tiny piggy eyes darted everywhere, noting everything. He was the first to spot us.

"Shush, guys. We've got guests." The fat man quickly gathered the cards and hid them in his pocket, signaling our arrival.

"I've got business with you," I said, figuring he was the one in charge around here.

This quest was testing my patience. First spiders (the mere thought of which makes my skin crawl) and now these shady goons who remind me of that Sullen jerk back in meatspace. I burned with the urge to clean up this dump.

"I don't do business with the law," the fat man declared.

"What makes you think I'm the law?"

"I can smell you a mile away..." he boasted to his buddies, taking a loud sniff. "The Whisperer tells me you're not our kind."

"Not your kind at the moment," I said with a shrug, "but give me your god's blessing and I'll be your kind just fine."

"Look at that!" The group giggled. "The law wants a freebie! Pay up, copper."

"How much?" I asked, unfazed.

Most of my capital was with Simba, but maybe I could offer them something from my inventory.

"Shiloh, check out the chick with him," one of the hoods said blatantly. "She'll do for us."

"Hand over the girl," Shiloh said matter-of-factly. "Then I'll bless you."

"The girl?!" I asked in surprise. "Are you losers that desperate? Don't you have girls of your own?!"

"Don't talk to us like that," Shiloh sounded offended. "We get plenty of women. Just that they're busy, taking care of our homes while we hustle out here, solving problems. We're opening a monastery. So they can serve our god, the Whisperer. Don't be stingy now. It's for a holy cause."

CHAPTER 24

"THEN SEND YOUR OWN WOMEN to the monastery," I reply.

The hoods casually circle us from the sides, surrounding us. Acting just like goons do. Let them try something — I'll take them all down. The strongest among them is Level 8.

"What did you say?!" One of the hoods tries to get tough. "You talking shit about our women?!"

"You could go serve your Whisperer yourself," I shoot back. "With that ass, you could pass for a woman."

I'm deliberately provoking them to throw the first punch. You can't just let this kind of behavior slide, or they'll walk all over you.

"Chill, Shnur... Don't start nothing..." Shiloh restrains his man. "Let's play a game with our guests. If you win, I'll bless you."

"And if we lose?" Sibyl asks.

She's looking around curiously, clearly amused by the situation.

"You can go on your way," Shiloh smirks. "Come on, Shnur, count us in."

Shnur steps forward, raising a hand with a shiny gold ring on his finger. Typical instance of flash over cash.

WHAT'S THAT RUSTLING AT THE WINDOW...

THE WHISPERER'S FOOTSTEPS ON THE PROWL...

THE WHISPERING GOD WILL COME FOR YOU...

ANYTHING HE FINDS, HE'LL TAKE...

The ring sparkles in his hand, drawing all eyes as Shnur counts around the circle, moving his hand faster and faster.

MONEY, CLOTHES, AND YOUR WIFE...

YOU'VE LOST THEM ALL TO THE WHISPERER...

Gotta keep an eye on the hand... it's important. Don't know why, but can't take my eyes off the shimmer... the shimmer...

GOODBYE, PUNK...

YOU'VE BEEN CLEANED OUT!

His hand stops moving, and it's like I'm shaking off a bad spell. I squint to dull the blinding gleam, and when I open my eyes — the square around me is empty. Shiloh's gone, Sibyl's gone. It's just me and Shnur, and Shnur winks at me and vanishes into stealth.

THE WHISPERING GOD THINKS YOU'RE A

PUNK AND REFUSES TO WHISPER TO YOU.

QUEST FAILED: "DELIVER THE INVITATIONS FOR THE MAYOR'S BALL."

REPORT YOUR FAILURE TO THE MAYOR.

* * *

Damn! They played me like a... punk! I whip out my katana. Its blade whistles through thin air. In response, all I hear is quiet laughter. Looking for the invisible thief in this square is like looking for the wind in a field.

I force myself to calm down. This bastard's still here. Maybe he wants to rob me or just mock me. How can I catch him? None of my skills will help me here. I need to level up my detection ASAP. If these jerks gain power in the city, I'll have to watch my pockets. Hindsight is always 20/20. But what now?!

Why bother trying to look for him though? I should just throw some attacks and see if I hit him. I perform a *Whirlwind*, exploding with strikes in all directions — and get another giggle for my trouble. It sounds like this creep's having a blast.

Shame there's no explosives here. Or magic grenades or something. Although, there is one thing...

I pull out a capsule of Lolf's Dreams and toss it at my feet. It pops with a soft *pffft* and a barely visible greenish cloud spreads across the square.

Thump! The sleeping thief materializes from nowhere, hitting the pavement headfirst. Poor guy's been knocked out. First thing I do is take the gold ring off his finger. Just as I thought, fake. A trinket. I'll give it to Sibyl later, as compensation for emotional distress.

Then I try to message her.

SUBSCRIBER TEMPORARILY UNAVAILABLE.

The notification pops up at every attempt to send a chat message. What's worse is that all the quest markers that displayed the high priests' locations have disappeared from my map.

The only silver lining is that I have here someone who knows where to find Sibyl and Shiloh. But how do I get this guy to talk? Asking is useless. Death threats won't scare him. And if I try to torture him, the AI will register it as an attack and I'll become an outlaw. Then again... What if it's not me that does the torturing?

I hoist the unconscious thief over my shoulder. In real life, he would be heavy, but here, my Strength and Constitution make it possible to run with such a load. A few minutes later, I'm knocking on the door of the familiar gothic mansion.

Silence comes from the other side. They're all lying in wait for the unwary fly to enter their web.

"Come out, Theophilia!"

"Who's there?" asks a cautious voice from behind the door.

"It's me. I've brought you a fresh sacrifice... for your eight-legged spider mommy."

A plump, pretty priestess peeks out from

behind the door and then disappears.

"Come in!"

A welcoming committee waits for me in the entryway. Theophilia is holding her gas grenades just in case. Seeing me, she gasps in surprise.

"Who's this?"

"Name's Shnur," I reply, dumping the body on the floor. "He's eager to offer himself up to Lolf. The moment he heard my tale of the great goddess, he fainted from sheer ecstasy."

The priestess shakes her head, clearly doubting my story.

"And what do you want in return?" she asks.

"Just to chat with him before... before the spawn of Lolf start snacking on him."

The priestesses whisper excitedly among themselves. Then they deftly drag the thief down to their cellar. Seems like this is more than just entertainment for them. A new deity dishes out perks to its followers for each sacrifice. I need to adapt to this new world order. At least I'm now in good standing with the servants of two gods. Time to start making connections with a third. But first, I need to find him.

By the time I get downstairs, Shnur is stripped and neatly packaged. The priestesses examine him, whispering and giggling. They look pretty scary in their war paint.

Theophilia waves her hand in front of Shnur's face. He comes to, looking around, turning his head. When he catches sight of the priestess's breasts, a dopey smile spreads across his face.

I shove her aside with my shoulder and lean over the captive.

"Good morning, kiddo," I tell him. "Let's sort this out quickly, we don't have much time. Where's Shiloh?"

"What, you brought more chicks, loser?" Shnur sneers through his teeth. "That's awesome. We could always use more chicks..."

"Release your little friends," I tell Theophilia.

She nods. Two priestesses slide a panel aside, revealing a semi-circular arched tunnel. Probably leads to the neighboring house, the last spider nest. A drain pipe or sewer, maybe. Or perhaps the priestesses imagined it, and the AI answered their prayers.

A grate blocks it at the moment. There's darkness beyond.

"Come, children of the Spider Mother!" Theophilia chants. "Come and accept our offering."

"Hey, are you nuts?!" Shnur begins to squirm anxiously. "What the... I was just kidding... I didn't mean..."

Rustling echoes through the tunnel. I see faint silhouettes in the dark. Small green eyes glinting. Unblinking. Stiff black legs reach through the grate.

"They do listen to you..." I say, genuinely amazed.

Theophilia shrugs. "I call them and they come."

"Talk, you bastard," I whisper into Shnur's ear, "or you'll be eaten alive, you fucker. You stole my girl. Do you think I'll feel sorry for you?!"

"Are you serious?!" The thief struggles, but the ropes hold him tight. "My bros will tear you apart! You trying to scare me with this weak-ass bluff, ya bitches?!"

One of the priestesses begins to slide the grate open. I back up to the wall and draw my katana. Spiders are no friends of mine.

"Hold on." The priestess turns to me, takes a jar of black paint, and traces something on my cheek with her finger.

Feels like a spider.

The grate slides open and the guests arrive. The spiders crawl in leisurely, hesitating as if sniffing around. One approaches my feet, nuzzling my boots like a stray dog.

Overcoming my instinctive fear, I reach out and stroke its back. The green fur is plushy and soft to the touch. The satisfied spider turns and begins "sniffing" Shnur's legs.

"You coven of whores!" Shnur's voice breaks into a howl. The spiders tickle him, scratch him with their claw-tipped legs. One, apparently satisfied with its inspection, sinks its fangs into Shnur's thigh. "Gaaaarrrhhh!!!" he shrieks.

I feel Theophilia's hand grab and squeeze mine. She's trembling slightly. I turn to her to sneak a peek. The priestess watches intently, her pupils dilated, lips parted, chest heaving. Damn, she's about to come!

The basement air fills with the scent of terror and lust. It's so thick you could cut with a knife.

The priestesses moan with impatience, shifting from foot to foot. The smell hits my brain like alcohol. I get a wild urge to throw Theophilia down right here on the floor and take her amid the victim's screams. The priestess pulls my hand toward her… places it on her thigh.

"Speak, dumbass!" I release her hand and squat next to Shnur. "This is your last chance."

"Get them off me! I'll tell you…" whines Shnur. "I'll tell you everything!"

"Then talk, and I'll let you go!"

"You'll let me go?!"

"Yeah, sure, you can leave peacefully."

"Turn right from the garbage dump… walk down the the alley… after two houses, turn left… there's a big… three-story house… that's our place… the bros' hangout…"

"Smart guy…" I pat him on the cheek. "Did you have to act all innocent?"

I'm actually happy. After the thief's words, a glowing dot reappears on my map. That's where Shiloh is. Is the AI giving me a chance to save my quest?

"Will you let me go?" Shnur looks at me pleadingly.

"I'm not the one holding you," I say, spreading my hands. "That's for you to negotiate with the girls. Have a good time."

I turn around and head for the stairs.

"Wait!" Theophila catches up to me, and when I stop, she presses her body against me and kisses me deeply.

"Oofff..." she says, releasing my lips. "A new blessing for you. To renew Lolf's buffs."

She winks at me playfully and returns to her sacrifice. Shnur is still screaming, but his voice is quieter. Seems like he's going hoarse.

I'm about 500 meters away from the Temple of Lolf when my chat explodes with messages:

"You're a dead man!"

"A bro for a bro!"

"I'll get you in meatspace!"

"Go ahead and hang yourself now!"

"We've got your IP address, fucker!"

"The bros are on their way!"

And that's how I learned that Shnur's time in the beta had ended, the goddess Lolf had accepted another sacrifice, and her spider spawn had had a nice, succulent meal.

* * *

The Monastery of the Whispering God's adepts is called "Bedtime Story." Two hooded goons, balancing on a tall, rickety ladder, are nailing a sign that says so above the entrance just as I arrive. As I walk by, I casually kick the base of the ladder and both goons come crashing down, breaking the rungs as they tumble.

"What the hell, shitbird!? I'mma make you pay for that!" They both start cursing after landing hard, but then seeing my level, they decide it's better to run away.

The building itself is notable in that it's a full

three stories tall and in a state of dreadful disrepair. The windows are so dirty that no light gets through, the facade is grimy from time and neglect, and the door hangs on one hinge.

I enter the temple with a kick. The door flies open, taking down whoever was on lookout. They weren't expecting me. Shiloh, along with his cronies, lieutenants, and hangers-on, turn around and freeze in surprise.

The interior is the epitome of "shabby chic." All kinds of junk found in the garbage dump has been carefully brought here. Worn-out couches, scratched tables, a bar counter with a big hole.

Shiloh and his closest associates are sitting nearby, while the rest of the rabble respectfully keep their distance. In the corner on a semi-circular couch, I notice several girls, including Sibyl, her hands bound with a rope.

My body automatically reacts to a hit I don't even see coming. *Alert* is a useful passive skill I noticed in Anna's build and picked up the last time I was at the training camp. It lets me automatically respond to any sudden attack, whether it's an archer's arrow or an assassin's dagger from stealth.

Coolly, without looking, I strike back with my wakizashi, holding it in a reverse grip, and only then do I turn around. One of the sign-hangers decided to come back for revenge after all. Thinking he could get me from stealth, he took advantage of my entrance to come up behind me. I twist the sword in his belly and he turns to ash.

"Do you know what '*casus belli*' means?" I ask the high priest of the thieves' guild. "Of course you don't, you fat fuck. It means 'cause for war.' Your hospitable friend just attacked me. Not only was that a stupid thing to do given that I have six levels on him, but I now have official permission to wipe you all out. You're in one big party together, aren't you, oh my bros?"

I see Shiloh's face go pale. He's not stupid. On my way over to him, I lean down and finish off the "hood" pinned by the door. The game's AI stays silent. I haven't been declared an outlaw for PKing inside inside the city limits. The law's on my side.

"I wonder, what happens to a god if all his servants are wiped out?" I approach the counter where Shiloh is sitting, grab my katana with both hands, and with a long swing, decapitate one of his subordinates. "A crit!" I quip. "What do you think? Can I do you with one swipe from your shoulder to your belly? Will my blade make it?"

THE WHISPERING GOD THINKS YOU'RE A RIGHTEOUS DUDE!

QUEST RESUMED: "DELIVER INVITATIONS TO THE MAYOR'S BALL."

THE QUEST REWARD HAS BEEN UPDATED.

"Oh, but this is a simple misunderstanding, no more!" Shiloh says with a smarmy smile. "It was just a joke... A test of your bravery... Just bro stuff... Nothing happened to your girl... She's been hanging out with us, warm and cozy... Seriously, she was just here, waiting for you..."

"Don't lie," I raise my katana above my head,

readying my next strike. "So, the other girls are just sitting around waiting for someone too? Hey, girls!" I shout towards the back of the room. "Thanks, everyone, you're all free to go!"

"Please, don't!" I'm nearly bowled over, hearing their pleas. The "unfortunate captives" rush towards me and fall to their knees, smearing tears and snot across their faces. "Don't kill our boys... Don't hurt the Whisperer... We're all here willingly... by mutual consent."

"They're role-playing," confirms Sibyl, approaching me. Her legs are free, only her hands are tied, and even the knot looks a bit decorative. "What took you so long?"

"Come on!" I object. "Where's my 'Oh, my hero! Thank you for the daring rescue!' Why do the neckbeards get all the role-playing girls?"

"Oh, my hero," Sibyl corrects herself, kissing me on the cheek, then squints suspiciously at me. "And where has my hero been? Did my hero purposely send me here to get a chance to frolic with the priestesses? How many orgasms do they draw that spider for, one or ten? Did you serve Lolf in all your glory?"

"Are you jealous?" I retort. "I wonder of whom? I saw you making out with Theophila. You're not fantasizing of going back, are you? To serve the spider queen with your body?"

"We can also serve... with our bodies..." Shiloh tries to interject, but meets our annoyed glances and quickly quiets down.

It seems to me that Sibyl is staging a jealous

scene, but there's a sparkle in her eyes, and considering we hadn't even kissed once, this is all definitely a show for our audience. And maybe a little for my ego too. Her faux jealousy will make everyone think that I really did bang the spider priestesses in various positions.

I'm caught off guard by this so much that my anger cools.

* * *

"Give a woman her freedom, and she won't let you live in peace," Shiloh shares his wisdom about the spider priestesses. "And the third goddess you mentioned, who is she?"

Shiloh turns out to be extremely inquisitive. While his henchmen clean up the mess I made, we have a seat on the cleanest, plushest couch in the place and begin discussing the game's new geopolitics.

"The third deity is Anima, the goddess of war," I share willingly. "My buddy is her high priest."

I didn't see any point in withholding this information. Everyone would meet each other tomorrow at the mayor's ball anyway. But Shiloh's reaction was interesting to see. He clearly disapproved of the spider women, but the idea of an alliance with Anima made him pause and think.

"Another woman, eh?" The prophet of the Whispering God shakes his head doubtfully. "Well, at least her servant is a righteous dude."

"Righteous indeed," I confirm. "Sharp and to

the point. And quite abrupt."

"Abrupt is cool too," Shiloh approves. "More abrupt than you?"

"Abrupter," I don't lie, thinking of Simba.

"We'll definitely have to hang out sometime." Shiloh looks over at the monastery's busted front door, through which the sun is now gently shining.

"So... Will you be coming to the mayor's ball?" I steer the conversation towards my quest.

"No choice there," nods Shiloh. "I'll be there."

"And the blessing?"

"Got anything?" Shiloh spreads his hands. "The Whisperer doesn't abide freebies."

"And the fact that I just spared your life? That doesn't count?" I'm astonished at his audacity. "You owe me, big time."

"That's how you do it!" Shiloh even seems pleased.

He scats some words to me and a notification immediately appears in my interface:

THE WHISPERING GOD FAVORS YOU! (+10% TO ALL STATS.)

"Could you untie me while you're at it?" Sibyl holds out her hands. She's been sitting there with the rope around her wrists, acting as if it wasn't bothering her one bit. I was amazed by this ability of hers to become completely inconspicuous at times. That alone is enough to make a fellow fall in love with her.

"You can keep the rope," Shiloh says generously. "It's enchanted by the Whisperer. Only the person who tied it can remove it, and it disables access to the inventory and the chat. Consider it a little souvenir."

* * *

The crowd in the square did not seem to be dispersing. Having visited the servants of the two other cults, I was pleased to note that our Anima was the most popular of all. I expect this will prove beneficial in the future.

Simba rushed over to me as soon as he saw me — however, instead of joy, his face was filled with worry.

"Have you seen Stacy?" he asked, stunning us.

"Isn't she with you?"

"No... She's nowhere to be found!" Simba looked around as if he had just noticed Stacy's disappearance and was still hoping to spot her in the crowd. "People keep coming and coming, I was busy blessing... Then I turned around... And neither Stacy nor the sacred club were nowhere to be seen... You gotta find her... I have to keep blessing here."

Indeed, the place on the statue where Anima's divine weapon should have been was now empty. The statue's hand was clutching at nothing now and looked like it was either making an "okay" sign with her fingers or trying to grab an invisible enemy by the nuts. Menacing but a bit crude.

"Are you coming to the mayor's ball tomorrow?" I quickly tried to get my quest objective out of the way.

However, when Simba said yes, the quest didn't update. Furthermore, the quest marker for Anima, which I assumed marked the location of our goddess's high priest, was not only outside of the city but was now moving further and further away as we spoke.

Sibyl and I took off at a sprint, running out of the square and then the city. We caught up to the quest marker on a country road that led to one of the wyvern's nests. AngelCake was sitting, knees tucked under herself, before a wooden idol in a forest glade — the very one that Sibyl and I had hastily erected to save Simba from his divine madness.

"AngelCake? What are you doing all the way out here?" I called out to her. "You got us worried!"

The girl turned around, but there was something odd about her features. Her posture, gaze, facial expression... Through a multitude of small, barely perceptible signs, I realized that this was no longer our Stacy.

Chapter 25

THE GIRL STOOD UP GRADUALLY and deliberately, as if conscious of and relishing her beauty and strength. The way her ample chest swayed slightly made her seem even more impressive. She looked as if she had grown taller, so proud was her posture and so haughty her demeanor. It wasn't AngelCake, but the goddess Anima herself who approached me.

Behind me, Sibyl gasped quietly and, judging by the sound, fell to her knees.

"We welcome you, Awesome Anima!" she said.

The goddess paid no attention to Sibyl.

"Do you know that this body adores you?" she said to me. "It desires you."

The goddess ran her hand under my chin, a gesture simultaneously tender and haughty.

"Where's Stacy?" I asked, ignoring her divine rizz.

I've had enough soul swaps for today. If AngelCake also gets stuck in the game, I'll reset the whole damn thing right now. The longer I wait, the less chance I have to pull a player out. Yet worrying about this is pointless right now too, since I have no idea how any of this is happening.

"And don't you fancy me in turn, hero?" The goddess let out a soft laugh that sent shivers down my spine. "Don't worry. Your AngelCake will be back soon. I'm not so powerful yet."

"Accept our prayers, Anima," Sibyl brown-nosed behind me.

I looked over at her. The healer was indeed on her knees. Anima thoughtfully twirled a club in her hand, then skillfully, with hardly a movement, smacked Sibyl on the head. The girl collapsed in one fell swoop, passed out cold.

"She was annoying me," Anima casually explained. "Too persistent. Always butting into the conversation, interrupting."

"So, you want to talk?" I asked.

"No respect for the divine," the goddess went on, shaking her head. "Another deity in my place would have incinerated you two by now. But I'm kind. I even tolerate the mark of another god on you." She pointed at my cheek, where the little spider was drawn. "But remember, hero: The gods are a jealous kind."

She brought her face very close to mine, as if she was about to kiss me, and her eyes flared.

"CHOOSE THE RIGHT SIDE, HERO." The goddess's voice reverberated as if carried by some echo. "ONLY ONE WILL REMAIN!"

Then Anima staggered, nearly falling, and I instinctively caught her.

"Andrew?!" Stacy looked at me as if she had just woken up. "Where are we? How did I get here?!"

I sat her down on the ground.

"I think you picked up some debuff." I didn't tell AngelCake the truth.

Not only would it scare her, but I wouldn't even be able to properly explain what happened. Sibyl's joke — creating a deity in the image and likeness of Stacy — had brought about some unforeseen consequences to say the least. And the crowd in the square, seeing a living incarnation, truly *believed* in her.

This is the work of the game's neural network — a world where your dreams come true. If you desire something strongly enough, it will be granted eventually, so be careful what you wish for.

Sibyl also woke up. The first thing she did was glance over at AngelCake to make sure the goddess had left. Unnoticed by Stacy, I put a finger to my lips and Sibyl nodded understandingly.

Together, we escorted AngelCake back to the city and handed her over to Simba. Although her stats were fine, Stacy was still a bit out of it.

"My head is spinning," she complained.

We sat her down at the base of her own statue.

"Look after her," I told Simba.

"Everything's fine," he nodded. "There's less people now. I've already blessed a good four hundred or so. Awesome Anima is the most awesome goddess!"

"Yeah, right," I grimaced. "Listen, can I take the club?"

"No problem!" he waved his hand. "It's only in the way here. Everyone's trying to sneak up to it to get a blessing for free."

I looked at the timer. The day's quest had given me four hours initially and I'd already spent almost three of them. I needed to hurry up.

Traveling to the fourth quest marker took us out of the city. As soon as we left the last street behind, I drew my swords, ready for action. Sibyl tried to frolic and pick flowers on the roadside, but I scolded her and made her walk behind me. Killing me isn't that easy, but at her Level 5, it wouldn't take much for her to get taken out by a well-placed arrow or a sneaky assassin.

She acquiesced to following behind me, but she wouldn't keep quiet.

"What did you talk about with Anima?" she insisted.

"Nothing much."

"That can't be," Sibyl didn't believe me. "She didn't knock me out for no reason."

"She was just jealous," I shrugged it off.

"Don't joke about that," Sibyl frowned. "Gods are jealous, but not like that. They might seem funny to you now, but they're going to become a real force soon. And they won't tolerate a rival. You may be immortal, but you're not divine. There's a difference."

Shoot, had she faked being knocked out? She was saying almost the same thing Anima had.

"Then why do they need me?"

"Don't you get it?" Sibyl even stepped in front of me, barring my way and looking me in the eyes. "You're a hero — an immortal who can do the gods' bidding. You can be their sword of vengeance!" she added dreamily.

I stayed quiet, as if flattered by the prospect. The sun was shining and I felt good. This part of the forest turned out to be particularly beautiful. Colorful flowers dotted the meadow and the air was full of fluttering butterflies and the piercing chirping of crickets. It was a fine summer day.

Somehow, I felt this tranquility wouldn't last long. The AI had had given us a respite, but it was gathering strength no doubt. Soon, the players would be set against each other once again. And the prospect of becoming trapped in here forever would become much scarier than being kicked out of the game.

But no, this chirping around me couldn't be crickets. It was music. It came from somewhere within the treeline: rhythmic, cheerful. Sibyl involuntarily nodded along to it and I couldn't help but smile awkwardly.

The quest marker was very close. We turned onto a path, made our way through a dense growth of trees and emerged in a large, sundrenched clearing.

A large dance party was under way here. Girls in frivolous dresses and guys without a hint of armor, with garlands of flowers on their heads, were dancing to a simple techno beat.

Thump-thump-thump... What I first took for a stump in the middle of the clearing turned out to be like a wireless speaker or something. While I stood there stunned, wondering how such an advanced piece of tech had made it into this medieval setting, two girls ran up to us, placed garlands on our heads and pulled us into the dancing crowd.

The crowd parted before us like the sea before Moses and we ended up at the foot of a large tree, its trunk entwined with vines that bloomed with large white flowers exuding a delicious fragrance.

Under the tree sat a man. He was older, tanned, and exceptionally gaunt. He squinted cunningly, bunching the deep wrinkles that furrowed his face and somehow reminding me of the Master incarnated in the game. However, whereas the Master had almost no hair, this one had enough for two Masters — a great heap of it braided into a myriad of thin braids.

"Hi there, travelers!" said this odd new character. "Come kick it with us!"

"MC Ji-Bo says he's glad to welcome you," one of the girls translated for us, "and invites you to join our ceremony."

There was no ceremony to speak of. The people in the clearing seemed to be enjoying some club beats, no more. They were passing around strange fruits, resembling bottles, and sipping from them.

"I came to deliver an invitation to the mayor's ball..." I started.

"Hit me," said Ji-Bo.

The girl stood up, plucked two fruits from a vine, resembling either pears or gourds. She broke off their stems, pulled them out like corks and handed them to us.

I sniffed the liquid inside and smelled something tropical, delicious, and fresh.

"MC Ji-Bo suggests performing a hospitality ritual first," said the girl. "We can talk business after."

"What's your deity's name?" I asked.

Firstly, I was genuinely curious, and secondly, I wasn't in a hurry to drink some unknown thing with unpredictable side-effects.

"The Eternal Groove!" proclaimed Ji-Bo.

"Mmmmm tasty!" said Sibyl. She had already tasted the fruit and was now cheerfully tapping her foot. "No debuffs, I checked! Cheers! Cheers all around!"

She clinked her bottle-fruit against mine and took another swig. Trusting her words, I also took a sip from my gourd.

THE BLESSING OF LOLF NEGATES THE EFFECTS OF THE "INTOXICATION" DEBUFF.

Ji-Bo instantly felt something. He twitched as if reacting to some foreign magic nearby. However, instead of becoming upset, he actually seemed to get more cheerful.

"Stay sober like a fool if you like," he said to me, laughing.

Sibyl, with a squeal, dived into the crowd and started to groove to the music energetically. *Thump-thump-thump,* echoed above the clearing.

"Are you coming to the mayor's ball?" I asked Ji-Bo.

"I'm down for whatever!" he confirmed lazily.

Somehow, I found myself sitting next to him. In my hand was my second bottle... or third... And on my lap was sitting that same girl who had been translating the party lingo to human for me. Her behind was round and firm. I checked a few times with my hand just to be sure it really was.

"How did you guys find this place?" I asked.

"The Groove brought me here... The rest just showed up..." Ji-Bo gestured around the clearing. "It's summer here... It's sunny... Life's too short to spend it on killing. Killing's a real downer, you know."

"What if someone comes to kill *you*?" I couldn't help but wonder.

"Give it a shot," the high priest replied calmly. "Go ahead."

I jumped up. My sword came out of its sheath and I took a step towards Ji-Bo...

"Alice, groove!" he ordered, seemingly in the direction of the tree stump.

Thump... Thump... — the music changed, its rhythm growing abrupt and aggressive. It resonated with something inside of me. I don't know what, but it reverberated in every cell of my body. *Thump...Thump...* The blood was pounding in my ears, pumping through my arteries to the beat.

Thump... Thump... The sword slips from my hand. The more I resist, the more violent grows the beat. My body jolts... flinches... And I find myself dancing along with everyone else.

"Yeaaaah!" Sibyl shrieks in delight at the sight of me.

She starts to strip, pulling up her tight skirt as it snags...

This rhythm is like an itch, like a crumb under your undershirt, like an annoying mosquito buzzing in your ear at three in the morning. It's impossible to ignore, it's impossible not to submit to it. The groove is in you, and you are the groove. The itch intensifies. I realize that I'll go mad if I don't give in. My legs break move on their own and I dissolve in the crowd of ravers.

"THE ETERNAL GROOOOVE!!!" Ji-Bo hollers.

"WOOOO!!!" the crowd responds in unison as if the DJ just dropped the beat.

The high priest (or maybe shaman or guru) holds up his hand and I instinctively high five him.

THE GOD OF THE ETERNAL GROOVE FAVORS YOU! (+10% TO ALL STATS.)

GROOVE DEBUFF REMOVED.

I'm struggling to catch my breath. Resisting something like this is absolutely impossible. So, the game's alcoholics and escapists might last a while. But I wouldn't bet on them keeping this pace up in the long run.

"Tomorrow," the priest salutes me with his bottle. "We'll be there."

"I wish I had an item like your Alice there," I say enviously.

"Here you go," Ji-Bo unexpectedly pulls another, smaller wooden stump from under the tree's roots.

"Portable," the priest boasts as if he made it himself. "Just keep in mind that Alice runs out of batteries fast. You'll get ten minutes max out of her."

"Thanks," I say, delighted.

"Don't mention it, broham," Ji-Bo waves both hands like windmills. "It's all good!"

It takes a bit of an effort to pull Sibyl out of the dancing crowd. Her dress is all hiked up and she resists and tries to pull away to dive back into the dancing mob.

"Let gooo...," she slurs. "I wanna daaance..."

"Byeee... byeee!" the partiers wave to us. "May the Groove be with you!"

As we walk away, I remove Sibyl's garland from her head and throw it into the bushes. Mine flies after it. The memory of the club pops up before my eyes. Honestly, I felt more at ease even with the spider goddess. At least everything was clear back there. There were priests and there were sacrifices. But here, everyone was nice and all — yet at the same time there was like a whiff of rot about that scene, like something putrid that emanates from overripe fruit.

In the end I had no choice but to sit Sibyl

down on the grass. It took her a whole five minutes to come to her senses. Until then, she kept crying, accusing me of abusing her, and trying to run away.

"Wow," she said at last, once her sanity returned. "What was that?"

She blushed and started to adjust her dress, which was perfectly in order by then.

"Feeling better, you party animal?" Sometimes a sharp word can snap you out of it as well as a slap.

"That groove hit me hard," Sibyl shook her head, still in shock. "I didn't feel the debuff at first. And then it was too late and I couldn't control my body at all — I couldn't even think straight."

"Divine magic," I shrugged. "I imagine we're about to see even more surprising stuff."

"And how did you manage to resist?" the healer asked me skeptically.

"Willpower."

At this point, Sibyl was the last person I was going to share my true thoughts with. If you think about it, all the weird stuff happening lately was somehow connected with Sibyl. The healing and resurrections which hadn't been in this game before, the first idol made from a tree stump, which led to AngelCake becoming a living goddess... Even this very quest I was on now — hadn't it been Sibyl who had wheedled it from the mayor?

So I tried to keep a cool head, despite Sibyl's flirtatious, and sometimes blatantly suggestive glances. At this point, even Theophilia, the high priestess of the spider goddess, seemed less threatening to me. I just couldn't shake the image of T-Rex's, Xavier's and Shugga's bodies rising from the floor like zombies.

Heading to the last quest location, we were forced to venture ever further away from the city. What kind of priest chose such a remote place for their god? Who's even supposed to get their blessing out so far afield? Mobs? There were plenty of those here too, by the way. A few times, I caught sight of curious furry faces peeking out from the grass and low bushes, observing us. The local random encounter mobs looked like lemurs, with slightly elongated noses and huge eyes.

Unfortunately they all seemed to be no stronger than Level 5. Too low for farming, although given enough time, you could conceivably gather a whole bunch into a train and then level up a bit. To Sibyl's credit, she didn't get all mushy and try to pet the cuties. Instead, she walked closer to me, looking around warily. Smart girl.

The country road we were on twisted and turned, sometimes climbing hills, sometimes dipping into shallow valleys, until finally, after yet another climb, I heard a familiar sound: the whistle of blades, the sound of steel hacking flesh and even a death rattle. Either there was a fierce battle happening on the other side of the hill or someone was enjoying a farm fest.

With a gesture, I signaled Sibyl to stay put

while I carefully peeked over the top.

It was none other than Anna and she was having fun. She must have had to run around the area quite a bit to gather such an impressive train of mobs. The big-eyed lemurs surrounded her from all sides. There were about thirty of them, angrily yapping and howling, pushing and climbing over each other, just to get at their assailant and sink their teeth into her coveted bare legs.

But in vain. Each sword strike sent the fuzzballs to their digital heaven. None could get close to Anna. She moved smoothly and precisely, like during a training session, and I couldn't help but admire her flawless technique.

While we were messing around with deities, our main opponent was busy leveling up. Anna was already at Level 22. I checked the map. The waypoint was pointing right at her. Confronting a deadly psychopath outside the city walls wasn't exactly appealing. But I had no choice. The quest needed to be completed. So, I stood up at full height and whistled casually as I descended the hill.

"Hey there, Your Holiness! Bless a lone pilgrim, will ya?"

"Damn it!" Anna turned around, and one of the creatures, leaping, clamped onto her wrist. "Ow! You're nothing but trouble!"

She flung the mob to the ground, vengefully finished it off, and then looked up again.

"Never thought you'd enter the priesthood," I approached, maintaining the pretense of casual conversation. "Doesn't seem like your thing... bowing down and offering prayers."

"What makes you think so?" Anna smirked. "Do I look like a priestess?"

"No, but I definitely know you're one."

"A quest then," Anna nodded understandingly.

"Of course," I didn't argue. "So, which god do you serve?"

"None," said Anna, still approaching and making no move to sheathe her blade. "I am a goddess myself."

"A goddess of what?" This time she managed to catch me off guard.

"Why, Death, of course. I've been running myself ragged around here, collecting these crumbs bit by bit... And then suddenly a juicy Level 13 comes to me all on his own." She even licked her lips in pleasure.

"Well, I've come on official business, to deliver an invitation for you..."

Not letting me finish, Anna struck the first blow.

CHAPTER 26

HOW IS SHE SO UNBELIEVABLY fast? Even with my *Alert* skill triggering, I barely managed to parry her attack. But Anna attacked again and again... She just didn't stop, unleashing a flurry of blows with both swords from multiple angles. It felt like instead of a sword in each hand, she had at least five.

If we were in the Gladiator Games on equal terms, she would still have the upper hand. It's not about talent, though Anna is undoubtedly talented.

Her movements were flawless. You can only refine such technique with hundreds of hours of training. A maniac, a nerd, a killing machine, and now a Goddess of Death to boot.

And yet she has weaknesses. Everyone has them. They may not always be visible... They may not always be critical... And some even consider them their strengths, but that's the only way to beat them. Study them, find these weaknesses and hit them where it hurts.

Anna was vain. A fight between a Level 22 and a Level 13 is like a leopard taking on a house cat. She could have killed me instantly. She could have simply set off her skills and the dps alone would have done it. A true predator thinks not in terms of beauty but in terms of efficiency. Anna, however, wanted more than just to win. She had to prove that she was better. That's why she didn't use her skills now, pressing me with her innate agility, strength and fencing technique.

I went on full defense, dodging or parrying her strikes, but even that wasn't enough. I went to block, but she was faster and her sword sliced my forearm. My health dropped to half and then began to replenish in bursts. Sibyl must be nearby, healing me. I only pray Anna doesn't notice her or it'll be the end for both of us.

As I retreated under Anna's onslaught, she followed me up the slope of the hill with a satisfied smile. I was covered in minor injuries and she was already triumphing, raising her swords to deliver the finishing blow, when…

She froze, dropping her arms. The swords slipped from her hands, fell to the ground and the goddess of war fainted at my feet. Theophilia hadn't exaggerated: Lolf's Dreams worked even on gods. The pale green gas was not as effective as on ordinary players, though — upon closer inspection, Anna wasn't asleep, just stunned.

I had to hold out a couple of minutes to lure Anna where I had crushed the gas capsules beforehand. I had hoped it wouldn't come to a fight, that we'd just step aside to talk, but the psycho struck first, and I had miraculously managed to lead her to the right spot without dying. The whole plan had hung by a thread, but in the end, it all worked out as planned.

Thunk! Anima's sacred club appears in my hand and comes down on Anna's head. She falls unconscious. Our duel is over. Another point for me.

I use the Whispering God's unbreakable rope to bind the Valkyrie's wrists and ankles. The item's divine attributes really do come in handy. In the end, Anna presents a nice little package.

"Hey, you can come out!" I call to Sibyl. "The danger's over!"

Sibyl cautiously peers from behind the hill and gasps at the sight of Anna lying there motionless.

"I think I'll just sit over here."

"Come on, come over. Don't be scared. She's going to be a good girl now, right, Anna?"

Anna has already woken up. Damn, how powerful she is! Sibyl was out for a good two minutes. But Anna's level definitely makes a difference, and she probably has some divine perks too. By the way, the question of how she managed to become a goddess still remains to be answered.

"I'll kill you wherever I find you," she hisses.

"I'll hunt you down and kill you... I'll turn your life into hell..."

"Scary," I shake my head. "You try to kill me every time anyway. How's that working out for you, by the way? How about we skip the threats and move on to more constructive dialogue?"

"I'll kill you, you son of a..."

"Let me introduce you to a friend of mine," I beckon Sibyl to come over. "This is our Goddess of Death, although she's still a bit weak and a bit daft. I can't decide whether to complete the quest or to gank her. Or maybe I should complete the quest and then gank her. Look at the gear on her. Want me to give you her panties as a gift?"

"What a gentleman," Sibyl snorted with laughter. "Trying to woo a girl with used panties."

"Just wash them! They're divine after all! Imagine the hidden perks that a pair of divine panties must have."

Anna fell silent as if listening, then started struggling against the Whisperer's rope, trying to get a glimpse of Sibyl, who deliberately moved behind her to avoid her gaze.

"Madam Goddess, I hereby officially invite you to a ball taking place tomorrow at the mayor's residence," I told her clearly and distinctly.

Nothing happened, however. There was no notification that I had completed the quest and when I checked, I saw that it was still listed in my quest log. Anna's quest location still glowed on my map.

"What, has the vaunted messenger failed in

his quest?" Anna grinned wickedly. "It's not enough to just deliver the invitation, dummy. I have to accept it."

So there it is... the catch. I guess, the game had hinted as much. Can't deliver the invitation until the guest accepts it. No wonder I had to get in touch with Theophilia and the followers of the Whisperer too.

And now we're at a standoff. I can't gank Anna because I'd fail the quest. And she can stall as long as she wants to save her life.

"How about we make a deal?" I offered. "Your life in exchange for accepting the invitation."

"Go to hell," Anna responded tersely. "Try to make me. You have about five minutes left on the timer. Think you can do it?"

Her helpless, thoroughly packaged appearance, in nothing but sexy lingerie, suggested the dirtiest thoughts to me. But, no. Violence is not our way. Everything should be given to us consensually, joyfully and with song and dance... Song and dance! Of course! That's it!

"Step aside," I told Sibyl. "You're too impressionable."

Anna watched me suspiciously, wondering what threat could possibly come from the small wooden stump I pulled out of my inventory.

"Alice: GROOVE!"

Thump... Thump... Thump...

Sibyl yelped and ran, hiding herself behind the hill. Ten minutes? According to Ji-Bo, that's how long the battery lasts. I don't think it'll take that long.

Anna squirmed... then convulsed. The ropes themselves weren't uncomfortable. Your muscles didn't get sore or hurt in the game. But now, her body demanded movement. Every nerve in her body rebelled against having to stay still. I remembered the unbearable itch... the withdrawal... the pain... *THUMP... THUMP... THUMP...*

I couldn't last two minutes last time; my body betrayed me. And Anna had no choice but to endure or give in.

"You bastard..." she wailed. "Stop it! Turn that crap off!"

"What? You don't like club music?" I crouched in front of her. "Don't they play this in Europe? Sorry, maybe my playlist is a bit outdated. ALICE, LOUDER!"

"You monster!"

She broke in less than a minute, before the beta round could end. Silently, without a word. I found out only when I received a system notification that the quest had been completed.

QUEST COMPLETED: DELIVER THE INVITATIONS TO THE MAYOR'S BALL.

PLEASE COLLECT YOUR REWARD AT THE MAYOR'S RESIDENCE.

"Alice, stop!"

"Just kill me," said Anna, looking at me with loathing.

I drew the wakizashi, bringing its blade close to her eyes.

"You like to break promises. You promised me information, then you vanished..."

My gaze slowly traveled over her body. It stopped on a lace garter on her thigh — the kind that brides throw at weddings to unmarried guests. I lowered my sword and snapped her garter with the blade.

"I'll just take this... as a keepsake." I waved the satin ribbon in front of her face.

"TargetAi," Anna's voice was surprisingly calm. "This rope you tied me with, it's not ordinary, is it? Will it still be binding me tomorrow?"

"I don't know," I shrugged. "You'll find out tomorrow."

"Untie me... please."

I waited until the timer was on the last second and then I pulled the knot, freeing Anna.

* * *

Back in the locker room, standing in the shower, I pondered why I hadn't killed Anna. Everything suggested I should have cut her down as soon as I completed the quest.

I wonder how much XP killing her would have given me? I could have gone up three, maybe four levels, and picked up some unique weapons and gear in the process. And that's not to mention the kind of bonuses the game would give me for killing one of the gods.

I'd like to know why I trusted my intuition and

left her alive. It wasn't just a display of weakness or pity. I've always trusted my intuition, considering it to be the same as thinking logically, only faster.

When you train your intuition, it starts to take into account many factors that the brain doesn't even have time to process. In battle, there's no time to think, you have to trust your reflexes, and it was the same here.

I've always just done things in life and only understood why afterwards.

Anna is the kind of person who keeps her word. Probably not because of her integrity or her particularly good upbringing. More likely because of her pride. She wants to play by the rules. That way, she proves to everyone that any victory isn't the result of chance, but a demonstration of her absolute superiority. And she's accustomed to winning and can't even imagine a different outcome.

So, as a result, it was advantageous for me to keep Anna indebted to me. The game doesn't end with one victory. If I killed her, I'd instantly wipe out any moral debt she might feel toward me. Anna was peculiar and unpredictable. Her closeness to the MosTech executives, her mysterious past, her unique game skills... She was too independent to become someone's ally, but her arrogance would naturally lead her to get hooked. At least, I hoped so.

Marina intercepted me in the hallway. She grabbed my sleeve without saying anything and dragged me to her office.

"Marina, I'm in a hurry," I said, figuring that she wanted to revisit the morning's arguments, something I had no patience for.

"Just five minutes... please," she said softly.

This didn't seem like a bout of jealousy, so I couldn't help but feel intrigued.

"Go on."

"Would you like some coffee?" Marina immediately took control as soon as we entered. "Sit down, I'll make it quick. I have a new coffee machine, better than any coffee shop... Or would you like tea?"

"Marina," I felt a bit sorry for her, seeing her fussing over me. "I really have to go. And it's business, not some other girl, as you might be imagining."

I was bending the truth a bit here. Marina might well consider Sibyl one of the bitches, but my rush to meet with her wasn't for romantic reasons. I was curious why Sibyl was so persistently avoiding real-world interactions. And I was especially curious if today's rendezvous would even happen.

"Remember how you asked me to find out about someone this morning?" Marina glanced around nervously, as if afraid we might be overheard. "Well, there's almost no information about her, but I did find something."

She proudly handed me her tablet. An article from some European newspaper was on the screen. The browser helpfully translated the text for me: It was about a car accident that had occurred a few years back. At first, I didn't see the connection, but the more I read, the wider my eyes grew.

"Did I do good?" Marina popped up in front of me like a student awaiting praise. "Is this useful?"

"Good job," I confirmed, and — surprising even myself — kissed her.

"M-m-m," the blonde purred and pressed her body against mine.

Regrettably, I pulled away.

"But really, I have to go."

"Will you call me tonight?" Marina asked hopefully.

"Sure," I agreed. And why not? It seemed like she had learned her lesson.

* * *

"Beer?" Simba greeted me at the entrance to the MosTech building.

Stacy, standing next to him, stomped in the cold, her whole demeanor endorsing the idea.

"Cool jacket," she observed. "Did you pick it out yourself?"

"Yep," I lied. "Have you seen Sibyl?"

"She's a flake," Simba stated flatly. "You know she won't show up."

I scanned the surroundings. Should I wait or bail? The chances of meeting the elusive Sibyl were dwindling. Then, from the parking lot, a dark figure on a black sports bike waved at me. Could it be? If not one meeting, then another.

"There's still time to get a beer later," I hurried. "I'll call you in a bit!"

"Wow..." Noticing where I was looking, Simba craned his neck. "Smooth! Well, have a good night!"

The snow crunched underfoot. Only the most hardcore fans of two-wheeled transport hadn't traded their bikes' saddles for the cozy, heated cabins of cars by this time. Anna, it seems, was one of them.

"Ever ridden on a bike before?" she asked, handing me a helmet.

"Only in VR," I replied honestly.

"Then hold onto me, press close, and shift your weight with mine."

"Are you trying to seduce me?" I settled in behind her, wrapping my arms around her waist.

Anna didn't respond, the bike's engine roared to life, and we rocketed off the parking lot like a missile.

Honestly, I relished the eroticism of the situation for about five minutes. Then, my stomach climbed into my throat as Anna began weaving her bike through the tiniest gaps between cars.

And later, when I got used to her daredevil driving style and started to enjoy it, we burst out of the city and sped along an almost empty road, a blur of snow-covered trees lining either side. That's when I truly started to feel the cold; my much-praised jacket did nothing against the oncoming wind. By the time we arrived at a house standing alone in the forest, I was freezing.

From my description, it might sound like this house was some forest cabin or hunting lodge. Not at all. In front of us stood a spacious, high-tech style mansion with a flat roof and panoramic windows, surrounded by a tall fence with massive gates. It was surrounded by forest, with no other houses or even infrastructure in sight — a sort of 21st century witch's hut.

Anna opened the gates with a remote, roared up the driveway in front of the house, and wheeled the bike into an underground garage. From there, a small door led us into a spacious hall.

Once again, stepping into a strange home, I couldn't help but feel a sting of inadequacy. My family's entire two-bedroom apartment could easily fit into this living room, maybe even twice over.

Anna clicked another remote, and a huge screen on the wall started blurting out stock market news in German.

"Want some hot chocolate?" She gestured at a supple gray sofa, inviting me to sit down.

I wouldn't have said no to something stronger, but I wanted to keep my head completely clear. Getting into Anna's house and being alone with her seemed like a quest far more challenging than anything the game had faced me with.

Anna was in no hurry. First she went to the coffee machine, fiddled around with it for a while, then came back with two large, cozy mugs.

Judging by the smell, it was some hot chocolate with espresso. She handed me one and settled into a chair opposite me, taking a sip and savoring it. Only then did she get down to business.

"So what was it that you wanted to find out?" she asked.

"*Everything,*" I wanted to say. What the hell was going on with this game we were playing... Why its AI was kidnapping people... What could we do to stop it... Why was *she* in the beta at all... But I decided to start by beating around the bush first.

"A few years ago, there was an accident in the Alps," I spoke slowly, as if quoting the newspaper article. "A German citizen, Elsa Falk, and her husband, a mathematician named Sergei Zvyagin, died in the accident. Only their daughter Anna survived. And although you always call yourself Anna Falk, your passport lists your full name as 'Anna Sergeyevna Zvyagina,' which means Sergei Zvyagin was your father."

"You did your homework," Anna snorted as if amused, "but it's all lies."

"What do you mean?"

"That whole article is a lie. And everything the journalists wrote later, too. And everything that my father's *coworkers* said later as well." She said the word "coworkers" with a palpable sneer.

I listened without interrupting, afraid to interfere with her telling her story.

"I did hit my head pretty hard in that accident," Anna paused, as if it was difficult for her to talk about it. "And it took me a very long time to recover. But my memory is fine now. The thing is — it was just my mother and me in the car that day. My father wasn't there at all."

END OF BOOK TWO

Thank you for reading *Kill or Die!*
If you like what you've read, check out other sci-fi, fantasy and LitRPG novels published by Magic Dome Books:

Reality Benders
a LitRPG series by Michael Atamanov

The Dark Herbalist
a LitRPG series by Michael Atamanov

Perimeter Defense
a LitRPG series by Michael Atamanov

League of Losers
a LitRPG series by Michael Atamanov

Chaos' Game
a LitRPG series by Alexey Svadkovsky

War Eternal
a LitRPG series by Yuri Vinokuroff

The Hunter's Code
a LitRPG series by Yuri Vinokuroff & Oleg Sapphire

An Ideal World for a Sociopath
a LitRPG series by Oleg Sapphire

The Healer's Way
a LitRPG Series by Oleg Sapphire & Alexey Kovtunov

Kill or Die
a LitRPG series by Alex Toxic

The Way of the Shaman
a LitRPG series by Vasily Mahanenko

The Alchemist
a LitRPG series by Vasily Mahanenko

Dark Paladin
a LitRPG series by Vasily Mahanenko

Galactogon
a LitRPG series by Vasily Mahanenko

Invasion
a LitRPG series by Vasily Mahanenko

World of the Changed
a LitRPG series by Vasily Mahanenko

The Bear Clan
a LitRPG series by Vasily Mahanenko

Starting Point
a LitRPG series by Vasily Mahanenko

The Bard from Barliona
a LitRPG series
by Eugenia Dmitrieva and Vasily Mahanenko

Condemned
(Lord Valevsky: Last of The Line)
a Progression Fantasy series
by Vasily Mahanenko

Loner
a LitRPG series by Alex Kosh

A Buccaneer's Due
a LitRPG series by Igor Knox

A Student Wants to Live
a LitRPG series by Boris Romanovsky

The Goldenblood Heir
a LitRPG series by Boris Romanovsky

Level Up
a LitRPG series by Dan Sugralinov

Level Up: The Knockout
a LitRPG series by Dan Sugralinov and Max Lagno

Adam Online
a LitRPG Series by Max Lagno

World 99
a LitRPG series by Dan Sugralinov

Disgardium
a LitRPG series by Dan Sugralinov

Nullform
a RealRPG Series by Dem Mikhailov

Clan Dominance: The Sleepless Ones
a LitRPG series by Dem Mikhailov

Heroes of the Final Frontier
a LitRPG series by Dem Mikhailov

The Crow Cycle
a LitRPG series by Dem Mikhailov

Interworld Network
a LitRPG series by Dmitry Bilik

Rogue Merchant
a LitRPG series by Roman Prokofiev

Project Stellar
a LitRPG series by Roman Prokofiev

In the System
a LitRPG series by Petr Zhgulyov

The Crow Cycle
a LitRPG series by Dem Mikhailov

Unfrozen
a LitRPG series by Anton Tekshin

The Neuro
a LitRPG series by Andrei Livadny

Phantom Server
a LitRPG series by Andrei Livadny

Respawn Trials
a LitRPG series by Andrei Livadny

The Expansion (The History of the Galaxy)
a Space Exploration Saga by A. Livadny

The Range
a LitRPG series by Yuri Ulengov

Point Apocalypse
a near-future action thriller by Alex Bobl

Moskau
a dystopian thriller by G. Zotov

El Diablo
a supernatural thriller by G.Zotov

Mirror World
a LitRPG series by Alexey Osadchuk

Underdog
a LitRPG series by Alexey Osadchuk

Last Life
a Progression Fantasy series by Alexey Osadchuk

Alpha Rome
a LitRPG series by Ros Per

An NPC's Path
a LitRPG series by Pavel Kornev

Fantasia
a LitRPG series by Simon Vale

The Sublime Electricity
a steampunk series by Pavel Kornev

Small Unit Tactics
a LitRPG series by Alexander Romanov

Black Centurion
a LitRPG standalone by Alexander Romanov

Rorkh
A LitRPG Series by Vova Bo

Thunder Rumbles Twice
A Wuxia Series by V. Kriptonov & M. Bachurova

Citadel World
a sci fi series by Kir Lukovkin

You're in Game!
LitRPG Stories from Our Bestselling Authors

You're in Game-2!
More LitRPG stories set in your favorite worlds

The Fairy Code
a Romantic Fantasy series by Kaitlyn Weiss

***The Charmed* Fjords**
a Romantic Fantasy series by Marina Surzhevskaya

More books and series are coming out soon!

In order to have new books of the series translated faster, we need your help and support! Please consider leaving a review or spread the word by recommending *Kill or Die* to your friends and posting the link on social media. The more people buy the book, the sooner we'll be able to make new translations available.

Thank you!

Till next time!

www.ingramcontent.com/pod-product-compliance
Lightning Source LLC
LaVergne TN
LVHW010050170826
845678LV00012B/2098
* 9 7 8 8 0 7 6 9 3 4 7 0 2 *